THE BEST dEFENSE

Nonfiction books by Ellis Cose

Color-Blind
A Man's World
The Rage of a Privileged Class
A Nation of Strangers
The Press

THE BEST dEFENSE

ELLIS COSE

HarperCollins*Publishers*

HarperCollins books may be purchased for educational, business, or sales promotional use. For information please write: Special Markets Department, HarperCollins Publishers, Inc., 10 East 53rd Street, New York, NY 10022.

FIRST EDITION

Designed by Elina D. Nudelman

Library of Congress Cataloging-in-Publication Data

Cose, Ellis.
   The best defense / Ellis Cose. —1st ed.
     p. cm.
   ISBN 0-06-017496-X
   I. Title
PS3553.0738B4 1998
813'.54—dc21   98-16838
                                                                                   CIP

98 99 00 01 02 ❖❖❖ /RRD 10 9 8 7 6 5 4 3 2 1

For Lee

Acknowledgments

Writing a book is always, in at least one respect, a humbling experience. For it forces you to confront the depths of your own ignorance. Happily, ignorance is not a terminal condition, but can be remedied through the kindness of friends.

In the course of crafting *The Best Defense*, I had more than my fair share of help from some of the brightest minds that have ever focused on criminal misbehavior. Defense attorney Laura Miranda took any number of late-night calls to verify fine points of law and bounce around ideas. Judge Carol Berkman, Judge Nicholas Figueroa, ADA Patricia Gatling, ADA John Irwin, Bronx District Attorney Robert Johnson, Mary McClymont, Leslie Moore, Judge Dianne Renwick, Judge George Roberts, ADA Alberto Roig, ADA David Strachan, ADA Marcie Waterman, and ADA Jim Williamson were much more generous in sharing legal wisdom gained in countless years before the bar. Detectives Guy Laieta, Thomas Lombardo, and Scott Wagner gave me insights into police thinking and procedures that I never could have acquired on my own. John Dillon, forensic consultant first class and former chief of the FBI Laboratory firearms unit, provided an essential mini-course in automatic weapons. Doctors Stuart Kleinman and Jennifer Smaldone generously tutored me in psychiatry and psychology.

Acknowledgments

Doctors René Davis and Alan Small likewise helped to fill in gaps in my medical knowledge. Deborah Allen, LaVerne Cose, and Betty DeRamus similarly clarified the many mysteries of beauty shops.

Help provided in the editorial arena was just as important. My agent, Michael Congdon, was, as always, a source of counsel, ideas, and support from the earliest stages of the project. My editor, Carolyn Marino, and her assistant, Robin Stamm, gave invaluable editorial feedback and advice. Assistant District Attorney Peter Kougasian served double duty, not only as an indispensable legal advisor but as a reader of the manuscript in an early stage. And then there is Lee, my wife, house counsel and muse, who, in addition to lending her legal expertise and editorial advice, was always a source of confidence and strength whenever mine began to waver.

Prologue

John wiped the sweat from his brow as he sipped the Scotch and water. The heat and crowd had long ago overpowered the feeble air conditioning, giving the bar the feel of a dank, gloomy marsh. But the weather was not to blame for the fire devouring his intestines. Those flames fed on despair, a mounting sense of loss, and on anger as pure and intense as a laser.

He considered calling Linda but instantly dismissed the notion. Their discussions of late had become painful, full of awkward pauses and unspoken reflections. They rarely lasted long enough to say anything substantial. It was as if she not only wanted to end the marriage but to erase him from her life. Yesterday, after a few minutes of halting conversation, a male voice had sounded in the background; she had hastily hung up, saying she had company. John thumped his glass on the bar and imagined smashing it against the face of Linda's "friend." *If killing him would bring her back* . . . The thought trailed off as he glanced at the pretty brunette seated down the bar to his left. She quickly looked away, prompting John to glower. *Who in the hell was she to reject his gaze?* But even if he'd had the nerve to approach her, he lacked the appetite. Tonight, his heart had no room for romance.

"Another Scotch," John barked at the bartender.

"Coming right up."

A fat man in his late twenties wearing a Yankees baseball cap eased into the seat to his right. He ordered a beer and, turning toward John, asked, "So, what's up, buddy?"

John shrugged. "Not much—'cept I've lost my goddamn job."

"Sorry," the man said, oozing phony sympathy.

"So am I."

"I guess so," his new chum replied, nodding agreeably, "But, hey, I'm sure things'll work out." The man smiled and held up his beer bottle as he made a toast: "To better days, and easy women."

John silently stepped away from the bar, loath to be around anyone so irrepressibly cheery. He gulped his drink and reflected on the situation at work. Roughly four months ago the rumors had started—talk about Computertronics being on the block. Initially, management had made the usual denials and John had paid the scuttlebutt little attention. But one morning a notice had gone up inviting all employees to a midday meeting, at which they were told Computertronics was being acquired by the much larger Infotect.

John had assumed he was safe. He had spent eight years at Computertronics, starting in word processing and eventually graduating to accounting. No one on staff was better at training than he. Certainly no one had his gift for demystifying computerized ledgers, or for making small businessmen understand the necessity for accurate data. He had composed a little speech that he gave many of his clients about the importance of good information in decision-making. Good information, he would say, was the difference between being dropped in a strange land with a map and a compass and being stranded without a clue. Sometimes, when he felt particularly eloquent or was striving to impress, he would contrast Computertronics's *Numberperfect* to the competitor's *Account-right*. "Our program is as big a step beyond *Account-right* as a computer is beyond an abacus," he would declare. "And when you're crunching a lot of data, an abacus just won't do."

From the moment John had transferred to accounting, he knew he had found a home. He delighted in the way the software turned endless columns of numbers into income statements and balance sheets. Order, control, triumph over confusion, the virtues he so valued in life were precisely what his product delivered to his clients.

John had done well enough to be promoted to training director for his division—a nice management job, complete with bonuses, corner office, and stock options. His new bosses, he had assumed, would understand the centrality of Computertronics to his world—and, more important, his value to them. The bosses, however, had turned out to be fools. And he had spent the last seven weeks looking for work.

Even though there had been offers, there had been nothing approaching the pay or rank of the position he held. With one week to go before being kicked out on the streets, he was past the point of despair.

He ordered another drink and touched the glass to his lips, barely tasting the Scotch as it trickled down his throat. It was bad enough to lose a job—and to have prospective employers ignore his calls and overlook his track record. But it was galling to watch Francisco García, who had half his experience and a fraction of his ability, being kept on. In fact, word was that Francisco was up for a promotion. That was nothing short of an outrage.

John sighed, wallowing in his anguish. His efforts, his plans, his existence counted for nothing in their eyes—nor, it seemed, in Linda's, who, without reason, had rebuffed every attempt at reconciliation. He had tried to persuade himself that it was all for the best, but the last two months had convinced him only that life was crueler and more capricious than he had ever imagined.

He caught the bartender's eye and pointed toward his glass, having long ago lost track of the number of drinks he had consumed, but certain he needed at least one more to strengthen his resolve.

John finished his drink and picked up his pile of cash from the bar. He left five dollars for the bartender and quietly slipped into the night. The air was only slightly less sultry than earlier, but a gentle breeze blew from the west. John turned in the zephyr's direction, picturing himself in a desert, strolling in the endless sand toward everlasting tranquillity.

It was odd walking New York City's streets on Sunday night

when so few people were stirring—like watching a gigantic and forbidding roller-coaster at rest that needed only a jolt of electricity to bring it to life. Every city, he imagined, had its own distinct nocturnal mood. Some years ago, as part of a computer training exercise, he had spent several days in Tokyo. He had been struck by the city's lack of menace, its feeling of absolute safety, even after dark.

A shout rang out ahead. Two men suddenly came into view. In the darkness and from a half-block away, John could not decipher their conversation, but something seemed amiss. One was yelling and shaking his fist. The other, who appeared to be in retreat, was also screaming.

Normally, John would have crossed the street to avoid drawing their attention. At five feet nine, one hundred and fifty pounds, and naturally bashful, he was accustomed to fading into the background. But tonight he felt reckless, and utterly beyond their grasp.

They were now some thirty feet away, but their words, slurred and accented, were not much clearer. Their voices, nonetheless, sounded friendly, and their elaborate gestures seemed less threatening than comical.

As he sauntered by, the squabbling stopped. "Hey, man. Hold up," one of them shouted.

John's muscles tightened as he turned. The men had clearly become more interested in him than in continuing their dispute, and he doubted their intentions were benign. Still, he did not even think of running. He wasn't in such great shape. And with his luck, he would stumble after a couple of steps and end up with a broken leg. Besides, he was in no mood to back away from a fight. If they were looking for trouble, he'd be glad to oblige.

Sweat dripped into his mouth and down his chin. His breathing quickened as he slipped his right hand into the canvas pouch strapped around his waist.

The light from a nearby neon sign revealed the men to be perhaps half his age: early twenties, with baggy casual clothes. One was more than six feet tall and at least two hundred and twenty-five well-muscled pounds. The other was shorter and slender. Both had black hair and appeared Latino—either Puerto Rican or, more likely, Dominican. They did not look like beggars. Neither had the demented, desperate look of men who had lived too long on the streets or were strung out on crack. But obviously they wanted something—probably money—and they no doubt intended to take it. Still, maybe they were just beggars. It wasn't as if panhandlers wore uniforms. A show of compassion, John decided, would not be out of line.

"Luh . . . uh . . . look," John sputtered, his tongue thickened by alcohol, focusing his attention on the bigger of the two. "I don't have much money, but I might have some change."

He reached into his pocket, pulled out an assortment of pennies, nickels, and dimes, and thrust them toward the man more forcefully than he had intended, gently hitting him in the chest as the coins clattered to the ground.

The man gaped in apparent astonishment. "What the fuck—," he shouted. "What do I want with this shit, man?"

John knew the question was rhetorical, but also realized it demanded an answer. "Look," he blurted out, "if you don't want it, that's fine. But that's all I got to give. Anyway, I got to go."

"Where the hell you got to go to?" screamed the giant. The man, his angular face twisted into a scowl, glanced at the sidewalk, shaking his head. "Can you believe it," he said to his friend, "this drunk fool is throwing pennies at us." The bully laughed, but his voice suddenly turned cold. "Take your damn pennies, man," he commanded. "Do you know who won the fuckin' game?"

John's "no" did not conceal his annoyance, nor his befuddlement at the man's question. *What game was he talking about? Was the question some kind of trap? Could these loud, loathsome men with malice in their eyes be strung-out homicidal fiends?* John backed away, eager to end the encounter.

A passing car slowed but quickly sped up. John considered screaming out but thought better of the idea. To cry for help would only anger them. And by the time anyone arrived—assuming anyone did—who could say what would have happened to him. He would have to handle this alone.

"What's with you?" the man snapped. "You don't like my company?"

"Look, I got to go," John murmured. "I really have to go."

"What wrong with you, man? Why don't you show some fuckin' respect?"

"Respect?" John, suddenly angry, glared at the man with contempt. "I don't even know you. Why should I respect you?"

"Why you dissin' me, man? You don't like my company?"

"Look, uh . . . Forget it," John replied.

As John continued to back away, the man's companion maneuvered himself slightly to John's left. They were playing with him, like wolves with a deer, blocking his escape route, slowly circling for the kill. Not today, John said to himself, taking several shallow breaths in rapid succession. He suddenly realized that the man to his left had stopped walking and was reaching for something in his belt. At that moment, John's mind became utterly clear. He had to beat his tormentor to the draw.

"Fuck," the bigger man said as John's gun grazed his chin. He froze, along with his companion, and stared at John for several uneasy seconds, then he slowly retreated as he mumbled, "Chill, man. Okay? I didn't mean nothing. *Okay? You hear me, man?*"

John looked into their terrified faces, enjoying the sensation of absolute power, savoring the shift in their attitudes. It would be so easy to pull the trigger. And who could blame him?

"Do you want to die?" he asked softly. Both men shook their heads. The smaller, heretofore silent one, whispered, "No, sir."

John pointed the gun at the larger man's head and parted his feet in what he took to be a shooter's stance.

"Oh, shit," gasped the prospective target, who abruptly whirled around and took off at full speed, tracing a zigzag pattern down the street. His friend immediately followed, leaving John triumphant and alone. The jubilant mood passed as quickly as it had come; and the familiar heartburn-like sensation returned as John strode off in search of a taxi.

* * *

The building guard made no secret of his surprise at John's arrival. "Don't usually see you around at this hour," he said.

"Don't usually have a reason to be here," John shot back as he autographed the sign-in sheet and headed for the elevator.

John used his card key to enter the common area and crossed the carpet to Francisco's private office. He tested the door and, finding it unlocked, pushed it open and walked in. The desk was a portrait of neatness. A few papers were stacked in one corner, a legal pad was in the center, and photographs of an attractive dark-haired woman were on either side. In one of the pictures she was holding a young girl, who clung to a tiny doll. John slid into Francisco's chair and picked up the legal pad. He had thought a great deal about what he wanted to say, but his hands were trembling. He stared at the paper for several minutes and finally began to write, addressing the note to Stan Rothstein, chairman of the board.

> *Once upon a time I had a job I enjoyed, and I thought I had a future here. I had planned to spend the rest of my productive years serving Computertronics's customers, and I dreamed of retiring and spending time with my wife. I no longer have my job, and I no longer have my dream. I no longer even have a wife. I have lost everything, through no fault of my own.*
>
> *I was never so foolish as to believe that life was fair; but I did believe that years of dedication and good work counted for something. Though I have tried, I don't understand why I should be sacrificed for sins I did not commit.*
>
> *I am not an illiberal person. I understand that some people might need a break. I know that some people have suffered unjustly. But America never persecuted Colombians. So why do we owe anything to Francisco García? I hope you will think about that, Mr. Rothstein. And I hope you will see how ruining lives like mine can only bring the company and the country down. Please wake up. PLEASE WAKE UP, NOW.*

John underlined the last phrase three times, put the paper in the center of the desk, and flung the pen across the room. *Damn them all.* He trudged into his own office across the way and retrieved the small bottle of Scotch from the bottom drawer of his desk. He sipped straight from the bottle, savoring the feel of the liquor stinging his throat. He returned to Francisco's office, bottle in hand, and placed the gun on the desk.

Depression washed over him. He felt adrift in a boundless ocean, tossed any which way by waves too powerful to resist. Tears spilled from his eyes, mingling with the sweat on his cheeks, and he dug his fingernails into his forehead, trying to counteract the pain inside.

He picked up the gun and stared in awe at the lightweight, black polymer frame. So much power in such a small object. He was ready, and yet he was afraid. He thought of calling Linda but quickly changed his mind, and took another sip from the bottle just as the door swung open.

Francisco García entered, a look of astonishment on his face. "Wha . . . What in the hell are you doing?" he stammered.

John looked up, placed the bottle on the desk, and held the gun tightly as he said, "This is all your goddamn fault."

1

Geneva Johnson was on the verge of leaving when the messenger arrived, but as soon as she realized what the package held, she redeposited her purse on the sofa. "Come on. Come on," she said, hunching over Felicia. "You are soooo slow, girl. Just rip the blessed paper off."

Felicia finally got the magazine out, and gasped as her eyes took in the cover. The portrait was nothing short of stunning: an image so much more glamorous than the stylishly conservative thirty-nine-year-old professional who generally resided in her mirror. This woman was a vision from a fashion photographer's fantasy, with dark caramel skin, long jet-black hair, a white silk blouse, and a playful smile that stopped just short of a sneer, with lips slightly parted, as if to whisper "I dare you."

Geneva shook her head in wonder, causing her neatly braided hair extensions to flick against her face. "Damn, you look hot," she said. "Is this *really* you?"

Felicia grinned, staring at the cover line. FELICIA FONTAINE: LAWYER OF THE YEAR. The words were practically as large as the *Manhattan Woman* logo. In slightly smaller type, the magazine proclaimed her "The most innovative and unpredictable defense attorney since William Branegan."

"Interesting company they put you in," said Geneva. "Branegan, as I recall, was something of a nut."

"He wasn't a nut," said Felicia. "He was just, well, *different*. The polite word, I suppose, is eccentric. But he was also probably the best lawyer I ever knew. His defense of Darnell Guilliam was absolutely brilliant. Maybe one other lawyer in the city could have gotten Guilliam off."

"Who."

"Me, of course," she said, beaming. "But even I wouldn't have had the nerve to do what Branegan did. I mean, when you have a dope-dealing convicted felon for a client and he's executed two plainclothes detectives, it takes real chutzpah to put him on the stand to testify that he thought the cops were hit men out to assassinate him."

"That's right. I remember now. He did do that."

"Yep. By the time Branegan was done, he had the jury convinced the cops were contract killers working for some Colombian drug lord."

"Were they?"

"Who knows? I doubt it, but anything's possible. Still, his closing argument was so good, he nearly had me convinced that Guilliam had performed a public service. If I had been on that jury, even I might have let him off . . . And I was a prosecutor at the time."

Felicia sighed, her expression suddenly serious. "You know, I miss talking to him. We didn't agree on much of anything, certainly not on politics. And his style was way too flamboyant, even for me, but we had something of the same attitude—a sort of subversive approach to jurisprudence. He also had the best sense of humor of just about anybody I've ever known. But then his clients were so wretched—terrorists, religious fanatics, demented killers—that he probably needed to keep laughing just to get him through the day."

"So this is the man whose shoes you're going to fill?"

"Be serious. Branegan was one of a kind. Plus, he lived for the law. I have other priorities."

"Like paying for this big-ass place."

"That's one of them."

"Well, girlfriend, congratulations. You are definitely on your way. But don't let this stardom stuff go to your head. Just like they can build you up, they can take you down. And believe me, they can do it in the time it takes to blink. Anyway, got to run. Got a hot date."

"Really?" asked Felicia, feigning astonishment.

"Yeah, with my two sons. Think we're going out for pizza. Talk to you tomorrow."

After Geneva left, Felicia opened the magazine to the beginning of the profile. The photo inside was almost as striking as the cover shot. Wearing a lavender blouse and a dark blue power suit, she was holding her glasses in her left hand, looking both scholarly and seductive. "Felicia Fontaine: Nobody's victim," read the caption. The spread went on for ten full pages, hitting every highlight of her career. There was criticism to be sure. "A showboat, all flash and no substance," one unidentified "former colleague" called her. But the barbs were few, and they were more than balanced with the sort of lavish praise normally reserved for eulogies.

She tossed the magazine to the center of the cocktail table, letting loose a chuckle of delight. *Manhattan Woman* might not be the big-time, but it was more than respectable. "Yep. You're doing all right for yourself, girl," she said, savoring the satiny sound of her voice.

What would Branegan make of her modest fame? she wondered. At the very least, he would find it amusing. And he would probably warn her—just as Geneva had—not to take it terribly seriously. "Find a suitably modest way to declare your superiority, but never make the mistake of believing you're as good as you claim," Branegan had once advised with a wink. The suggestion was not particularly original, but it certainly summed up his own approach to life, and she had tried to follow it as best she could.

She had never been quite sure what had drawn Branegan to her. At first she had assumed it was sexual attraction, but he had made it clear, in myriad subtle ways, that he had no interest in sleeping with her. "I'm a sixty-six-year-old man with a young wife at home. She's all I can handle," he had joked. Perhaps he merely admired her audacity, she had concluded, which mirrored—albeit faintly— his own. By the time she and Branegan had become devoted, if somewhat wary, chums she had been practicing law for nearly a decade. She had already mastered the art of making a powerful impression, having realized that image, especially for those in the public arena, is a source of power; that perception, in the realm of human affairs, is invariably more important than reality. Her first high-profile case, the prosecution of Geoff Jay, had driven that lesson deep into her bones.

Jay was a handsome, successful stage actor, who had savagely beaten his male lover. And though all the evidence—including the victim's fractured orbital socket and broken eye vessels—pointed to Jay's guilt, she had lost the case. The jury had simply concluded that Jay was too nice a man to do the awful things she had proven he had done. Winning a case, she had learned, sometimes required more than simply having the facts on your side.

At least one good thing had come of that case: a relationship with Frank Conroy. After all these years, she was still not certain what had possessed him to come to the courtroom day after day and to sit in the front row—generally reserved for cops, the press, and practicing attorneys. He had said his interest stemmed from having followed Geoff Jay's work on stage, but she had believed from the beginning—and did still—that his real interest was her. They had met briefly a few weeks before the Jay case, when Frank had dropped by to visit Sam, the assistant district attorney with whom she then shared a small, cluttered office. Frank had taken her hand as if to shake it but instead had merely held it as he gawked, an unintended gesture which had totally undone his affectation of nonchalance.

Felicia gazed at the intricately carved Carrara marble fireplace that anchored the living room. She had purchased it in Florence on a whim, for $25,000, the kind of money she had taken six months to earn only a few years ago. She considered it a symbolic investment in the lifestyle she felt she deserved, in a lifestyle she had more than earned. What was it that Frank had once said to her: "We never seem to get our due." The "we" Frank had in mind were black Americans, but she had heard much the same elsewhere—from other women, from Latinos, from a whole motley tribe of the so-called disadvantaged who were unsure of how to get ahead in life. Her response rarely varied. "We get what we know how to demand," she had told Frank. She had repeated the phrase to the *Manhattan Woman* writer who had used it as the caption for a huge photo. Frank would get a kick out of seeing that.

If only he were a little more clever, a tad more exciting, a bit more prominent, Frank might be a perfect match. He was good-look-ing—in the sense that he had no conspicuously unattractive feature. His stomach was not exactly flat, but neither did it obviously pro-trude. His chin, though weak, was covered with a nice, scholarly gray beard. He had made a nice name for himself in a not particu-larly fascinating field, as a law professor specializing in sentencing issues. He was passionate about his work, clearly enamored of her, a very good buddy, and a sensitive, if less than dynamic, lover. If only he ignited half the sparks in her that she seemed to set off in him. She picked up the phone from the table at the end of the sofa and dialed his number. As she heard his voice, she felt a surge of affection. Without bothering to say hello, she murmured, "Frank, honey, why don't you let me buy you a drink."

Frank arrived a half hour later, wearing a boxy, light gray suit and carrying a bulky briefcase. Felicia pushed a glass of white wine into his free hand as he entered the living room.

"I'm one drink ahead of you," she said. "So you have a bit of catching up to do."

She stepped back to inspect him as he dropped the briefcase on the carpet. "You look like a banker," she said, a look of fake con-sternation spreading across her features. "That suit has no shape or character whatsoever."

"I have to wear *something* to work tomorrow, honey. Plus, I don't want to get the co-eds too excited. So I'm striving to look as unappetizing as possible," he said, smiling. "Call this my undesirable professor look."

"Well, what about getting *me* excited? Don't you feel the need to wear something sexy for me? Or don't you care about that anymore?"

"Ouch!" Frank whispered, grimacing. He took a sip of wine, his eyes lingering over Felicia's clingy summer dress, as an exaggerated leer formed on his face. "I always figured you were sexy enough for the two of us," he said.

"Flatterer," she responded, suppressing a grin.

"Yes, I am. But it's sincere flattery . . . By the way, don't you have a magazine to show me?"

"I was waiting for you to ask."

As they leafed through *Manhattan Woman*, Frank's face displayed an expression of purest pleasure—a reflection, Felicia presumed, of his pride in her. That was pretty much what she had expected. His supportiveness, she had concluded some time ago, was perhaps his best feature. Indeed, it was the one thing that sometimes made her believe that they might even have a future.

As Frank became aware that she was watching him, his expression turned to one of almost boyish bashfulness. There was something very warm and comforting, almost seductive, about him—at least tonight, thought Felicia, as she drained her third glass of wine.

After placing the empty glass on the table, she turned toward him and, smiling dreamily, kissed him lustily on the lips. She held his lips captive for nearly a minute, simultaneously stroking his beard with her fingers. Then, without a word, she lifted the magazine from his hand, placed it on the sofa, and led him into the bedroom.

Felicia swiftly undressed him, even as he undressed her, planting kisses on each area of his body as she exposed it. As he stood naked before her, she reached behind him and yanked the plush comforter from the king-sized bed, allowing it to fall in a lump to the floor. She gently pushed him backward onto the sheets, instantly falling down beside him.

Frank tried to maneuver himself on top, but Felicia shook her head and firmly held him down. And after gently massaging his already awakened penis, she nimbly positioned herself astride him. Guided by her hand, he entered her easily, emitting a low moan as he did so.

Felicia stayed in charge, moving slowly at first, then more forcefully, slowing down whenever she sensed he was about to lose control, expertly easing him down from the heights only to swiftly carry him back again. As she writhed above him, Frank's breathing grew frenzied. "Please don't stop," he gasped, whenever she slowed the pace.

Felicia came first, her torso exploding in ever-quickening undulations, as waves of pleasure pulsed throughout her body. All the while, she pressed his hands tightly into the mattress, holding him helpless against the sheets. Frank came immediately thereafter, letting loose a loud, feral growl that seemed to emerge from some hidden part of his soul. She stared at him for several seconds, sighing heavily before collapsing against his chest; and as she gently drifted toward sleep, she smiled, imagining his face on the figure of a tender, cuddly angel.

The ringing hit her eardrums with the force of a locomotive, causing her to lurch forward and nearly knock the phone off the table. She had been in a state of blissful tranquillity, not quite asleep, not totally awake, floating across a fog-filled sea. The scent of the ocean water lingered in her nostrils as she mumbled a sullen "Hello." At first all she heard was an unintelligible whimper, but it quickly became a vaguely recognizable voice: male, high-pitched, filled with trepidation.

"I'm so sorry to call so late, Ms. Fontaine. Please forgive me. I didn't know who else to call."

The sleepiness lifted, as the name leapt into her mind: Mike Orbach, her first big client as a private attorney. A software code writer, Mike had been accused of illegally copying and selling programs owned by the small start-up company where he then worked. Though he had faced all-but-certain conviction, Felicia had turned things around by trying the company in the media. Women who were being sexually exploited, old-timers who were being eased out, expectant mothers denied rest breaks—all showed up, thanks to Felicia, on the nightly news. Under the barrage of bad publicity, Pipe Dreams Software quickly backed down, awarding Mike a settlement of $150,000, from which Felicia had triumphantly taken her one-third share.

"I think he's being charged with murder."

The words snapped her back to the present. "Slow down, Mike. What in God's name are you talking about. Who's being charged with murder?"

She could hear Mike fighting to control his breathing as the story tumbled out. "John, John Wisocki. We used to work together. He called a few minutes ago from the police station. He shot somebody at work, by accident."

"He works Sunday night?"

"No. Yes. Uh . . . I don't really know. He's been really hurting lately, and . . . I don't know, but I told him you could help, that you would be his lawyer. I hope that was all right."

"Do you know where he's being held?"

He gave her the information along with his testimonial: John, his good friend, had never harmed another human being. John abhorred conflict in any form. John couldn't possibly be guilty of murder. Felicia grunted sympathetically as Mike babbled on. The last thing she felt like was picking up a possible homicide tonight; but she owed Mike, or felt she did. And what the hell, it probably wouldn't hurt her image to handle an arraignment the very day her face was plastered all over New York City. "Go to bed, Mike," she ordered. "I'll deal with it."

As she hung up the phone, she glanced across the bed at Frank, who was resting on his elbows. "So what was that all about?" he asked, a hint of concern in his voice.

"I'm not quite sure, but it sounds like a murder case." She leaned over, kissed him lightly on the cheek, and rolled out of bed. "Go back to sleep," she whispered. "I'll use the phone in the living room."

Felicia called the precinct, identified herself as Wisocki's attorney, and demanded that any questioning cease. Having accomplished her main objective, she briefly debated whether to stay at home. A soft bed with a warm lover was certainly a lot more inviting than a precinct station full of uncaring cops. Nonetheless, she decided to go—not only to reassure her new client, whom she expected to be terrified, but to reinforce her hands-off warning to the cops.

During the taxi ride to the station, Felicia found it impossible to concentrate on what little she knew of the case. Her mind insisted on dwelling on Frank and on their love-making of the evening. That level of passion was rare for them, especially of late. And she found herself alarmed at the thought that maybe what had ignited it was not anything about Frank, but rather her joy at being *Manhattan Woman*'s star of the moment. She had a lot to sort out, she concluded—but not tonight.

The minute Felicia entered the precinct, all thoughts of Frank evaporated. Instead, she focused on taking charge of the case and limiting any possible damage Wisocki might do to himself.

The police were holding him on the second floor in a small, barren room often used for lineups. They had parked Wisocki there while they filled out the paperwork because they thought he would find it more comfortable than a cell, a detective explained to her. The real reason, she suspected, was that such a setting allowed them the access they needed to interrogate him without appearing to do so.

The detective in charge, Billy O'Rourke, smoothly turned aside her request for a more private place to meet with her client. "He's in the most private, secure place we got right now, 'less you want to meet with him in the men's room," said O'Rourke.

"To tell the truth, it wouldn't surprise me to find you even have peepholes in the can," replied Felicia, who consented to see Wisocki in the lineup room. She had no hope, after all, of holding a truly private conversation anywhere in the precinct.

Wisocki, wearing a disheveled dark suit and a vacant expression, did not stir when she walked through the door. He remained in his chair, staring dead ahead. She was surprised they had not yet taken the clothes she presumed he had been wearing when arrested. "I guess they have other priorities," she said to herself.

As she approached, she smiled at Wisocki and, extending her hand, softly said, "Hello. I'm Felicia Fontaine, a lawyer. Your friend Mike called me."

Wisocki leapt to his feet, suddenly animated, his features flush with gratitude and relief.

"Thank God," he said, seizing her hand. "When do I get out of this place?"

"Whoa. Not so quick," she said, extracting her fingers from his grip as she fixed him with a somber yet sympathetic expression. "There's a lot of process stuff that has to be dealt with before we can talk about sending you home."

"But I didn't mean to—"

"*Don't*," she ordered sharply. "Don't say a word about anything. *Not a word.* The walls around this place have very sensitive ears. I already told the cops not to question you, and if they have any sense, they won't. They might, however, try to talk to you, to lure you into explaining what happened tonight. *Don't.* Until you hear something different from me, don't discuss what happened with anybody— not a lover, not your wife, not your best buddy, and certainly not with anybody you meet in this joint. What you say to me is privileged. What you might say to anybody else is not, and no matter how innocent, it might come back to hang you. Understand?"

He nodded, although she could tell from his lost and worried expression that he had only the vaguest notion of how much trouble he was in. She drew a deep breath and continued her lecture: "Starting from this moment on, I'm your new best friend, maybe your only friend. I'm also your best hope of getting out of this place. If you forget that, you might end up forfeiting not just your freedom, but your life."

Taking note of his muffled gasp, she judged that her words had struck home.

"What happens next?" he asked, timidly.

"First, they have some hoops for you to jump through here, then they send you to central booking. The most important thing, coming up, however, is your arraignment. That will probably be tomorrow. And we have to make sure we get some of your family to that. So I'll need numbers for any close relatives that live in the city."

He stared at her, nervously clenching and opening his fist. "The only family I have here is a mother and a wife. And I'm not sure my wife is talking to me," he mumbled.

"Well, I suspect she'll talk to *me*," said Felicia, as she whipped out a pen and pad of paper.

Senior trial counsel Mario Santiago's beeper went off just before two in the morning. The time registered in his brain as he leapt up and grabbed the alarm clock, which in his sleepiness he took to be the source of the sudden noise. He immediately realized his mistake and snatched his trousers (with the beeper in the pocket), hanging from the bedroom door, intent on silencing the racket before it awakened María Cristina. He stumbled into the corridor adjoining the bedroom, the telephone in one hand and rumpled pants and a fresh white shirt in the other.

Mario had come to think of the beeping in the middle of the night as the sound of death. A summons to the aftermath of mayhem. He pulled on his clothes and dialed the number of the cop on duty: a lonely sentinel watching over the city from behind a metal detector at the District Attorney's office at 1 Hogan Place. The cop picked up on the first ring. His gruff voice did not mask his youth and inexperience, both of which became increasingly apparent as Santiago pumped him for details. He knew virtually nothing. A murder suspect was being held at the Midtown South Precinct on West Thirty-fifth Street. Apparently, the perpetrator had been arrested at the scene.

In the old days, that is, when he had started a decade ago, the DA's desk was staffed with veterans who knew what in the hell was going on; with cops who, as a point of pride, had every relevant fact on a case before they made the call. Now, the desk cops were little more than clerks.

He dialed the precinct and got through to Billy O'Rourke, the detective in charge, who fed him a few relevant facts. Yes, they had the shooter. Yes, he had been found at the crime scene—some kind of computer company office on West Thirty-fourth Street—along with an incriminating note. No, they had not questioned him. "He lawyered up right away. Shut us down cold."

Mario grimaced. It was always so much easier without the defense attorneys involved. In the immediate aftermath of a crime when the perpetrator was typically at his most voluble, confessions could often be coaxed by simply offering a sympathetic ear. This, unfortunately, was not to be that type of case. "Can you spare somebody to pick me up?" he asked.

Mario gave his address, hung up the phone, and picked up the briefcase he always kept packed with the paraphernalia of the trade: grand jury subpoenas, search warrant forms, the penal law and criminal procedure manual, Miranda warnings in English and Spanish, numbers of detective squads, interpreters, and other ADAs—materials, for the most part, he would have no use for, but felt the need to carry, just in case. He tiptoed into the bedroom and gently kissed María Cristina on the lips, provoking nothing more than an indecipherable grunt, and quietly slipped out the door.

The cops took less than five minutes to arrive, but Mario had already grown impatient. "Hey, guys," Mario said, as he slid into the car. "If it's all right with you, let's swing by the scene before heading to the precinct."

As they sped through the streets, he tingled with anticipation. It was similar to what he had felt as a teenager while waiting his turn to walk on the mat during Tae Kwon Do competitions: eagerness tinged with caution, with awareness of a million things that could go wrong. He had seen so many cases lost for the stupidest of mistakes—the failure of a cop to disclose a conversation with a suspect, the failure of an ADA to establish the chain of custody of evidence. Better to be on top of everything from the beginning.

By the time Mario arrived, the crime scene unit had pretty much wrapped things up. The body was long gone, as was the video unit. Much of the evidence, including the gun, was en route to the precinct. A detective gave him a quick summary of the facts of the case and then pointed to the blood-splattered carpet behind and to the side of the desk and muttered, "Looks like he did him right here. The victim was dead when EMS got here, probably died instantly." Mario walked around to the back of the desk and glanced at the picture of the females he presumed to be García's wife and daughter—she couldn't be more than four or five. Tonight, he imagined, would be the worst day of their lives. He was glad he was not the one charged with giving them the news.

As he looked around the room, committing its contours to memory, he wondered why, if Wisocki had come here with murder on his mind, he had waited until García was right on top of him to fire. Why not shoot him from a safer distance? Maybe, he reasoned, Wisocki had shot him from farther out and then dragged the body to the spot where he was found. Maybe García had rushed Wisocki but died before he could grab the gun. The technicians should be able to come up with some likely scenarios fairly quickly. But who in the hell knew when Wisocki had composed that note? The crime scene would yield few answers tonight, he concluded. He turned to Shaughnessy and Ortiz, the detectives who had picked him up, and asked to be taken to the precinct.

Detective O'Rourke had begun to pull things together. A twenty-year veteran with massive shoulders, a small diamond stud in his left ear, and a breezy, unflappable manner, he took Mario into the kitchen area in the back—out of earshot of those milling around out front in the detective squad room—and concisely summed up what they knew. The victim, a male Hispanic named Francisco García, had suffered a fatal wound to the chest. The shooter, a male white named John Wisocki, was in custody. They had a nine-millimeter automatic, two spent bullets, and an incriminating note. "Looks to be pretty open and shut to me," said O'Rourke. "Wisocki hated Francisco, saw his opportunity, and took it. Slam dunk. Nobody shoots at someone two times by accident."

"No case is open and shut. You know that, Detective. But you may be right. We've probably got his ass. Any priors on this guy?"

"Not a thing, Counselor."

"Any statement?"

"Not here. We must have spent two or three hours processing him, trying all the time to get him to tell us what happened. All he would say was that he didn't mean to kill nobody. Cried like a baby for much of the time. Then he started hollering about a lawyer, so we backed off. His attorney showed up pretty quick. Whirled through here like a tornado, taking down badge and tax ID numbers of every officer in sight. Had a long chat with the sergeant, too. Pretty feisty broad. If we even thought about questioning her client, she said, she'd haul us into court. But she did it in a nice way, if you know what I mean. Had a smile on her face the whole time. Not that there is any question about Wisocki's doing it. Told the arresting officers the gun went off in his hand, supposedly by mistake."

"So he admitted that he did it?"

"Yeah. Also admitted it was his gun."

"To whom?"

"Kelly and Strachan. They were first on the scene."

"I'll want to talk to them."

"Yeah. I know the drill, Counselor."

"Any other witnesses?"

"Nobody saw the shooting, but we got the lobby guard who saw him come in. There was also a cleaning crew and a couple of them heard some things. The building, though, was pretty much deserted."

"Who called it in?"

"The perp. He called nine-one-one."

"How's he doing?"

"Probably asleep by now. You know, all these lowlifes fall asleep when they come down from the homicide high. It's like, 'Do a murder, take a nap.'"

"I thought that was only when they confessed—and had a load lifted from their chests."

"To be honest, Counselor, I think what it really is is that they are so weary after hours of processing, and being pumped full of every noncaffeinated drink we can give them, that they just collapse from exhaustion."

Mario smiled grimly and pondered his next move. He couldn't question the suspect, nor review the DD5 police reports—or "pinks," as the cops called them—since they were far from done, but there were scads of people he could talk to. Assuming O'Rourke had done his job, many of them would be on hand. But before beginning his interviews, he would look in on Wisocki. He might not be able to interrogate him, but at least he could fix the man's image in his mind.

Mario briskly walked the several steps to Wisocki's cell. He had passed the cell on his way into the squad room, but had been in such a rush to speak to O'Rourke that he had not paused to take the measure of the man. Now Wisocki had his full attention. The cell, located at the entrance to the room, was perhaps ten feet by eight, smaller than the holding cell downstairs where run-of-the-mill offenders were kept. Wisocki, a small man with a face that seemed almost cherubic, was hunched up on the bench in the back of the cell. Contrary to O'Rourke's assumption, he appeared to be wide awake, and was staring intently at the wall to his right. He wore a sweat suit, given to him when his own clothes were taken for evidence, that was way too big, making him look even punier than he might otherwise. He was not the sort of man, Mario knew instantly, who would adjust well to life in prison. The gangs—black, Latino, and probably white as well—would label him a pansy and then proceed to bang away at him until there was nothing left but a shell.

Before beginning his interviews, Mario again sought out O'Rourke and asked that Wisocki be extensively photographed. Such documentation could be invaluable during the trial. "Also," added Mario, "I'm going to want this guy's fingernails scraped and a blood-level reading. I'll have the warrants in a few minutes . . . By the way, you wouldn't happen to remember the defense lawyer's name?"

"Shit, who could forget her," replied O'Rourke. "Felicia Fontaine. I met her when she was in the DA's office. Kind of snooty, but a real babe. You should see the butt on that woman. A piece of prime . . . Ummm . . . Uh . . . You know what I mean."

Had Mario been hooked up to a heart monitor, alarms would have blared. As it was, the only thing that betrayed any emotion was the sudden tapping of his finger on the detective's desk. It had been several months since he had seen Felicia, and nearly three years since they had had an extended conversation. Generally, when he spotted her, he managed to walk in another direction. The thought of seeing her again—especially under these circumstances—filled him with foreboding. "Just what I need," he muttered, as he fished in his briefcase for his notepad. Yet even as Mario shrank from the idea of becoming reacquainted with Felicia, the prospect also fired his imagination. Over the last several years, he had spent countless hours recalling the times they had spent together and the confidences they had shared, all the while telling himself that some memories were better left buried—and some secrets left undisturbed.

By the time Mario headed home, New York wore an ethereal glow as the sun gently made its presence felt. Too weary to savor the beauty of dawn, he focused instead on what he had accomplished—and the countless tasks yet to be done. He had touched base with the Emergency Medical Service unit, with the Night Watch detectives, and with the crime scene folks dispatched from the Bronx. He had written and served subpoenas for several cops at the scene, but there were many more to be served. He would also have to order the 911 tape and leave a message briefing Irene Riley, chief of the trial division.

Mario shifted his satchel from his right to left hand as he nodded a greeting at the doorman and headed into his lobby. His briefcase always felt heavier after the initial work on a case. That was mostly because he was tired, but also because, if only in some metaphorical sense, new information was weighing it down: phone numbers, preliminary statements, impressions gathered from the myriad sources that converge whenever there is a murder in Manhattan.

Though he had not yet spoken to John Wisocki, he already had a very clear picture of the man he would be prosecuting: a lonely, bitter soul, filled with self-pity and hatred, especially of Latinos; a man who blamed everybody but himself for his life being such a mess. His mind flashed back to the note: "I no longer have my job, and I no longer have my dream. I no longer even have a wife. I have lost everything, through no fault of my own." A flicker of pity coursed through him, but was immediately supplanted by loathing. "What a sick, sorry fuck," he mumbled, as he stepped into the elevator.

2

Mario awakened, still clinging to sleep, with a mildly painful throbbing in the back of his head and with eyes that felt as if studded with tiny specks of glass. After less than three hours of fitful slumber, he looked forward to the day ahead about as enthusiastically as he might look forward to getting hit by a bus. Still, he willed himself out of bed and into the bathroom.

Even without looking in the mirror, Mario knew his eyes were bloodshot. Not much he could do about that. He dashed some water in his eyes anyway, and splashed some more on his face. It was a face that, even covered with stubble, was more than passingly attractive. The cheekbones were high and so unyielding they looked as if carved from sandstone. He had his mother's full, expressive lips and his father's wavy, jet-black hair and brown eyes capped with long, curly lashes that virtually flirted on their own. His complexion was marred by pockmarks, which neutralized, in large measure, the prettiness of his features. People, especially women, tended to find him appealing, and he had learned to use that gift to his advantage, particularly when talking to juries.

Shaving and dressing—in the same clothes he had discarded and left hanging on the chair a few hours earlier—took only minutes. Mario tossed down the lukewarm coffee and headed out, grabbing the two daily tabloids at the corner stand en route to the subway.

The subway platform was even muggier than the streets above, so he inhaled with relief when the train doors sprang open and a refreshing air-conditioned breeze spilled out. He gracefully squeezed into a seat a young boy was vacating, leaned back, and closed his eyes, as his mind settled on Felicia. He tried to imagine facing her in court, but his brain would not cooperate. Instead his mind fixed on her long, slim legs, and on the silky texture of her skin pressed against his. "Lord help me," he muttered, opening his eyes.

As Mario exited the subway station and headed north, the aroma of Chinese and Indian spices sweetly caressed his nostrils, causing him, momentarily, to put his anxiety aside. He loved downtown Manhattan, the myriad scents, sounds, and cultures converging to form one gigantic jumble of new possibilities. A few summers ago, while visiting Tio Miguel in Río Piedras, Puerto Rico, he had searched for a phrase to explain the ethnic stew that was New York and had finally settled on *"la ciudad que le roba algo a cada cultura en el mundo y luego la hace mejor."* The cultural total really was so much more than the sum of its parts.

Mario stopped a block short of his office on Hogan Place to contemplate the pronouncement neatly printed on a separate small placard under the Worth Street sign: "Avenue of the Strongest." It had never occurred to him to find out just what the message meant, or who had asked that it be inscribed; but today, he decided to read the words as an omen from God, as a promise that God would be with him, giving him strength for the unpleasant battle that the Wisocki case would surely become.

The car service limousine dropped Felicia at Hogan Place and Centre Street, a few steps from the front of the building that housed the district attorney and the arraignment courts. For several seconds she stood outside, gazing at the ongoing parade—a boy on Rollerblades, another dribbling a basketball, hordes of bustling professionals in business suits. She smiled as she glanced at the bushes outside the building. Every day, long before nightfall, that foliage would be loaded with hidden weapons, the greenery having become a garbage dump of opportunity for thugs who came to be arraigned and realized, upon approaching the building, that they would never make it armed through the metal detectors. Once or twice a day, court officers sifted the bushes, prospecting for knives, brass knuckles, and the occasional gun. A nice resale business could be put together simply distributing their recovered weapons.

She looked up at the tall, dingy, stone-faced structure whose surface was studded with air-conditioning units, and was briefly transported to the time, a few years back, when that building was the center of her world.

Her time as an assistant district attorney had helped her to realize just how privileged her life had been—just as much of her previous life had driven home the magnitude of her deprivations. Not that she came from especially humble circumstances, but she had been consistently outclassed at the Holbrook School. Most of her fellow students in the Chevy Chase, Maryland–based institution were second-, third-, or fourth-generation gentry, whereas her own parents, who worked as civil servants, had come of age in poverty. They took pride in the fact they had risen into the middle class and could send their only child to an exclusive, all-girls prep school.

Holbrook had taught her she would never totally rise above her origins. It had shown her the difference that breeding—or, more accurately, background—could make. The rich kids were no smarter than she, but they arrived knowing the world was theirs, and that there was nothing in it they could not have. Bright and driven as Felicia was, she realized that she could never compete on their terms; for their fathers owned the clubs she would be begging to make her a member.

By the time she entered Harvard, she had made a strategic choice. Since she could never win at the insider's game, she was exempt from their rules. So she would use her insider credentials—Holbrook, Harvard, and later New York University Law School—to demand a seat at the table, and then use any trick her conscience would accept to walk away a winner.

Felicia flashed her ID and walked into the building. She had learned from an ex-colleague in the DA's office that Mario would be standing up on the case. That news had brought a certain amount of suspense. She was curious to see whether marriage had changed him, whether he had begun to put on weight, whether he was less intense, and whether he was still angry with her. His courtroom presentation would be thoroughly professional. He would die before he would betray any hint of personal involvement, but he was an intensely passionate man who could not always hide his emotions.

Felicia slid into the clerk's office outside the felony arraignments courtroom where she quietly filled out the notice of appearance, an official form that would set in motion Wisocki's transfer from the holding pens in the basement to the smaller pen behind the judge's bench in the courtroom. "Almost show time," she whispered, as she straightened her red Jean-Paul Gaultier "TV suit."

As she strode purposefully into the courtroom, Felicia stared straight ahead, silently taking notice of the substantial press presence and of the whispers that her entrance had provoked. A photographer rose and snapped her picture. A reporter began to approach, but she waved him away, and he rejoined his sundry colleagues in the front row. A television videocamera had been set up near the front, a few feet away from the heavy removable chain that separated the spectators from the action.

The judge, a relatively young ex-prosecutor named Dorothy Phillips, was listening closely to the arguments of a legal aid lawyer as the assistant district attorney stood silent. The scene was illuminated by huge rectangular overhead lights, which, despite their harshness, could not altogether compensate for the lack of light from the perennially dirty windows. On normal days the courtroom—with its stark lighting, plain wooden benches, office-blue furniture, and humorless functionaries—seemed much like a factory, a place where idealistic fantasies of jurisprudence gave way to the reality of assembly-line justice; but today, at least to Felicia, the courtroom had the feel of a theater.

Felicia squeezed into the front row, taking time to smile a greeting at several of the reporters she recognized. She was under no illusion that they had come for her; they had come for her client, but since she was his voice, that amounted to the same thing. The arraignments paralegal, whose presence she acknowledged with a nod, was familiar—a gregarious black woman who had been extremely helpful during Felicia's days as an ADA. Mario had not yet appeared, but it was only a matter of time.

For several minutes, Felicia sat on the bench, tuning out the proceedings before her, rerunning in her mind last night's brief meeting with Wisocki. With his balding head, round, delicate chin, and thin lips, which seemed to fade into his face, he appeared both mournful and kind. He looked—or would in the eyes of a jury—not at all like a murderer. That was something to be very thankful for, given that juries generally paid more attention to appearances than they did to the facts of a case.

Felicia glanced around the courtroom, and spotted Mike a few seats back to her left. Apparently true to his word, Mike had by his side a white-haired woman she presumed to be Wisocki's mom. Given Wisocki's brief synopsis of the state of his marriage, she had thought it better to leave the wife alone—for now—but had called the mother first thing in the morning. After recovering from her initial shock, Mom had quickly agreed to come and Mike had promised to pick her up.

Felicia slid out of her seat, waving back a reporter who seemed poised to follow, and took a seat next to Mike. In whispered tones, Mike introduced Felicia to Wisocki's mother, who was wearing a dark brown suit that seemed much too heavy for the summer heat.

Felicia took the old woman's hand in hers and said, "Your presence here is more important than you can conceivably imagine. Thank you so much for coming." The woman, who seemed to be on the verge of tears, squeezed her hand in return.

Sweetly smiling, Felicia smoothly freed herself from Mrs. Wisocki's grip, rose, and walked to the front of the courtroom. Steeling herself for the meeting with her new client, she slipped through the chain barrier and flashed her ID, before walking through the door to the judge's far left where the holding pen was located.

As she slid into the booth and called out Wisocki's name, she imagined herself on the other side of the thick metal mesh divider. If she narrowed her field of vision enough and blocked out the bodies lounging around in the cell behind the partition, she could believe, at least for a moment, that she was the one in the cage; and she could feel, if only dimly, the sense of forlornness incarceration engendered. She thought back to Wisocki's despondent expression of several hours ago. A night in jail and in various prisoner transport vehicles would not have put him in a better frame of mind.

Wisocki appeared and slipped into the seat on the other side of the booth. He seemed about as comfortable in his new environment as a Brooks Brothers suit salesman at a nudist camp. His jumpiness, she suspected, had much to do with his new associates—low-level thugs and hustlers—in the holding cell.

"Thank you for coming," he said, his voice quivering.

"I promised I would be here," said Felicia. "We won't have much time before the arraignment, but that's fine. We'll have plenty of time to talk later. The arraignment, as I told you, is pretty much a formality. They are going to read the charges against you. They will offer you a chance to appear before the grand jury. And they will set bail and a court date. That's about it. It's all pretty much pro forma, except for the details."

She paused before going on, steeling herself for what she had to say next. "Before, I wouldn't let you talk because I knew the cops were listening," she said. "Here things are a bit more private. And I need to know, before we go on, what happened last night in that office."

John nodded, as he nervously clenched and opened his fists. "I'm not totally sure, myself, Miss Fontaine . . . I . . . I do know that I didn't mean to shoot Francisco. It was . . . Jesus, it was a nightmare. I went there . . . and you have to believe this. I went there. I mean, I took a gun because I was depressed and . . . I—"

"A gun from where?"

"I got it from a friend, for protection. A couple of years ago I was beat up pretty bad. A couple of men robbed me on the street and . . . well, they left me in pretty bad shape. I was in the hospital for two days."

"Fine. Go on. About last night."

"I went there. It was late, after eight, maybe nine. And I . . . Everything seemed so screwed up. I just wanted to . . . You know, it's like my life was kind of ending anyway."

"Meaning?"

"Everything seemed so hopeless. I've spent eight years at Computertronics. Everybody will tell you, I'm the best trainer they've got. Anyway, they were getting ready to give me the boot . . . And when García—"

"Francisco García?"

"Right."

"And what's his relation to you?"

"Francisco? He was the man who . . . Jesus, I didn't mean to shoot him. He wasn't supposed to be there . . . I . . . Anyway, Francisco walked in. I had the gun. The gun was . . . uh . . . Francisco sort of . . . I mean, he figured out right away what was going on. I begged him to leave, but he wouldn't. He kept coming at me. He—we—he tried to take the gun. He kept pulling on it, and it, it just went off. It . . . and . . . God. It was horrible. It—"

Felicia murmured, "Take it easy. Take a deep breath. I'm with you. Your note, assuming the papers got it right, hints at some kind of corporate policy that benefited García. Is that the way you see things?"

John nodded, his expression glum. "They—the new owners— had some kind of . . . Well, I guess what they call a diversity program. Francisco was a part of it."

"You mean you believe he was kept on just because he was Hispanic?"

John cringed, shame spreading across his face. "I'm . . . I mean, I'm for everybody. I . . . What, I mean, is I don't . . . I'm not a prejudiced person. I have nothing against the Spanish, or anybody else. It's just that. Well, I mean, I did have a lot more experience than he. And, well . . . Like I said, I'm not prejudiced or anything, but, well, bottom line, I think I was better qualified than he was. And, I mean, I even heard he was up for promotion."

"You said you're separated from you wife, right?"

"Kind of. We're sort of separated. Not official, but—"

"How long?"

"Well, earlier this year she moved out. But . . . she's still my wife."

"Good. I'll be in touch with her. I don't think it'll be too hard showing her why it's in her best interest to help out. By the way, I took the liberty of having Mike bring your mother down. As I told you, it's important to show the judge that your family is behind you."

Frank nodded, his face gloomier than ever. "I want you to know, Miss Fontaine, that I appreciate what you're doing. Also, I hope you understand, I really didn't mean to kill Francisco. I didn't mean to kill anybody. I mean . . . I've always—"

"I think I understand," said Felicia. "The district attorney won't be half so understanding. You know, it's not their job to believe you're innocent. They automatically assume you're guilty. They're going to do their damnedest to show that you set out to kill García and that you then cooked up a cockamamie story about an attempted suicide. They're going to charge you with murder two, a weapons charge, and God knows what else. In their eyes, you are worse than scum. You're going to have to help me prove them wrong. How are you feeling, by the way?"

"I've felt better," he said, managing a smile. "But this place. I mean, these guys. There are a lot of scary, creepy people in here. How long . . . I mean, when can you get me out of here?"

Felicia grimaced and shrugged, making her best effort to look sympathetic. "I'm not going to bullshit you, John. You may be here for a while. I'm going to do everything I can to get you out. But the DA is going to play hardball. They are going to try to make you out as a cold-blooded murderer. I know that's not how you see it, but, to be blunt about it, they don't give a damn. They have a body, they have the press kicking up a fuss, and they have a political angle. Some guy on radio is already calling this the affirmative action murder. They need a villain, and, as far as they are concerned, you're it."

A look of stupefaction swept across John's face. "Wha . . . What? It was an accident. I—"

"I know, John, and it's our job to convince them of that. I'm on your side, dear. One way or another, we'll get through this. If we can't get you out of here right away, we can certainly make sure that no one does you harm. I understand you're scared. There's nothing wrong with that. But you're going to have to keep yourself together. Can you handle it?"

"I guess I have to," he said, blinking furiously as he suddenly wiped his hand across his eyes.

When the call came, Mario was seated at his desk, looking, for the umpteenth time, through the Criminal Justice Agency report on Wisocki. No priors. No outstanding warrants. At his current address forever. At his current job nearly as long. Not a hell of a lot to work with. Had the crime been anything less serious than murder, no judge in New York would have denied Wisocki bail. But it was murder, and no sane judge, least of all Dorothy Phillips, would be so foolish as to set him free, particularly when the press stood ready to pounce.

He glanced at the *Inquirer*, which lay open to page five. A banner headline across Jake O'Hare's "Streetlife" column asked DID "DIVERSITY" KILL FRANCISCO GARCÍA? The *Daily Journal* had covered it in a front-page news story: LAYOFF LEADS TO VIOLENT DEATH. Well, press or no press, he had to make the argument, and he had to face Felicia. Mario pushed his papers in his satchel and headed down.

He spotted Felicia the moment he entered the courtroom. She was seated in the front row, as striking in her bright red suit as a rose in a field of lilies. She was turned slightly to the side, intently focusing on some papers in her lap. Her face, or what he could see of it, seemed as delicate and beautiful as ever. He did not allow his eyes to linger, but, ignoring his racing heart, walked quickly and decisively past the spectators' section and took his place behind the barrier, next to his colleague handling arraignments, and turned his attention to the case.

Certain prosecutors, Mario supposed, might have been somewhat sympathetic to Wisocki. He didn't, after all, fit the profile of a typical felon. He seemed so desperately unhappy, so distraught, so out of his element, that the prospect of beating up on him in court seemed almost sadistic. But he had certainly done the crime. And something in Mario rejoiced at the prospect of prosecuting a middle-class white guy, particularly one who seemed so bitter and odious. He was tired of looking into faces that reminded him of his childhood and sending people to jail who had never had much of a chance at a decent life. With so many black and brown people going through hell in this city, why should Wisocki get any sympathy from him? He thought again of Wisocki in his cell last night, and of his visceral reaction to the man—and he again felt like wringing Wisocki's throat.

As Felicia waited for the case to be called, she studied Mario's profile. She had always thought he had a strikingly noble carriage and a silhouette that belonged on a coin. Had he not wished to work, Mario no doubt could have made a living on his looks, and left a string of lovesick women in his wake. She looked away from Mario and recalled the anxious, miserable face of her newest client.

She tried to put herself in John's mind. His resentment of Computertronics and Infotect, she easily understood. For she, too, hated being disregarded as an individual and being treated merely as a member of a race. At Harvard, white students with half her brains had routinely questioned her right to be there. If she had not been black, they had said (by their looks if not their words), she would not be at an Ivy League institution. Many professors were no better. One she had gone to for assistance in calculus had smiled broadly and said, "Why, Felicia, you're doing perfectly fine. You don't need any help." She had stormed out in a fury. From her perspective, he might as well have said, "We don't expect black girls to make anything better than a B. Begone and be happy."

She had found attitudes much the same in law school, and at the white-shoe Washington law firm where she had interned for a summer. Though she and Wisocki saw the problem from different angles, she did not doubt that they sipped from the same pool of frustration. But was that frustration enough to make him kill a man? She doubted it, and, for the moment at least, would take him at his word.

She glanced at the bench near the holding pens and noted that Wisocki had been brought out. A few minutes, she reckoned, as she glanced at the judge.

It was her bad luck that Dorothy Phillips was presiding. A former assistant district attorney who had never psychologically left her old office, Phillips was notorious for favoring prosecutors in felony cases. She also was not the brightest bulb on the bench, nor the most courageous. Getting any break from her today was out of the question.

The court officer called out the docket number and noted the charges. Mario spoke first. "Good morning, Your Honor. Mario Santiago, for the people."

Felicia, after fixing Mario with a lingering, noncommittal stare, cleared her throat and in a loud, clear voice said, "Good morning, Your Honor. Felicia Fontaine appearing for Mr. Wisocki. We waive the reading of the rights and charges." She also served notice of John's intent to appear before the grand jury—a right she could later decide not to exercise if testifying seemed not to be in his best interest.

"The people serve felony grand jury notice," announced Mario. "The people also serve statement notice. At the time and place of arrest, the defendant, in substance, told arresting officers Jack Kelly and Dave Strachan that he had fired the gunshots that resulted in the death of Francisco García. The defendant also made written statements, copies of which will be provided to the defense with the people's Voluntary Disclosure Form." Given that the "suicide note" had already appeared in the press, the promise, though proper, was essentially meaningless, as Mario well knew. He then proceeded to lay out his argument, briefly describing what he called "a violent, callous, coldly calculated murder" and strongly argued against bail. "The defendant has committed a bloody, heinous crime as casually as a camper might flick away a fly. He admits to firing not one but two bullets and to shooting a human being—a man with whom he worked—totally without provocation. The weapon has been recovered and the defendant has, in effect, confessed. He has shown little remorse and is demonstrably unstable. He is a desperate man, without a job, without close community ties, who is likely to flee the jurisdiction. The people are requesting that the defendant be remanded. In the event that bail is set, we ask that it be set at a reasonably high level, at least two million dollars."

"Your Honor," Felicia forcefully interjected, "I respectfully submit that 'the people' have taken leave of their senses. I request that you release my client on his own recognizance. As the court is aware, Mr. Wisocki has no criminal record. In fact, he has never previously been arrested in his life. The prosecutor can search heaven and hell and will not find as much as a jaywalking conviction attached to his name. We're talking here about John Wisocki—not John Dillinger. No job? That's simply not true. (Felicia saw no purpose in acknowledging that the job would soon evaporate.) And he is certainly not a candidate for flight. As we all know, he did not run last night when he had the chance. Instead, he—my client—called the police. If he did not flee then, he certainly will not flee now. He waited at the scene and cooperated. If the people seriously believe he might abscond, my client would be willing to surrender his passport, and even to consider some arrangement that would constrict or monitor his movements; but there is absolutely no reason to keep him in jail. He has deep ties to this city, and to his community. His mother, as you can see, is here in court, seated in the third row. If Your Honor would permit it, I would ask Mrs. Sophie Wisocki to please stand."

Felicia turned dramatically to face the courtroom and, smiling encouragingly, motioned to Mrs. Wisocki to rise. The old woman, assisted by Mike, slowly rose to her feet, and energetically waved her right hand high over her head.

"Yes, I see you. Thank you, very much," the judge said icily to Mrs. Wisocki. "You may be seated now."

Felicia went on for several minutes more, portraying Wisocki as an utterly decent and innocent man victimized by an evil corporation. "No conceivable purpose would be served," she concluded, "by keeping him in jail."

A smile danced across Judge Phillips's lips as she spoke. "Thank you. The court will remand the defendant."

"Your Honor," Felicia said, "in light of the special circumstances surrounding this case, the huge and unfavorable publicity it has already received, and the easily understandable emotional distress of my client, I request a suicide watch and protective custody for my client."

The judge glanced at Wisocki and shrugged. "I am marking the papers to so indicate. The case is adjourned."

Felicia had already tuned the judge out. She stared at the inchoate smile forming on Mario's obviously tired face, and acknowledged it with a slight bow. As she watched his hand rise slowly to his chin—a nervous tic she recalled from years ago—she whispered to herself, "This is only the beginning, lover."

3

Never having prosecuted a high-profile case, Mario had not realized how profoundly the news media altered everything they covered. Since John Wisocki had fallen into his lap, he felt forced to peer into a parallel universe, one over which he had no control. In that universe dwelt versions of himself and Wisocki that bore no resemblance to what he considered reality. He was a taciturn prosecutor whose favorite phrase was "no comment." And Wisocki could be just about anything: a raging bigot, a hapless victim, a wrongly displaced worker who had finally gone over the edge. To some demented souls, he had even become a hero. Jake O'Hare, the columnist for the *Inquirer*, seemed determined to make Wisocki into a symbol of righteous indignation over social policies run amok.

Mario plucked the latest *Inquirer* from a pile of papers on his desk, and skimmed O'Hare's column. Wisocki's tragic plight was "a warning to all who would make a mockery of the concept of merit," proclaimed O'Hare. "Who needs this garbage?" muttered Mario, as he flung the newspaper into the wastebasket. The *Journal*, to his horror, had been even worse. Citing an unnamed source, it claimed that Mario had boasted in the precinct, "We're going to kick this guy's ass. A slam dunk," in reference to Wisocki.

Mario tried to concentrate on his upcoming grand jury presentation, but instead of focusing on the names of his witnesses and a summary of the physical evidence, his mind flashed back to last night's news. Channel 3 had presented a long feature on Wisocki, interviewing childhood friends, neighbors, and anyone else producers could find who claimed a connection, however tenuous, to the man of the moment. They had been unified in their description of him as a shy, studious saint who wouldn't harm a fly. The reporter's conclusion had been stunning in its banality. "Who knows," she had uttered, staring sorrowfully into the camera, "whether any of us, under similar circumstances, might follow in John Wisocki's footsteps."

Channel 10 had been equally idiotic. Their reporter, camped outside the home of García's widow, had prattled endlessly about the "unimaginable pain that has plagued this noble immigrant family." "Where do they get that shit?" Mario asked himself.

Part of the answer, he supposed, rested with Felicia. She had always known how to work the press and had never been averse to planting stories favorable to her clients. And the Wisocki case was tailor-made for her talents. Glib, attractive, spirited, self-righteous—she was everything reporters adored. She was also the most exasperating, and the most exciting, woman he had ever loved. Though Mario did not believe in love at first sight, he had been drawn to Felicia from the moment of their initial encounter.

At the time, she had occupied an office down the hall from where he now worked. She had stepped out into the anteroom to rifle through a huge stack of files precariously stacked in a large cardboard filing cabinet. He had been rushing to a meeting with his boss. So preoccupied had he been that he had nearly run her down, stopping barely in time to avoid a collision, and to mumble an apology.

When he looked up to acknowledge her acceptance, he found himself unable to look away. Mostly to prolong the encounter, he hastened to introduce himself. She was not merely attractive, but appealing in a very sensual way; so much so, that he was forced to thrust his hand into his pocket to hide the too evident evidence of his sudden arousal.

Felicia's keep-your-distance aura and her relatively senior status quashed any notion of sweeping her off her feet. For several months they warily circled each other, neither exactly expressing interest, but managing to cross each other's paths much too often to attribute it all to coincidence. At the office Christmas party, held in a historic refurbished mansion, they had finally crossed the line. They kissed, after toasting the future; a kiss so ardent that it melted the wall of reserve—behind which lay passion powerful enough to reduce them both to tears.

From his pocket, Mario pulled a slip of paper on which he had written her name and office phone number. Since the arraignment, he had carried it with him, certain he would have an occasion to use it. He was somewhat disappointed, and yet also relieved, that the opportunity had not yet come.

The door flew open and María Cristina breezed in, a dazzling vision in a white pantsuit. "How goes it, honey?" she asked, flashing a huge smile.

"Bad question," he replied, stuffing Felicia's number back into his shirt pocket.

Mario and María Cristina had met four years ago, shortly after her arrival as a rookie assistant. He had been assigned to talk to her class about evidence as part of the orientation for new ADAs. Her dark, attractive features and her name—María Cristina Balboa—had led him to assume she was Mexican American. During a break, when he had approached her and began chatting away in Spanish, she had grinned and replied, "Sorry. *No hablo español.*"

Too embarrassed for a graceful recovery, he had beamed sheepishly and mumbled, "Oh. I had just assumed that you would."

"It's a common mistake," she had replied. "Balboa comes from my father, who is Filipino. My mom's Latvian. And I'm, well, glad to meet you." That encounter had led to dinner and, two-plus years later, to marriage.

"What's the problem?" she asked, depositing herself in the armchair in front of his desk.

"No real problem. I'm just ticked off at the press spin on this thing. You'd think, from some of this shit they're coming up with, that this guy deserved a medal. And then there's this nutty quote they're attributing to me."

"I know. But you can't let it get to you."

"Yeah, but it would be nice to be able to respond. It's frustrating as hell. My name is being bandied about, and there's not a damn thing I can do except call up the guy I believe leaked this inaccurate bullshit and give him hell. Meanwhile the press reports any damn thing it feels like, never mind whether it's true. And Felicia Fontaine. Why is she involved in this, anyway? I can't figure out her angle."

"You never could, from what I can tell," she said. "Jeez, honey. Her interest is as clear as day. She's a media whore and this case is getting her major, major TV coverage. You're a brilliant man, baby, but you do have your blind spots."

"But even Felicia—"

"She's a whore, Mario. End of story."

"Yeah, I suppose," he mumbled, thinking it wise to change the subject. "You know, I have a meeting with Mrs. García later this afternoon. She seems like a very sweet person."

"How's she holding up?"

"I'm not really sure. She's been through one hell of a lot in the past few days. It's bad enough to have your husband murdered, but then to have all this weird attention from the press. And, of course, she has to explain it all to the little girl. What a mess."

The phone rang. Mario picked it up and immediately placed the voice as one of his investigators.

"Hey, Enrique. *¿Que se cuenta?* What's up?"

"A lot. There's a very interesting story floating around about Wisocki. If you're not sitting, take a seat. I need to fill you in."

The maître d' at Smith & Wollensky, the ritzy East Side steak house where politicians dined to be seen, greeted Felicia effusively before showing her to her table. Her lunch date, Jake O'Hare, was already seated. He rose as she approached and, in an exaggerated show of gallantry, took her hand and lightly grazed it with his lips. "Finally, we meet in person," he said. "The pleasure is most definitely mine. Is it all right if I call you Felicia?"

"Of course." She smiled, delicately withdrawing her hand. She noticed that he had already finished half his glass of red wine. His age, she guessed to be in the mid–thirties, a bit younger than she had expected. He was also somewhat more attractive—albeit, a bit chubby. She had imagined him to be a repulsive, wizened older man, with ill-fitting clothes and a curmudgeon's personality; but with his trim, dark hair, neat mustache, and elegantly cut suit— Paul Stuart, she guessed—Jake seemed intent on looking, and acting, like a big-time operator. In a rather crude way, perhaps he was. In the few seconds it took her to squeeze into her seat, he had managed to wave and call out a genial greeting to people at two separate tables; but he obviously had not quite mastered the art of casually being noticed. There also was an aura of pomposity about him that was out of sync with his relatively hip appearance.

"I didn't realize reporters hung out in such pricey places," she teased.

He grinned. "Occupational hazard. I aced Expense Accounts 101 my first week on the job and have been practicing diligently ever since. It's important to maintain a certain standard when you're courting the rich and famous."

"Well, that excludes me," she said, with a laugh.

"I'm not so sure about that. Seems to me your star is definitely on the rise. The cover of *Manhattan Woman*. A hot court case. You're definitely a poor candidate for obscurity."

"Fair enough."

"Just in case you're not a regular here, they serve plenty of things other than steak. The seafood and the vegetables are excellent. Everything's very fresh. And—"

"Yes, I know. So, to what do I owe the pleasure of this get-together?"

"I'll be very blunt, Felicia. I find the saga of John Wisocki fascinating. And so do other people at the *Inquirer*. His story, on its face at least, is a perfect prism through which to explore some of the most important issues in society today. I think that story needs to be told. And I would like to tell it."

"Are you talking about a series of columns?"

"Maybe something much bigger. At any rate, I think it's in our mutual interest to get to know each other better, and to see where things might lead."

"You realize my client is not making any statements at present."

"Yes, I understand that."

"You should also know that that policy is not going to change. Nor will I be making many statements that can be attributed to him. Most of what we have to say, we'll be saying to a jury and the judge."

"I understand that as well. Nonetheless, I think there may be a way to tell his story."

"I'm not inclined to disagree," she said sweetly, as she turned her attention to the waiter offering a menu.

Felicia had scheduled the press conference even before she'd had lunch with Jake, but their conversation had set her mind humming. The press could never take the place of a good defense, Branegan had told her, "but it sure as hell can help." And Jake had helped to open her eyes to just how much of a player the press was likely to be. In more than one sense, that was a blessing. The DA's office, she knew from her own experience, would remain almost utterly mum. The less said about a case, they assumed, the less chance of getting into trouble. The result was that her side would be the only side the press would hear, other than what they picked up from leaks and in open court. And that, theoretically at least, gave her one hell of an advantage.

Felicia leaned back in her chair and took several deep breaths, struggling to focus her mind. The objective, she reminded herself, was to see to it that everyone understood that this case was primarily about an attempted suicide gone wrong, but also that it was about much more. She glanced at her watch: a quarter to four, fifteen past when the press conference was scheduled to begin. She would give it another ten.

"How do you feel?" The question came from Stephanie Kaufman, her partner, who had poked her head in the office.

"Fine," responded Felicia, "just composing my thoughts."

"I'll leave you alone. Break a leg."

Felicia stared at the wall for several minutes, reviewing the points she intended to make. Then she took a deep breath and rang Tracy on the intercom: "How does it look?"

"You've got about thirty people in there. I think they may be getting a little restless."

"Good."

Felicia pasted her most seductive smile on her face and sauntered down the corridor and into the conference room. She shook hands with several of the reporters she knew as she made her way to the front. The television lights were warm, comforting; she felt as if she were being hugged by a host of luminous angels. She glanced at her watch—four o'clock, plenty of time to make the evening news and the morning papers. Fixing her eyes straight ahead, she cleared her throat and began.

"Thank you for coming, my friends. And let me get right to the reason we're all here. As you know, I am defending John Wisocki, who is tormented beyond words by the turn of events that thrust him into the limelight. Unfortunately, there has been some loose speculation that Mr. Wisocki may be some kind of homicidal lunatic. Nothing could be further from the truth. As you will discover, he is a gentle, caring, normal man, with no criminal record.

"Mr. Wisocki is now behind bars simply for one reason: because, in a fit of despair, he tried to kill himself. He is an innocent man drawn into a tragic event that he had no way of foreseeing. If there is a culprit in this case, it is Infotect, which created the condition that led to the appalling tragedy of the other night. Once the district attorney has an opportunity to fully investigate this matter, he should understand that. It's my expectation that Mr. Wisocki will be vindicated completely. I'll be glad to respond to any questions you may have."

Immediately a cacophony of voices erupted, but one rang out above all the rest: a booming, Spanish-accented baritone belonging to Jesús Gómez, a rangy, pugnacious, investigative reporter for *La Nueva Prensa*.

"If I may, Ms. Fontaine," he shouted at the top of his lungs, and the other reporters grudgingly gave way. "Ms. Fontaine," Gómez continued, "we have heard that the same night Wisocki shot Mr. García, he was seen waving a gun around and menacing two men, who also happened to be Latino, near East Harlem. Would you care to comment on that?"

"Do you know the source of that rumor, Jesús?" she asked, hopeful his question was nothing but a bluff.

"Yes. The men who say Wisocki attacked them have spoken to one of our reporters. We are preparing a story on their charges. I am interested in getting Wisocki's response to them."

Felicia swallowed and waited for the nausea to pass. The hot lights suddenly seemed hostile, evocative of the atmosphere in a police interrogation room. Yet even as her confidence shriveled, Felicia conjured up a smile and smoothly replied, "I'll be glad to provide a comment on that after discussing the matter with my client."

Once Felicia arrived, it took nearly half an hour for the guards to retrieve Wisocki and bring him to the Twelfth Floor Bridge—the secured area in the 100 Centre Street Building where lawyers met their incarcerated clients. All the time, Felicia sat fuming, fury feeding on fury. Had Wisocki not been behind a mesh metal separator, she would have tried to throttle him. Instead, she sat, glaring at him for several seconds, before finally blowing up: "What in the hell is wrong with you?"

His face was a picture of wounded innocence as he stared, uncomprehending, but she continued on the attack. "Why, in the name of God, didn't you tell me about running around pointing a gun at people? Are you totally nuts? This kind of stuff inevitably comes out, John. Why in the world didn't you tell me?"

"Oh. That had nothing . . . I mean, I didn't think it was important. And I wasn't pointing a gun at people. I was pointing one at some hoodlums who were threatening me. I was just trying to protect myself, for God's sake."

"You didn't think it was important. So you're a lawyer now? You're deciding what evidence is relevant. It's not your damn job to decide what's important."

"Look, Miss Fontaine."

"For God's sake, call me Felicia."

"Look, Felicia, I'm not an idiot, all right. I would appreciate it if you would treat me with some respect. I appreciate your being here. And, okay, I made a mistake—a big mistake. I should have told you about that incident. But the fact is, I was just trying to defend myself. What's wrong with that? Let's face facts. I'm obviously not the toughest-looking guy in the world. How else am I supposed to protect myself if not with a weapon."

He took a deep breath as his body rocked to and fro. When he continued, his voice was trembling. "If I hadn't had a gun, I think they might have killed me. They said they were going to. I was scared. Taking out the gun was a last resort. I'm sorry I didn't tell you about it. Obviously, I screwed up. But you don't have to talk to me like a child. You don't have to use that tone with me. I'm a very bright man, but these are not the kinds of things I typically deal with. This is not my world. I'm not in my natural element, all right. So I might come off a little weird. And I might not be so quick to make some connections. But I'm all here. All I'm asking is for some understanding, and a little respect."

"Fine. Fair enough," she said, her anger spent, as she stared at her obviously distraught client. The last thing he needed, frightened and off-balance as he was, was her screaming at him. "I shouldn't have come down on you so hard," she said, softening her voice. "So please forgive me. But the fact is we have some serious damage to repair. So you need to tell me, taking it from the top, exactly what happened that night. Everything." Suddenly conscious of the other lawyers locked in with her in the relatively small meeting space, she smiled self-consciously and added, much more faintly, "And, John, please keep your voice down."

Speaking in a tone barely above a whisper, John methodically recounted, to the best of his ability, the longest Sunday night of his life. In his gray jail-issued jumpsuit and shoelaceless shoes, he had the lonely, timid look of a lost child. Felicia had an impulse to reach out and hug him, and would have, if not for the mesh wall between them. She was glad she had demanded that John be put under suicide watch, glad that he was away from the general population. She wondered whether, if convicted, he could survive in prison. Her job, she reminded herself, was to make certain that things never reached that point.

In a legal sense, the situation was simple. The grand jury would certainly indict him, and with whatever charges—including murder two—that Mario felt like bringing. Then the inexorable march toward a jury trial would begin. The jury would either accept or not accept Wisocki's story about what had happened, and either accept or not accept her explanations for how to understand it; and on that basis, he would either be imprisoned or set free. A case like this, however, raised other questions that had nothing much to do with the law. Many people would find Wisocki hard to take simply because they disagreed with his view of the world. Others would not be able to get over the fact that he had killed a man whom he disliked—or certainly resented—at least partly for racial reasons. Even if she succeeded in making Infotect the enemy—which would not be all that hard—the liberal press would lynch Wisocki and vilify her. Some people already saw her as an ambitious opportunist. She took that to be the price of not fitting the mold, of not being the sort of self-effacing female who went out of her way to put others at ease. Even some former allies would perceive her role in this case as stepping across an invisible line. Instead of giving her points for being an independent thinker, they might denounce her as a traitor.

John had fallen silent and was obviously waiting for a response, which Felicia calmly supplied. "Let me tell you something, John. This is going to be a tough case, but I think we can win it. I wouldn't be here if I didn't. Just promise me, no more surprises."

"I'll do my best."

"By the time this is over, John, total strangers will know who you are. Some of them will hate you. You are on your way to becoming a very famous man. The process will be tremendously exciting, maybe even frightening, but it won't necessarily be pleasant. This trial may be the hardest test you will ever endure. It will change your life in ways you cannot now imagine. It's important that you understand that going in."

"I believe I do, Ms. Fontaine . . . Felicia. I don't expect this to be easy. Lately, not much has been," he said, as a slight smile crossed his lips.

"That's true. But it's also important that you understand that you have a lot going for you. I'm going to be very straight with you. The fact that you're a middle-aged white man callously kicked out on the street can buy you a certain amount of compassion, and we need to milk that for all it's worth. The press and a lot of ordinary people—people like those who sit on juries—will sympathize with your situation, even if they don't approve of your actions.

"Jake O'Hare, at the *Inquirer*, loves you already and Quentin Varner, the *Journal* columnist, calls you 'a human sacrifice to corporate and social engineering'—whatever that means. Jurors read. Judges read. And they aren't going to sequester any juror during the trial phase, not in New York City. During deliberations, maybe. But not while we're making our case. And we'll be making the case not only to the jury but to the press. The more coverage we get, the better, provided it's the right kind of coverage."

She grinned ruefully and added. "The right kind of coverage, incidentally, my friend, is not a surprise report about a client pointing a gun at strangers in the street."

She dismissed her own comment with a wave of her hand as she said, "But I'm sure such surprises are a thing of the past. And as for the future, they really don't have much. Attempted suicide is not a felony. And the fact that García was killed accidentally during your foiled attempt still does not make it a crime. That fact will obviously not stop the DA's office from playing this thing out. At this point, it's hard to say just what they're after. They can't be serious about this murder rap. At least I don't think they are. But they may try to hang you with involuntary manslaughter and reckless endangerment. We will need to inoculate you against responsibility for anything that happened in that office."

"Inoculate? Sounds like you're prepping me for a doctor's appointment," said John, trying to sound a good deal more jocular than he could possibly feel.

"I wish it were so simple," Felicia replied. "Unfortunately, this is not such a neat and easy process. I will need you to understand that, at times, it may get extremely disagreeable, maybe downright dirty."

John nodded, in what Felicia took to be a sign of assent, or at least of comprehension of what she was implying.

"There's no real question of getting bail before the grand jury acts," she said. "After that, we'll see. The indictment will come pretty soon. When a defendant is held on a felony complaint, the authorities only have one hundred and forty-four hours to indict— or show damn good cause why they haven't. Your clock started running Sunday night, and it's soon due to run out.

"In the interim, we have several things we need to discuss. One is money. Another is your wife."

"My wife?" he asked, unable to conceal his astonishment.

"Yep. We're going to have to patch up your marriage. And I have some ideas about how."

The visit to Wisocki and a rash of phone calls from reporters left Felicia no time to focus on more mundane matters, until Stephanie stuck her head in the door and inquired, "Isn't this your tutoring night?"

"Oh shit," replied Felicia, glancing at her watch. Fifteen minutes past seven. "Thanks for the reminder," she mumbled. Flashing a sympathetic smile, Stephanie retreated as swiftly as she had appeared. With a shrug of resignation, Felicia stuffed the papers on her desk into her briefcase and headed for the door.

The weekly tutoring session was one item on her agenda that Felicia held sacrosanct. She had not missed an appointment in the year since she had signed up—after meeting the program's founder at a Gracie Mansion banquet—and was determined not to be late today. Muriel, a high school junior from Washington Heights, had an adolescent's casual approach to time. She could profit, Felicia felt, from an adult example of reliability and punctuality—an example she was not likely to find at home.

From what Felicia could surmise, Muriel's home life was something of a shambles. The father, she gathered, was a former drug dealer who had a hard time holding on to a steady job; the mother, only fifteen years older than Muriel, worked as a supermarket cashier and was the principal source of support for Muriel and her two younger sisters. Neither parent had much of a sense of life's grander possibilities, or of how to foster Muriel's intellectual development. So Felicia had resolved to do what she could to ensure that Muriel did not fall through the cracks, her academic ability stunted by lack of nurturance.

To Felicia's relief, a taxi pulled up as she left the building. Careering though traffic, they made it to the activities center on 106th Street at seven-thirty precisely. Muriel was nowhere to be found. She arrived at five minutes to eight, blue jeans and a sheer blue halter top covering her lanky form.

Felicia fixed her with a chilly stare and snapped, "You must have lost the watch I gave you. Do you have any idea what time it is?"

"Sorry, Miss Fontaine. I was on the phone and—"

"So that makes it all right to sashay in here a half hour late?"

"I didn't mean to be late," she sputtered, twisting her mouth into a pout. "Anyway, I said I was sorry. I mean, this isn't like school or something."

"That's my point," said Felicia, trying hard not to sound prissy, "this is exactly like school *or something*." She sighed and added, "I wouldn't be so bothered, if I didn't believe this was important. This is not just about my having to wait. And it's not just about you getting a better grade in English. It's about not getting in the way of your own success. I know this may not make much sense to you, but believe me, these little rules matter, more than you can imagine. Trust me on this, Muriel. If I didn't care about you, if I didn't believe in you, I wouldn't ride you the way I do. But if you're not serious, I'm just wasting my time. And I don't have time to waste."

"But I am serious, Miss Fontaine."

"So that means you won't be late again."

"I don't think so."

"You don't *think* so?"

"No. I won't."

"You won't what?"

"I won't be late."

"Good. So let's take a look at that English paper of yours. Did you stick with Alice Walker?"

"Yeah, I did. But I'm not sure I totally understood it."

"Well, let's see what we have here," said Felicia, taking the paper from Muriel's hand.

4

In more than a decade as a prosecutor, Mario had learned the futility of trying to make sense out of death's judgments. The one consolation, when it came to murder at least, was that more bad people than good people made themselves into targets. Nonetheless, decent people, innocent people, died every day. Fairness didn't necessarily enter the equation. Knowing that did not make García's death any easier to take.

At García's wake, which Mario had attended with Detective O'Rourke (who, en route, denied responsibility for the "kick this guy's ass" leak to the press), Mario found himself deeply depressed. How could God allow a loser like Wisocki to assassinate someone like García?—who, it was obvious from the hundreds who came to mourn him, was a good and well-loved man.

On his way out, Mario hugged Mrs. García and promised to be in touch. Friday he called and made a date for Sunday. That visit to her home was his third time seeing her and the second seeing her five-year-old daughter, Blanca—who grinned ecstatically when he handed her a lollipop as he came through the door.

The apartment, in a brownstone in Chelsea, was comfortingly familiar. It reminded him of so many of his own relatives' homes. The porcelain knickknacks strewn throughout the living room were virtually identical to those collected by his maternal grandmother. The intricate lace curtains could have been taken from his Tía Elsa's place.

Isabel García showed Mario to the kitchen, where she served him cookies and coffee and asked straightaway, "Can you tell me what will happen to the man who killed my husband?"

"I expect we'll be able to get a conviction."

"He deserves to die," she shot back with unexpected fervor.

"I would very much like to tell you that was going to happen. I can't. But what I can promise you is that I will do everything in my power to make sure he spends a long, long time in jail. By the time this is all over with, he will surely wish he was dead."

She nodded grimly. "He deserves worse, but I guess that will have to do. That man, when he killed my husband, he put a bullet in me, right through my heart."

"I'm sorry," said Mario. "I know he was a good man."

"He was my heart," she said, dabbing at her eyes.

"How did you meet?" asked Mario.

Mrs. García smiled, wiping a tear away. "At City University. We both came from Bogotá, but we met in New York. That was fifteen years ago, and we fell in love."

For much of the next two hours, as Blanca's giggles periodically issued from the living room where she was watching a video, Isabel reminisced about Francisco and their lives together—years spent redefining themselves and rediscovering their love as they strove to fulfill their American dream.

When night fell, Mrs. García thanked Mario for his time and for caring. As he rose to leave, she grasped his hand tightly and pleaded in Spanish, "Please don't let that evil man get off." Then she released Mario and walked him to the door, bidding him farewell with a subdued *Que Dios le bendiga.* It was a customary blessing, one that he regularly heard—in its familiar variant—from his mother, but in Isabel García's mouth it took on the character of a personal prayer. Mario smiled diffidently and swore to himself not to let her down.

The Best Defense

* * *

Felicia read the indictment—murder in the second degree (two counts) and criminal possession of a weapon in the second degree—as a study in indecisiveness. Mario was out for blood, but he was also playing it safe. That he was asking the jury to decide between two different theories of murder meant he was uncertain he could prove either one. That he was throwing in the weapons charge meant that he was further hedging his bet; even if he couldn't get a murder conviction he didn't intend to walk away empty-handed. His strategy, she suspected, reflected pressure from above. With so much press coverage, the eighth floor would be demanding a conviction, even if it was on a less serious charge.

Given the involvement of his bosses and given Mario's own stubborn streak, Felicia suspected the odds of cutting a good deal were virtually nil. Mario would want a scalp to show for his efforts, and she was not prepared to offer him one. Still, she felt compelled to reach out to him, to see what sort of plea he would be willing to consider. Any good defense lawyer, she told herself, would do the same. Yet, professionally correct as contacting Mario might be, a good part of her motivation was personal. She wanted to see him up close, to determine whether the fires still burned.

The intercom buzzed and Tracy informed her that she had Mario on the line.

"I seem to remember a time when you placed your own calls," said Mario. "I guess you've really risen in the world."

"I don't know about that," Felicia replied, struggling to sound casual. "It just seems to be a little more efficient this way."

"So, to what do I owe the honor?"

"I could just be calling to say hello," she said.

He laughed. "And I could be the king of Spain."

"Truth be told, I was thinking we should talk about our case, explore whether we can avoid a trial," said Felicia.

"I see," he said, his tone totally noncommittal. "Well, my door is always open."

"Is it?" she asked in a voice that was not quite flirtatious but nonetheless hinted at possibilities beyond the matter at hand.

They sparred for a few minutes more before making a date; and when Felicia replaced the receiver, she realized that she was breathing more rapidly than normal and that she had unconsciously been flexing the muscles in her legs. *This case is definitely going to be interesting,* she thought. For if her history with Mario hadn't complicated things enough, the press coverage surely had.

Working with so many reporters buzzing around was like trying to function on a movie set, where any phrase could be picked up, distorted, and amplified by a thousand mikes. Even Tanya, the paralegal, was unnerved.

The only person in the office who spoke Spanish, Tanya—after hearing Wisocki slammed on Spanish-language radio following his arrest—had voiced an objection to having a "racist killer" as a client. As Felicia walked through the door Monday morning, Tanya greeted her with *La Nueva Prensa* and with her best "didn't I tell you?" look. A huge picture of Wisocki was on the front page, along with a startling headline: ASESINO AMENAZÓ DOS LATINOS CON PISTOLA. The story, as Tanya explained it, suggested that Wisocki was a paranoid, gun-crazed, Latino-hating killer. An accompanying front-page editorial jumped to the editorial page, where it ran alongside an English translation. One paragraph grabbed Felicia's attention:

"It is the good fortune of the Latino community that the Manhattan DA's office has a strong Puerto Rican prosecutor fighting on our behalf. Mario Santiago, according to published reports, has promised to 'kick Wisocki's ass.' We may not approve of Counselor Santiago's graphic language, but we heartily endorse his sentiments."

Felicia shook her head. "So this is why we have freedom of the press," she murmured.

A freelance investigator she sometimes used had alerted her over the weekend that the story would be in Monday's paper, but he was confident they could easily knock it down. "It's thinly sourced," he had said, "like most of their stuff." Not that she was particularly concerned about the Spanish-language press. But she wanted to preclude any possibility of the story being picked up by the so-called mainstream media.

She rang Tracy on the intercom. "Get me Hector González, please. After that, I need to talk to Jake O'Hare. And could you call and confirm the meeting tomorrow morning with Linda Wisocki. Then call Frank and tell him I'm going to be late for dinner. This is going to be one crazy day."

Whoever it was who said a prosecutor could indict a ham sandwich was not too far from the truth, mused Mario. The real work was not in convincing a grand jury—where, after all, the prosecutor ran the show—but in proving a case in court against serious opposition. Felicia had some very large flaws. That they were no longer together was, in his mind at least, evidence of that fact. Yet numerous as her flaws might be, inability to persuade jurors was not among them. She was one of the best lawyers he had ever met. To forget that, or to let his continuing—though stifled—attraction toward her interfere with his handling of the case, would be tantamount to courting prosecutorial malpractice.

Irene Riley, chief of the trial division, had already given him heat when he had pushed for dropping the weapons charge. "At least that way we get him for something," she had said.

"I don't want him for *something*," Mario had replied, "I want the bastard for the murder he committed. To give them the weapons charge is to give them the option of compromising by convicting on the lesser charge. If I can't get him on murder, I don't need to be doing this job."

Riley had remained unmoved, insisting, in her quietly infuriating way, that they indict on every charge they could, including criminal possession of a weapon. She had also questioned his objectivity, citing his prior relationship with Felicia. "That will have nothing to do with how I try the case. If anything it gives me an edge, since I know how she thinks," he had assured Riley. The words sounded hollow even to Mario, who doubted he could ever be truly objective as far as Felicia was concerned. Nonetheless, his arguments, or perhaps his passion, had backed her off; but he was clearly on notice that the bosses were watching.

Earlier this morning he had been summoned to District Attorney Richard Schneiderman's eighth-floor office—a sumptuous sanctum that bore roughly the same resemblance to his own office as J. C. Penney did to Neiman-Marcus. There Schneiderman had presided over a combination pep talk and strategy session. Several of Schneiderman's key lieutenants had attended, including the bureau chief, the press spokeswoman, and Riley. Schneiderman had not delivered any edicts, but he did make two things clear: that he didn't want the office embarrassed and that Wisocki—as part of any plea bargain offer—should serve serious time.

To Mario's exasperation, Schneiderman refused to consider allowing the office to issue a statement denying the "kick this guy's ass" remark. "Once you start confirming or denying things, you inevitably get drawn into the press's game," he pronounced. "We make our cases in court, not in the pages of the *Daily Journal*." On Mario's way out, Schneiderman had placed his hand on the younger man's shoulder and somberly advised, "Remember, García's widow is depending on us."

There was no chance that he would forget. Mario was haunted by her sorrow, by the desperation in her voice, and by the laughter of her little girl. He resolved to carry the image of Blanca in his head until Wisocki was convicted of murder.

The phone rang and even as he picked it up, Mario knew it would be the guard, telling him Felicia had arrived. "Send her in," Mario ordered and braced himself for the emotional impact. He hastily cleared some papers from his desk and positioned himself by his office door. Felicia appeared seconds later, in a stylish dark blue dress just tight enough to show off her svelte figure.

"Well," she said, taking in the clutter of the outer office, "I see this place is as ratty-looking as ever."

Mario shrugged and replied, "Yep. I suppose it is. One of these days all these old files are going to tumble over and set off an earth-quake."

Felicia grinned as she walked into his office. "The earthquakes I remember occurring in this place had nothing to do with legal files," she said. "As I recall, we set off tremors on more than one occasion on the purple sofa in my old digs. I'm not sure my back has recovered yet from those evenings on the couch."

Mario blushed as he closed the door, uncomfortable with the turn the conversation had taken. His mind flashed back to a very late evening, years ago, when, overcome with desire, they had ravished each other in Felicia's office. That no one had discovered them had only emboldened them to do it twice more, each time disrobing just enough to facilitate their objective. The lovemaking had been fast, frenzied, exhilarating—their senses heightened by the need for vigilance. If not exactly romantic, it had been exceptionally erotic, and was in no danger of being forgotten.

"That was a long time ago," Mario finally said, reminding himself of his earlier resolution to stay focused on the Wisocki case.

"Yes, a real long time ago," agreed Felicia. Nothing with Frank, or anyone else, had quite matched the intensity of that period with Mario; and perhaps, she told herself, that was for the better.

Felicia smiled ruefully. "Too bad when we finally do get together again, it's for official business."

"The unavoidable fact," Mario said evenly, "is that's the only kind of business we have."

"Touché. I guess I had that coming."

"I didn't mean—" he began and cut himself off. No point, he reminded himself as he fidgeted behind his desk, of lingering any longer in the past.

Felicia repositioned herself in the armchair, delicately placing one leg over the other. She waited several seconds for Mario to continue his thought but was rewarded only with silence. Finally she spoke again.

"Getting down to business, Mario. Don't you think it was a little much indicting on two counts of murder?"

"Not really," he replied, suddenly sounding sure of himself. "Wisocki obviously committed murder, with full intent to do so, but the grand jury, in its wisdom, wanted to provide alternatives. If we don't get him on intent, we get him on depraved indifference. Either way, he loses, which is the way it ought to go."

"So what kind of offer are you prepared to make my client?"

"Wasn't it you who once said, 'I don't make offers on violent crimes'? Murder seems plenty violent to me. But just for the sake of discussion, what do you have in mind?"

"I could live with criminally negligent homicide."

"Be real, Felicia," he said, grinning sardonically. "Going from an A to an E felony?"

"So dismiss the murder charges and we deal on CPW in the second degree. Criminal possession is a C and—"

"Whoa, honey. The old man would have to sign off on that one, as you know. And there's about as much chance of that as of me being elected mayor."

"Maybe your political future is better than you think, love," said Felicia. "Anyway, you can't prove either one of your murder theories. Why embarrass yourself in court? I'll tell you what, talk to the old man, drop the murder stuff, and we go from CPW to reckless endangerment. You get to claim victory, and everybody's happy."

Mario laughed, shaking his head in apparent wonderment. "Reckless endangerment? That's not an offer, that's unconditional surrender. That gets him, what, probation? Why not just give him bus fare home and let him go right now? Be serious. If I was to consider a plea, it would have to be to a real felony with some real time, not some reckless endangerment nonsense."

"Manslaughter?"

"First degree?"

"Second."

"Not in this life. Think about it. Manslaughter One gets you down to a B felony."

"That still amounts to an admission of murder," pointed out Felicia, a touch of impatience in her voice.

"That's what he did. That's what he has to admit to. But to show you how generous I can be, I'd consider, say, ten to twenty years. And if you say please, perhaps even nine to eighteen. He'll get out of prison in time to collect some of his Social Security."

"You've gotten very unreasonable in your old age, Mario."

"That, I guess, makes two of us."

"Which means?"

"Felicia, you've got a lunatic racist for a client and bullshit for a case. Face it. You waltz in here with garbage and I'm supposed to jump because you say so. Doesn't work that way. Not anymore, lady."

"What's that supposed to mean?" she asked warily, sensing a shift in Mario's mood that could only bode ill.

"Simple. If you want an offer, I've got an offer. Tell Wisocki to admit the crime, be prepared to do time, and we can deal. Otherwise, we have zip to talk about. Is there some part of that you don't understand?"

"Yeah," she replied, fighting to keep her temper in check. "There's a lot about it I don't understand. So tell me, what are you really saying, Mario? That because *we* didn't work out, you're going to be a prick?"

"It's not that we didn't work out. It's that . . . Hell. Why am I even getting into this with you?"

"It's obviously an issue. We might as well get it over with now."

"Get it over with? Get what over with, Felicia?"

"Look, Mario, I loved you, okay. But I didn't see a future for us. We're just too different. You . . . We just wanted different things. My idea of heaven is not the DA's office. We're just different people."

"We sure as hell are."

"Plus, I think you have real problems with strong women. You've got this macho thing going that—"

"You are a piece of work, Felicia. That's one thing about you that apparently hasn't changed. Like I said, you've got bullshit for a case. And you've got bullshit for a memory. It's not *us* that didn't work out. It's *you*. To hell with you."

"So that's all you've got to say?"

"What else do you need to hear?"

"Not a thing, Mr. Santiago. See you around."

She whirled, bolted out of the office, and quickly disappeared, and as Mario sat, fuming, staring at the chalkboard on his wall, he whispered to himself, "You didn't handle that too smoothly, Mr. Santiago. Get a grip."

Felicia sat in the car, enveloped in a bubble of gloom, suspended between rage and regret. She had always known her leaving had hurt Mario, and that her manner of doing so had made it even harder to take; but not until today had she realized how painful it would be to face his anger. She had never been quite as serious about him as he had been about her, which, in retrospect, was perhaps the fundamental problem. But she had cared about him, deeply. She had even—albeit fleetingly, and not very seriously—entertained the notion of being his wife.

One problem was that he was perfectly content being a civil servant, which meant, in her opinion, he was aiming way below his potential. The more serious problem was that he couldn't understand why she couldn't be content subordinating her desires to his—subordinating herself to him. Their entire relationship, impassioned as it was, was filled with acrimony. They bickered almost constantly, for no ascertainable reason. He was proud of her accomplishments and yet felt compelled to denigrate them. Part of the reason, she had always suspected, was that he was fazed by her Ivy League credentials. Also, having started three years earlier than he, she was always, in the unofficial status rankings within the DA's office, situated somewhere above him. Although he had never said so directly, that had clearly not sat well with him. He apparently had felt even more threatened when she had decided to leave and open her own practice. Instead of providing her with support, he had peppered her with arguments, with countless reasons why she should stay where she was, fighting the so-called good fight, instead of crossing over to "the other side."

To make matters worse, she had long harbored apprehensions about Mario's family, at least the part that remained in Puerto Rico—apprehensions she attributed to a trip they had taken together to visit his paternal grandparents. The couple, in their mid-eighties, lived in a modest brick home on the outskirts of Ponce, and had a beautiful garden out back in which flourished an array of delectable fruits and vegetables. The week-long trip had been pleasant, if somewhat boring, until she overheard his grandfather suggest to Mario, in a whisper much louder than the old man could have imagined, that she was perhaps too dark for him. She had not understood much of their conversation, but had picked up enough Spanish phrases here and there—including something about bettering the race, *"mejorando la raza"*—to know the old man was concerned about the color of his yet-to-be-conceived grandchildren. Mario had told the old man he should lay aside his silly ideas, but she did not think he had done so emphatically enough. She felt he had, in some sense, failed to defend her, which had led to a deep sadness that, however irrationally, she blamed on Mario. Concern about his family, in itself, would not have driven her away; but it was another bad omen in a relationship that already had more than its share.

She had concluded, after one particularly long and pointless argument, that she could not battle him and her own fears, doubts, and insecurities at the same time. So she had told him—knowing it would enrage and estrange him—that there was someone else. And, in a sense, there was. Winston, a charmer and an investment banker, had launched a full-scale assault on her resistance. His flowers, calls, and endless adulation were wearing her down. She had even convinced herself that the match made sense. Given his good education, money, and blinding confidence, he would certainly never feel overshadowed by her, and would, therefore, presumably feel no need to undermine her or tear her down. What she hadn't reckoned on was the shortness of Winston's attention span, which reflected a more fundamental problem: he had no long-term interest in anyone other than himself. After several months, she had cut things off with

Winston and settled into a comfortable situation with Frank convinced—the Winston letdown notwithstanding—that the breakup with Mario had been in the best interest of them both.

The taxi pulled up to her Madison Avenue office, where she found Hector and Stephanie chatting in the anteroom.

"How did it go with Mario?" asked Stephanie.

"It didn't. I'll give you the play-by-play later."

She turned to Hector and said, "If you don't have good news, I don't want to hear it."

"I think you'll want to hear this," he said as he followed her into her office.

Hector González, a former cop, had spent most of his career as an undercover drug detective working so-called buy and bust operations in poor inner-city neighborhoods. He loved the streets, and he also loved media folks. He often spoke of his dream of joining their ranks as a best-selling crime novelist. Felicia had assumed he would be perfect for checking out *La Nueva Prensa*'s report. His haste to share his news told her that her assumption had been correct. González's words began tumbling out the minute the door swung shut.

"*La Nueva Prensa* has dick. This is the deal. Some Dominican guy named Angel Martínez apparently saw a picture of Wisocki in the paper. He begins telling folks that Wisocki pulled a gun on him and his buddy. No one seems to know who the buddy is, and this Martínez character has disappeared. Now here's the kicker. From what I hear, the reporters from *La Nueva Prensa* never talked to Martínez or his buddy. They got their reports secondhand from some of Martínez's homeboys. And it gets better. Martínez has a rap sheet a mile long. Mostly petty stuff—drugs, farebeats—but at least a couple of assaults and there's a warrant out on him for armed robbery. And get this. He doesn't even have a green card. He's fuckin' illegal."

Felicia grinned and surprised him with a peck on the cheek. "Hector, baby, I love you."

Rather than obsess on the fiasco of a meeting with Felicia, Mario tried to focus on his work, on the subpoenas—for phone logs, witnesses, and a million other things—still to be drafted, and on the continuing pressure for information from the eighth floor. In the past when he had prosecuted important cases, he had always felt reasonably free to call his own shots. The fact that this was a press case, however, had put people on edge; none more so than trial division chief Irene Riley, who, when he had called to report on the rapid breakdown of plea bargain talks had seemed distinctly displeased.

"Are you certain you'd rather try this case?" she had asked. He had assured her that he was. "Are you positive this is not a personal battle between you and Felicia?" He had assured her it was not.

The next step would be Wisocki's arraignment before the Supreme Court (where New York County felonies are tried). There, he imagined, Felicia would use essentially the same arguments for bail as she had at Wisocki's criminal court arraignment. Since the Supreme Court judge was not likely to be quite as accommodating as Phillips had been, Mario might need some new ammunition to keep Wisocki in jail. In the next several days, he intended to interview everyone he could find who could shed any conceivable light on the relationship between García and Wisocki. He particularly wanted to know whether Wisocki had ever threatened García, or, for that matter, anyone else. Already he had dispatched investigators to follow up on the *Nueva Prensa* story and to canvass Wisocki's neighbors and try to uncover any other public weirdness in his past.

The phone rang and the caller identified himself as a reporter for the *Daily Journal*. Mario cut him off before he could get his question out. "Sorry, you know I can't comment on anything. Try the press office."

Seconds later the phone rang again. Mario grimaced and picked up the line, ready to slam the phone down the moment the reporter opened his mouth.

"ADA Santiago."

"Hey, honey. Was wondering whether you're going to take lunch today."

He exhaled in relief at the sound of María Cristina's voice and replied, "I don't know. I have a lot to do."

"I think you need a break. What about a quick bite at Forlini's."

"Sure. I probably do need to get out of here for a while."

They agreed to meet at the police guard station on the first floor, and as Mario hung up, he realized how hungry he was. He was not sure, however, that he was in the mood for Forlini's, the restaurant and bar around the corner where prosecutors, judges, and others connected with the courts hung out, all of whom were certain to have opinions on his case.

As they stepped out of the Hogan Place exit, Mario turned to María Cristina and said, "I hope you don't have your heart set on Forlini's. You game for somewhere a bit more off the beaten path?"

"Like?"

"You decide. I'm too tired to make a decision."

"Well, why don't we just walk awhile."

As they descended the stairs, Mario became aware of shouts coming from the direction of Centre Street. After a few seconds, he realized it was a chant, though he could not make out the words. He and María Cristina walked in the direction of the din and noticed that police barriers had gone up. When they were a few yards from Centre Street, the marchers came into view, perhaps 150 people heading down the street, a few with signs held over their heads. JUSTICIA, read one placard. JUSTICE, read another.

As the crowd approached, Mario made out the leader: Nelson Flores, a community organizer and preacher from Washington Heights, a largely Latino community uptown. He had met Flores some years ago at a neighborhood function and had immediately liked him. Unlike some professional protestors, Flores seemed sincerely committed to the welfare of those in the barrio, and he was less interested than most in self-glorification. Though Flores could be an outspoken firebrand, he didn't jump on any sensational issue that came along but made an effort to choose battles that made sense.

Now, with the marchers nearly upon him, Mario could make out the words in the chant: "Justice for Latinos! Death for Wisocki! . . . Justice for Latinos! Death for Wisocki!" The chanters switched to Spanish: "*¡Justicia para Latinos! ¡Muerte para Wisocki!* ... *¡Justicia para Latinos! ¡Muerte para Wisocki!*" They then switched to a traditional unity message: "*¡Un pueblo unido jamás será vencido!* ... *¡Un pueblo unido jamás será vencido¡*"

As the demonstrators passed, alternately chanting in English and Spanish, Flores glanced in his direction. Mario thought he glimpsed a smile flash across his face but quickly turned away and Flores marched on. Seconds later, however, Flores lifted the megaphone to his mouth and shouted, "Thank God for our Puerto Rican brother who is fighting from within the office of the district attorney!" Then, raising his voice even higher, he led the multitude in a boisterous new chant: "Santiago, kick his ass! ... Santiago, kick his ass!" Mario recoiled, as his ear exploded with what seemed to be the sound of a million voices calling his name. He grabbed María Cristina by the arm and whispered, "I think it's time to go."

Felicia wasn't sure why she'd decided to have dinner at Café con Leche. A homey West Side eatery specializing in such Latin-Caribbean dishes as *mofongo*, *pernil asado,* and *arroz con chorizo*, it was not a place she customarily frequented. She had, however, gone there once with Mario and this afternoon when she had suggested it to Frank, he had enthusiastically agreed.

Frank ordered paella and she requested steamed vegetables, and as they awaited their food and sipped sangria, she reflected on the conversation with Mario and concluded the outcome, as far as Wisocki was concerned, had been foreordained; for neither she nor Mario saw much point in settling for anything to which the other would agree. Even if they were perfect strangers, their positions, she suspected, would be the same. Still, such a bastard.

"You know," she said, looking up at Frank, "I think this case is very personal with Mario. He made it clear he wouldn't even consider a plea, at least not to anything realistic."

Frank shrugged. "Are you sure it's the case, Felicia? From what I understand, you two have a lot of history."

"True enough," she agreed. "But that's no reason—"

"Anyway," Frank continued, "it seems to me that from any angle you view it, this case could be a real mess. Stephanie is not that enthusiastic about it. Much of the community is up in arms over it. The press, at least part of it, is making Wisocki out to be some kind of lunatic. Are you sure you need this headache?"

"Probably not. But to be honest, I think it's an important case. I truly believe there are some interesting and significant issues here. And I also believe Wisocki's story. I mean, you take one look at that man and know he could no more be a murderer than I could be a sumo wrestler."

"Interesting thought," Frank said, grinning. "I don't know. Put on a few pounds, you might get quite a reaction stepping into a sumo ring. I'd sure pay to see it."

"Very funny, Mr. Conroy."

"Talking about putting on weight. Looks like the food is here," said Frank. The waiter set several steaming plates on the table— their orders, plus huge platters of beans and rice.

"You sure don't go away from this place hungry," said Frank, as he spooned beans onto his plate. "I didn't realize how famished—"

"As I was saying," Felicia interjected, "Wisocki's just not the type to kill anybody."

Frank took a few seconds to chew before responding: "Strange sentiments coming from an ex-prosecutor, my dear. I thought the one thing they taught you folks in DA school is that anybody can be guilty of just about anything."

"Seriously, Frank. I don't think he meant to shoot the man. Also, to be perfectly honest about it, this kind of case can make a career."

"Or break it."

"I don't see it going that way."

"I hope you're right. 'Cause even if you win it, what in the hell does it mean? It means this sicko gets off. And what if you lose? That, sweetheart, could be a disaster—both personal and professional. People will take the fact of his conviction as proof that he is exactly what Mario says he is—a racist homicidal maniac, which inevitably raises the question of why you are on his side."

"Are you saying I shouldn't be?"

"I think there are better things you could be doing with your time. This is a classic no-good-outcome situation. If you win, you lose. And if you lose, you lose even more. Bottom line, baby, I will support you however you come down. But you might want to give some more thought to this thing."

Felicia sighed as she pushed her vegetables from one side of the plate to the other. "For the last week I haven't been able to think about anything else. I know some folks feel that this is not the kind of case a black woman should handle. But you see, Frank, that's one more reason I can't walk away from it. I don't intend to let anybody put me in a narrow little box."

"That I understand. *Believe me*, I do. But this might be the wrong case on which to make that kind of stand. I'm just worried you might find yourself walking off a cliff. The report on those two Latino guys, for instance. It seems—"

"Oh yes. *That*," she said, pouting. "That's one thing I wanted to tell you about. Hector turned up some interesting information, and afterward I had a nice chat with Jake O'Hare."

"With that right-wing nut?" Frank wrinkled his nose.

"One and the same. He's fascinated by the case. Anyway, I turned over Hector's information and he promised to follow up. Just before I left the office, he faxed me a copy of tomorrow's column. Reporters usually don't like to show their work in advance, but he's obviously trying to get on my good side."

"What you mean is that he's trying to play you."

"*Whatever*. Anyway, I'm sure I can handle him. But the point is this. In the column he puts the *Nueva Prensa* report in context."

"Meaning?"

"Meaning that it's a pack of lies. And he says as much. Wisocki didn't attack anybody. The real attackers were the guys he waved the gun at. O'Hare names one of them in the piece. He's a

Dominican guy who was in this country illegally, and who has a rap sheet a mile long—a lot of it pretty serious stuff, drug-dealing, robbery. Anyway, here's the column."

Frank took the article and scanned it quickly, lingering over the last paragraph:

> The American system of justice is rooted in the idea that every accused person is entitled to his day in court. It is an idea liberal apologists well understand when it comes to parasites, predators, and illegal aliens. Certainly, Mr. Wisocki, who is none of those things and who thus far has led an exemplary life, is entitled to no less.

Frank rolled his eyes as he handed the piece back to Felicia. "So, let me get this straight. Jake O'Hare, previously known as a hatchet man for the far right, has suddenly become a poster boy for press ethics, the Constitution, and rhetorical restraint?"

"Stranger things have happened."

"Not in the world of tabloid journalism. And this patronizing, right-wing rhetoric—it's offensive. Are you sure you want to be associating with this guy?"

"If he can get out the truth, why not?"

"Maybe you're right. What do I know? I'm just a law professor, trying to have a good meal with his girl."

"Girl?"

"*Woman*. Okay? Jesus, honey. Cut me a little slack."

Frank deftly steered the conversation toward less troublesome topics, and they relaxed in each other's company, bantering the evening away. That night, when they made love, Felicia noted that Frank seemed much more ardent than usual—even without her taking the lead. It was almost as if by clinging to her as to life itself, by thrusting deeply, repeatedly and without restraint, he hoped, by sheer force of love and passion, to burrow into her very soul and exorcise whatever demons might therein reside.

* * *

Felicia arrived at the East Ninety-first Street apartment building at 9:30 A.M., precisely as promised, but received no answer when she pressed the buzzer. After trying several times more, she whipped out her cell phone and dialed Linda Wisocki's number. Someone answered on the second ring.

"Hello, Mrs. Wisocki?"

"Yes."

"This is Felicia Fontaine. We have an appointment for this morning."

"Yes. I know."

"Well, I've been ringing your buzzer and—"

"Oh, my goodness. I'm sorry. It must be broken again. Sorry about that. But, uhh, I've been thinking. I'm not so sure I should get involved in this. You know, John and I are separated and I'm trying to get on with my life."

"Yes, I understand, but—"

"Getting involved in this thing would only make things more difficult."

"Let me ask you something. Do you believe your husband is a murderer, Mrs. Wisocki?"

"Of course not. I can't imagine—"

"Then, I think you owe it to John to—"

"I don't owe John anything. *Not one thing*," Linda shouted.

Felicia winced. "I'm sure you're right. But what about yourself?"

"I don't understand."

"Let me be blunt, Mrs. Wisocki. As I understand it, you are not yet legally separated, much less divorced. If your husband is convicted, there will inevitably be a civil suit. And if he is convicted, believe me, García's family will win that suit. The damages would be astronomical. Paying them off would consume any and all resources you have acquired together. That would destroy any chance you might have of getting your rightful proceeds of the marriage, and it would likely saddle you with a mountain of debt that you would never get over. I think that you owe it to yourself, if not to John, to think about that. You certainly have nothing to lose by talking."

There was a long pause before she replied.

"All right. I'll have to come down to let you in."

Felicia slipped the phone back into her purse and perched herself on the front stoop. Heat and humidity already hung in the air; the afternoon would be intolerable. She turned, as she heard the door opening, and a thin Asian woman, perhaps in her early forties, emerged.

"I'm Linda Wisocki," she said, extending her hand.

"Really?" said Felicia, her face lighting up. "I'm truly thrilled to meet you."

5

Linda Wisocki, to Felicia's delight, turned out to be eminently reasonable. It seemed she did not really hate her husband, but was simply tired of him. Six years of togetherness was, in her estimation, about five and a half years too long.

"Living with John is like trying to sleep with a dripping faucet. At first the drip is not too bothersome," she said, "but after a while it drives you crazy. A couple of years ago, things got so bad I began to run out of patience. I want to enjoy my life. I wasn't doing that with him."

With Felicia's guidance, it did not take Linda long to realize that her eventual happiness—or at least the money to maintain it—was bound up with the fate of her husband. Felicia also appealed to her sense of responsibility. If she was truly convinced of her husband's innocence—as she said she was—she owed it to him, in this moment of need, to stand by him. So Linda agreed to make a reasonable attempt to pretend to be happily married, through the current phase of John's legal troubles at any rate. Felicia assured her she was doing the right thing.

Since there was no time to return to the office and also make her noon interview with Channel 3, Felicia decided to take a taxi directly to the station. The driver had the radio tuned to an all-talk station that blared forth the voice of Dick Rogers, a conservative fanatic who took great pride in skewering people and causes he deemed too politically correct. Over the last several years, he had provoked howls of outrage from liberals who thought of him as a racist panderer. Today he was doing his typical shtick:

"Hello out there in radio land. This is the beast from the east, coming at you from eighty-nine on your A.M. dial. Today's quiz-line question is: "What's the best way to defend yourself against riffraff? One, run. Two, plead for mercy. Three, threaten the scum with deadly force. The subject comes up, as those of you reading the papers know, because of the adventures of one John Wisocki. Seems Mr. Wisocki played the role of Dirty Harry with a couple of illegal aliens engaged in illicit monkey business. They declined to make his day. I say Mr. Wisocki had the right idea. We have enough home-grown crooks already, thank you very much. That's my opinion. But what do you think? Taking calls now on the quiz-line. Okay, we've got George in Queens. George, you're on the air."

"Hello, Dick."

"Yeah, you're on the air, George."

"Whatever happened to that electric fence we're supposed to be putting up along the border to keep the illegal aliens out? Didn't Congress vote money for that a couple of years ago? If the fence was up, we wouldn't have these problems."

"Could you pleeeease turn that off?" asked Felicia. The driver instantly complied and they drove the rest of the way in silence. But though Rogers's voice no longer filled the cab, Felicia could not get his show out of her head. It was a disheartening reminder of how easily Wisocki's actions could be twisted into a xenophobe's fantasy. It was also, she feared, a harbinger of how much of the media would choose to portray her client; and her appearance on Channel 3 did nothing to reassure her.

The noon news producer had promised a nuanced discussion about the presumption of innocence in high-profile cases, but by the time she was led onto the set—which consisted of two high chairs and an ersatz New York skyline—it was clear that things had changed.

"Hope you're ready to mix it up a bit," said the host, an athletic-looking man with longish, blond-gray hair.

Before Felicia could reply, he silenced her with a gesture and turned to face the TelePrompTer.

"Ten seconds," shouted the producer.

The show's bouncy theme music blasted forth, and the host beamed at the camera and announced: "Good morning. I'm Peter Young and this is *A Closer View*. Our first subject today comes straight from the headlines. You have been hearing a lot about John Wisocki, the so-called affirmative action killer. Is he a hero? Is he a villain? Or is he just a victim? You decide. Today our guest is the renowned attorney, Felicia Fontaine, who is defending Mr. Wisocki. Welcome to our show, Ms. Fontaine."

"Thank you," she said, forcing a smile.

"This is a most interesting case. So let's get right to specifics. Did he really pull a gun on two strangers?"

"No sane person would do that without a good reason," Felicia replied. She similarly parried questions about Wisocki's intent, his work history, his prejudices, and his political views. She ended up, in frustration, lecturing the host on the importance of unbiased reporting and on keeping an open mind. Felicia left feeling she had given as good as she got, but annoyed at herself for not having realized that preparing for television should always mean preparing for combat. It was a lesson she promised herself not to forget.

"**V**ery interesting," Mario muttered as he looked up from the police detective reports on his desk. The pattern was indisputable. García had worked four of the last five Sundays before his death. That piece of news should carry a lot of weight next week when Wisocki was arraigned in state Supreme Court. And he could certainly use the ammunition.

Judge Martin Frankel, who would preside, was a one-time legal aid lawyer who had gone into private practice before being named to the bench. He was notorious for his bias toward the defense. He also routinely popped up on media lists of incompetent judges. But even Frankel would have to draw the obvious conclusion—that Wisocki's timing was not exactly coincidental—and would be hard-pressed to justify setting bail, especially with the press hovering about.

Mario picked up the phone to call Detective O'Rourke. He noticed, just as he began to dial, that Barry Frommer, the deputy press spokesperson, was standing in his doorway. Supposedly, Frommer had once worked as a real reporter, apparently for a tiny community newspaper on Long Island. After he had become something of a burn-out case, his friend Ann Massengill, head of the DA's public information office, had been kind enough to offer him a comfortable job. Though it was hard to imagine the grossly overweight Frommer chasing any kind of news story, he seemed to fit right in at the DA's press shop, whose principal function, other than polishing Schneiderman's reputation, seemed to be muzzling prosecutors. The theory seemed to be that refusing to talk about a case would make bad publicity go away. Mario had put in a call to Ann to see whether he could get her to bend the rule. So Frommer's appearance, he was certain, was not due to happenstance. He put down the phone and waved Frommer in.

"Ann couldn't get away, but wanted me to talk to you about this statement you want us to put out," said Frommer, who had entered the office but remained standing.

"Yeah, Barry. My issue is very simple. I want us to put out a short, to-the-point statement that corrects the record, that makes it clear that I never said anything about kicking Wisocki's ass, nor any of the subsequent statements attributed to me."

"I can understand your frustration," Barry replied, showing an expression of practiced empathy, "but, as you know, Mario, the policy is clear. If we let every assistant make a statement whenever—"

"Give me a break, Barry. Who in the hell is talking about every ADA whenever anything? We're talking about me, and a specific case. How many cases a year get this much press? How many times do protesters march up a street chanting an assistant's name? What is it going to cost us to correct the goddamn record?"

"What can I say, Mario? It's the policy."

"This is bullshit, Barry. So you can't make an exception to the policy? *An exception*, Barry. You do know what that is. It's when you use your brain, instead of simply referring to a list of asinine rules."

"Look . . . I understand how you might be upset."

"Might be! Barry, is this why Ann sent you over here? The damn policy makes no sense."

"Mario, can you at least try to see it from our perspective? The last thing we—"

"You don't have a perspective, Barry. All you have is a fuckin' policy, and one that clearly was not designed to cover situations like this."

"I'm sorry you feel that way, Mario. But there's nothing I can—"

"I don't need to know what you can't do, dammit. What I need—"

"*Gentlemen*. May I suggest you lower your voices?"

They both turned as Rosa Linares, a community affairs specialist, closed the door to the office. Linares, a former high school teacher, coordinated a host of educational and outreach programs to schools, community groups, and organizations that worked to improve the quality of life in the city's poorer neighborhoods. She was one of the few non-lawyers in the office toward whom Mario felt genuine affection. When she asked him to speak to a class or a youth group he invariably agreed, in large part because she seemed so thoroughly convinced that his presence could provide hope, perhaps even salvation, in places where both were difficult to come by.

He smiled and, looking somewhat like a bashful little boy, sheepishly admitted, "I guess I did get a bit carried away, but it bothers the hell out of me to have Flores and God-knows-who-else repeating adolescent threats and attributing them to me."

"I know," she said, in her most comforting tone. "In fact, Flores called me earlier today. He said you asked him to get in touch."

"Not exactly. When he called here, I told him I couldn't talk to him and suggested that he call you if he had anything to discuss."

"Well, he had a lot to discuss. He's going to be putting people on the street every day for at least the next week, with a huge march planned for the day Wisocki is arraigned. And, as you probably already know, he's getting a lot of editorial support from *La Nueva Prensa* and also from the Spanish radio stations."

"Just what I need," said Mario, his tone conveying his exasperation.

"I don't know what you need, love. But Flores is what you've got. And he apparently intends to be your new best friend."

"I give up," Mario said grumpily. Seeing no purpose to indulging in aimless chatter, he unceremoniously ushered both Rosa and Barry to the door and returned to his desk. He stared at the police reports for several minutes but was unable to make his brain focus. The office felt confining, suffocating, and Mario was in no mood for work. He finally acknowledged the futility of trying to concentrate and headed to the neighborhood gym, a bare bones and poorly ventilated facility that was popular among weight lifters in the area.

Once inside, he quickly slipped into his workout clothes and, ignoring the exercise machines and the huge stacks of free weights, headed straight for the heavy bag hanging by a long chain in a small room off the main exercise studio. He was glad none of his sparring partners were around; he would only have waved them away, not sure that, even had they donned full protective gear, he could pull his punches enough today to render himself safe. Instead, he conjured up images of Wisocki and Frommer as he attacked the bag with snappy combinations of punches and kicks. After a few minutes, he paused, panting and sweating, just long enough to catch his breath before falling upon the bag again. He kept the barrage up for several rounds—using roundhouse kicks, spinning side kicks, jumping front kicks—until he was exhausted and also in a slightly better frame of mind. As he spun around to kick the bag a final time, he screamed as they had taught him during his training in Tae Kwan Do, and was transported, momentarily, to a time in his youth when he felt that, if only he could properly choreograph his kicks, nothing could—or would dare try to—withstand his power.

When Geneva had called to suggest they go to the beauty shop, Felicia's first impulse had been to beg off. Her own appointment for a touch-up was two days off and there was no real reason to move it up. Plus the day had been so draining—with romancing Linda Wisocki, fencing with Peter Young on television, juggling calls from half a dozen clients, and making the long trek to Rikers Island to visit John—that she was not especially eager to spend the evening waiting ad infinitum in a beauty parlor.

The Rikers Island trek had been especially tiring. She could have had Wisocki brought into town and met him on the Twelfth Floor Bridge, but Rikers offered a private interview room, safe from the prying eyes and ears of snitches always on the prowl for something to trade with a prosecutor. The trade-off was that privacy required a trip to the Bronx, by way of Astoria Heights in Queens, and a commitment of several hours devoted to travel and to dealing with the bureaucracy of a place that warehoused 14,000 prisoners.

Wisocki, still under suicide watch, had seemed somewhat more upbeat than usual—largely because of the news Felicia brought about his wife. Linda had agreed to move back into the Wisocki co-op, at least through the trial, assuming she had no problem subleasing her current place. She had made it clear that she had no intention of sharing John's bed, or in making a second stab at being a real wife. As she had put it: "This is not about giving love, or John, a second chance." John, nonetheless, had behaved as if Felicia had brokered a reconciliation. For the first time since they had met, she had seen a look of genuine happiness on his face, a look that said, "Maybe I have a chance with Linda after all." He was also optimistic about the upcoming arraignment, especially after Felicia explained that his relationship with his mother and his wife might help to sway the judge. Mainly, however, his mood had been somber, particularly when she had mentioned García and inquired about their relationship.

"I know what many people have assumed," Wisocki had said, "but the truth is me and Francisco were all right. I never disliked him personally. And I certainly never wanted him dead. I also don't have any problem with Spanish people. My problem was always with Computertronics, and with what they did to me."

"So you're saying you and Francisco were good friends?" she had asked, skeptically raising her left eyebrow.

"Obviously, we weren't best friends," he had replied, with a grimace, "but we got along. I can't tell you how much I regret the way things turned out. I think about him every day. I relive those awful moments. And I hate the fact that I didn't have the strength to kill myself before he walked in. I hate myself for causing such pain to his wife and little daughter, and I beg God to forgive me."

Wisocki had not been able to go on. Tears had rolled down his cheeks, and within seconds he had been sobbing, shamelessly and without apparent affectation.

It was during the taxi ride back to Manhattan that Geneva's invitation had begun to seem attractive. After such a rough day, Felicia owed herself an evening of mindlessness, and nothing struck her as more mindless than the goings-on in a beauty parlor. So she had called Geneva on the cell phone and agreed to meet her at Julian's Tresses on 125th Street in Harlem.

Although Felicia sometimes had her hair done at a chic East Side salon, she preferred coming to Harlem. Not only was the skill level a bit higher, at least when it came to black women's hair, but the view of life was richer. Also, she looked forward to the chance to catch up with Geneva, whose goodwill and good heart she had never doubted since meeting her at Harvard. After Harvard, Geneva had worked for a while in an advertising agency and then had earned an MBA at Wharton. She was now a marketing manager for a specialty foods company, and was one of Felicia's few acquaintances who could make her own vanity appear inconsequential by comparison. Not that Geneva was fashion model material. After marriage, two children, a divorce, and an adulthood of lavish living, her body no longer looked like it belonged to a twenty-year-old; but neither did it appear neglected. Geneva looked precisely like what she was: a well-cared-for woman entering middle age gracefully, who seemed sensual even in a business suit. She never lacked for male attention, just for the right man desperate to marry her. But she was far from giving up faith that the perfect mate eventually would appear. "I'll recognize him by his hands. Sensitive men always have interesting hands," she had once told Felicia, with no hint that she was kidding.

Felicia arrived at Julian's at six twenty-seven, three minutes before her appointment. Julian shouted an enthusiastic hello, but it was clear from the unfinished coiffure of the woman sitting in his chair that he was running at least an hour—and more likely two—late. Geneva arrived a few minutes thereafter, to find her stylist similarly behind. "It's a law of nature that when you come to the beauty shop you wait," Geneva said with a shrug. "It's God's way of teaching you patience.

"So, child," she continued, "I've been reading about this case of yours and this Adolf Hitler wannabe. What's up with that?"

"You know how the press is always twisting everything around. He's actually a nice, normal computer nerd, who happens to be innocent," Felicia said.

"So he didn't kill this guy over some affirmative action program?"

Felicia laughed. "You can't believe everything you read, dear. No, he didn't kill him because of affirmative action. Truth be told, though, he's no big fan of these programs. But as you know, Geneva, I don't think so much of them myself."

"Don't I know that, girlfriend," replied Geneva, rolling her eyes. "But—how should I put this—I think your position is inconsistent with your history."

"Maybe," Felicia acknowledged with a shrug. "Don't get me wrong. I'm grateful for having gotten into Harvard, and I'm grateful for whatever made it possible for me to go there. I wouldn't want to deny that opportunity to anybody else. But I think we have to find another way."

"Like *what*?" demanded Geneva. "Do you really believe, Felicia, that things would be better if affirmative action didn't exist? Hell, most white folks didn't consider us qualified even before they invented affirmative action. At least now we have a chance of getting in the door. Are you really prepared to pay the price of wiping affirmative action out?"

"I'm not saying just drop it, Geneva. I'm saying that it's time we stop looking at it as a cure-all. The fact is, it doesn't work very well. It doesn't take a genius to see that."

Clara, a stylist who had been listening in, ran her hand through her short blond—formerly black—hair and let loose a derisive guffaw. "My goodness, Felicia," she chimed in. "We're going to have to start calling you Miss Clarence Thomas. I didn't realize you swallowed all that conservative double-talk."

"I don't swallow conservative anything, Clara. I'm just saying that we need to start thinking for ourselves."

"So what does defending that crazy white boy have to do with thinking for ourselves?" asked Clara.

"Maybe nothing directly," said Felicia. "But it's my way of saying I will do what's right regardless of how people are programmed to see things. I'm an independent woman with my own independent mind. It's not a conservative or liberal—"

She stopped in mid-sentence when the door noisily flew open and a large woman carrying two baskets entered with a young girl trailing behind her. "I got chicken sandwiches and ham today," the woman shouted.

"I'll take a chicken, Doris," cried a voice from the back. A few others chimed in with orders as well. Moments later, the woman was gone, but she had obviously set Julian to thinking. Leaning his bulky frame against a chair, he momentarily suspended his exertions on the head in front of him and declared to no one in particular, "You know, everybody but black folks makes movies about food. I mean, there was that movie about Italian food. What was it called, *Big Night*, or *Night Out*, or something like that. And there was the Japanese movie. I think it was called *Tampopo*. And there was that other movie, *Babette's Feast*, and *The Cook, the Wife, the Lover*, or some such. Even the Mexicans got into the act with *Like Water for Chocolate*. But you never see a movie about black folks and cooking. And we have some of the best food in the world. I mean, why don't they make something called *Sapphire's Chitlins*, or *Tyrone's Fried Chicken*, or *Mama's Sweet Potato Pie*?"

"You know, they did have a movie called *Soul Food*," said Geneva.

"I must have missed that one," said Julian, who was back to combing his captive client's hair.

"How could you have missed that? It was all over the place," said Clara. "That's the one with Vivacious Fox and—"

"Vivica Fox, love. Vivica," said Felicia, shaking her head and grinning.

"Vivacious, Vivica, whatever," replied Clara. "What kind of name is that anyway? What I was saying, though, is the movie also had Vanessa Williams. She was playing a lawyer, a lady a lot like you, Felicia."

"Don't get me started," snapped Felicia good-naturedly. "That woman was a real bitch."

"Exactly," screamed Clara, beaming, clearly tickled with herself for having dissed Felicia.

"All I know," injected Geneva, "is that Babyface did the music. Now, *that is one good-looking brother*. He can play my chimes any day. But I think that movie was less about food than about three sisters and their relationships. Right?"

"I'm not so sure," said Clara. "For a movie that wasn't about food, they sure had a lot of fried chicken, ham hocks, black-eyed peas, and God knows what else up in there. Talking about movies, I saw Billy Dee Williams the other night in *Lady Sings the Blues*. Girl, that man was fine in his time. Now all they let him do is that psychic hotline bullshit. Why is it that black stars, when they start getting wrinkled and raggedly, have to do the psychic hotline? Can't they find some respectable roles for our folk instead of forcing them to sit up there trying to get poor folks to spend all their money on that silliness? Billy Dee ought to just get his ass home."

"What about Denzel? He only plays respectable roles. And I don't see him pimping for no psychic," said the woman trapped in Julian's chair.

"I'm talking about old stars," said Clara. "Denzel can play whatever he wants to. He's still young and pretty."

"Tell me about it, honey," said the woman who was Julian's current project and was taking advantage of his latest rest break to nod vigorously in agreement. "And he just gets finer every day. But Denzel aside, there are plenty of old stars who ain't selling out. Sidney Poitier, for instance, must be seventy years old by now—maybe more—and he's still doing his thing. He wouldn't be caught dead pushing some phony fortune-teller at a nine-hundred number. But Billy Dee and the whole bunch of those fools just ain't got class. You know, I used to have some respect for the man."

"Got that right. It's not like he really needs the money," said Clara.

Geneva grinned and turned to Felicia. "What were we talking about?"

"I think Denzel," Felicia replied with a grin, as she leaned back in the chair and relaxed, savoring the sound of people who, looking past the barriers of education and class, joyously communed with each other.

Mario took a bite out of his hamburger and gazed into María Cristina's dark brown eyes, listening attentively as she filled him in on her hearing that morning. The hearing had concerned suppression of evidence recovered by the police from a drug dealer.

"The funny part," said María Cristina, "was that the defendant was screwed either way, as his lawyer knew. His argument was that he had not abandoned the bags, that he was, in effect, just parking them in the dumpster for a while and that the cops had no business confiscating them. But the only way he could win that argument was to admit that the bags were his. And since they contained two guns and three dozen glassines of crack, he really wasn't prepared to take that argument very far."

"I guess not," said Mario, amused at the absurdity of a defendant claiming he had no intention of abandoning his crack. "Who was the judge?"

"George Stevens."

"He's pretty good."

"He was pretty good today, at any rate. Told the defense counsel to stop wasting his time. What's happening on your case, by the way?"

"Mostly routine stuff," he replied, grabbing the Tabasco bottle to spice up his burger. "Dealing with a lot of paperwork, you know, filing the indictment, the voluntary disclosure form, reviewing the DD5s. But we did come up with something interesting. It seems that García usually worked on Sundays. And that was no secret. A lot of people apparently were aware of it. Also, until about a year and a half ago, García reported directly to Wisocki. So it's unlikely Wisocki didn't know what he was up to."

"Interesting," she said, nodding in agreement.

"Also, I talked to O'Rourke. Angel Martínez, the guy Wisocki confronted on the street, is in the wind. They think he went back to the Dominican Republic, but they might have some leads on the second guy. They're working on it."

"Sounds like things are coming together."

"We'll see," Mario replied, as he bit into the Tabasco-treated burger. He grimaced and immediately grabbed the water.

"I think I put a little too much sauce on this thing," he said. "Anyway, the wild card is the media. I've got a stack of calls from reporters, some as far away as California, and half of them from the Spanish-language press. I turned the whole stack over to the press office. Then, of course, there's Nelson Flores. He's talking massive demonstrations."

Mario paused long enough to scrape away a bit of the sauce from his burger, which he wolfed down before adding, "Also, had the strangest chat with Irene Riley today. She didn't come right out and say it, but she was throwing all kinds of hints around that, if I win this case, there might be a promotion in it—I suppose to deputy chief of the bureau."

"Wow," she said, her eyes suddenly wide. "Do you want that?"

"I don't know. But it would be nice to have the offer."

"Would you get a raise?"

"Not much of one, but it would give me a chance to learn something about management, which might not be a bad thing."

"Forget management," she said, with a smirk. "The way this case is raising your profile, you might soon be beyond work. You know, you can make a good living just being a celebrity."

"Yeah," he said, grinning. "I'm all set to become the next Marcia Clark."

"Would that be so bad?"

"I guess it depends. I sure as hell don't see the attention helping me win the case."

"So you become a millionaire and get a TV show—not a bad consolation prize. That is how things work now. Right?"

Mario laughed, as he pushed the sole remaining french fry around his plate. "Maybe I don't even get the consolation prize. Unless we can somehow tie O. J. Simpson to this murder, I don't see it generating millions."

"I guess you have your work cut out for you," she said, her tone now serious.

"Yeah, I suppose so. But you know, for all my bitching, this is really interesting work. I can barely wait to get Wisocki's ass into court."

"I'll tell Flores you said so," she said, grinning mischievously.

"You do and next week I'll have him chanting your name on Centre Street. Believe me, I can easily figure out a way to do it."

"I don't doubt it, love," she said, stroking his hand. "You can pretty much figure out a way to do whatever you want."

"Except how to avoid all the shit that comes with a case like this."

"It's the price of fame, my dear. Get used to it."

Having Felicia back in his life was definitely among the things Mario had not yet gotten used to. When she called, proposing they "demilitarize the relationship," he was immediately suspicious, and he found her explanation less than reassuring. "It's not going to do either one of us any good to conduct this trial like a war," she announced. "We need to separate the personal nonsense from what's pertinent to this case. We need, at the very least, to clear the air—and to do it somewhere private, without reporters, without co-workers, without snooping, prying eyes."

When she suggested they meet at her apartment, Mario objected, but not very strongly. For although he was leery of her intentions, his curiosity (and he wondered whether it was more than curiosity) was stronger than his caution. He wondered what kind of life she had made—or at least what kind of lifestyle she had adopted—since striking out on her own. He also sensed her regret at the turn the conversation in his office had taken. And he felt, as he was sure she did, a desire to begin the dialogue anew. So he went, determined not to lose his head.

Entering her apartment was like walking into a home-decorating magazine. The marble fireplace, the formal dining room, the fancy Upper East Side address with the white-gloved doorman—they suited her in the way a stunning designer gown suits a neophyte socialite. All the same, Mario looked upon the surroundings with a vague sense of disapproval. The environment was a bit too extravagant for his taste. Still, he couldn't deny that Felicia cut a most appealing figure silhouetted in the early evening light, in a simple white dress, holding a wineglass as she stood before a huge stained-glass window.

"Thanks for coming," she said softly. "Can I offer you a drink—wine, beer. I even have Stoli, which I assume is still your drink."

"Good memory," he said, smiling despite himself.

She was tempted to remind him of his earlier comment about her having "bullshit for a memory," but immediately thought better of the idea. Instead, she replied, in a hushed tone that was almost a whisper, "It's not that my memory's so good. It's that after watching you drink it a hundred or so times, even I can manage to remember."

"I think I'll pass on the drink," he said, plopping onto the sofa, into which he sank much deeper than he had expected.

"So anyway," he said, leaning forward, "what's on the agenda?"

Felicia coyly pursed her lips and joined him on the sofa. She took a sip from the wine, turned to face him, and said, "We are on the agenda. You and I. Obviously, we are adversaries. That's the nature of the game. It's our job to make each other's case look bad. As a professional, I accept that. But we can still be civil to each other. And we can certainly be bigger than the petty, personal stuff that can't do anybody any good."

Mario shook his head in a show of bemusement. "So that's why I needed to come all the way up here? To hear that we should try very hard to be nice to one another?"

"That's part of why I wanted you to come," she replied, smiling tightly. "The other part, to be perfectly frank, is that I think we need to deal with us, with the personal baggage we're carrying into this trial. We can't just pretend it's not there."

Mario shifted, not particularly comfortable with the direction of the conversation, yet wondering where she was headed. "So what exactly are you proposing, Counselor?"

"I'm not all that sure, Mario. But I do know that there's absolutely no point in us acting like hostile ex-lovers—even if that's what we are. What happened, happened. It's time to put it behind us."

"I can't argue with that," he said, pensively touching his lips. "So what do you want, for me to forgive you?"

"If that's what it takes to move on," she replied, her eyes searching his for a congenial response, but instead finding what she took to be the determined stare of a man tightly holding on to his sense of aggrievement.

"Fine. I forgive you," he said dryly. "In fact, maybe I should thank you."

"For what?"

"For helping me to understand why we never belonged together."

"Which is?"

"Which is that we never truly shared a love. Whatever there was between us—and I don't deny that it was something powerful—it wasn't love. It was some kind of unnameable compulsion. You forced me to recognize that. And in doing that, you did me a big favor. So I forgive you. I promise to be a gentleman in court. And I thank you for showing me the light. Anyway, as you said, it's well past time to move on."

As Mario stood to leave, Felicia stood as well. And before he could react, her lips found his, touching them with a kiss so light that it was almost chaste. She then leaned into him, moving her lips ever so slightly against his, sending a tickling sensation throughout his body. He could not force himself to move away and yet he dared not embrace her; so he stood, paralyzed, his heart beating wildly, blood surging toward his loins. The room seemed to spin, and he felt his body floating through space, as visions of Felicia in rapture shot through his head. The pressure of her lips increased, and his mind flashed back to a night when dinner had burned because they had been so caught up in making love. Instead of having beef stew, they had had peanut butter sandwiches; then they had tossed the pot into the sink and returned to making love again. There had been nights when, due to the crush of work, they had tried to resist their mutual desire; but they had invariably surrendered and ultimately collapsed, sated, into each other's arms.

As the memories flooded his brain, she pressed into him, and Mario responded despite himself, thrusting against and wrestling her tongue with his as his arms pulled her closer; yet, even as he savored the taste and the touch, and felt the tug of a deep yearning he had hoped was dead, he summoned up the will to break the embrace and back away.

"What was that all about?" he mumbled, still in something of a daze.

"I thought it was worth seeing just how much of this 'unname-able' thing between us had survived," she said, beaming. "It seems to me that something's still there."

"Proving what?"

"You tell me," she said, as she danced away and opened the door, flooding the apartment with the harsh light from the hallway.

6

Felicia had never intended to kiss Mario, at least not in any conscious part of her brain. It was an impulse that had suddenly come upon her that she had been unprepared to resist. And, now, as she sat on her sofa staring beyond the television screen, she decided she was glad that she had done it. The act, in a manner of speaking, had cleared the air in a way that words could not. It had forced a certain basic honesty into their relationship. Mario could no longer deny—and, for that matter, neither could she—that powerful emotions still connected them. Why it was so important that that be proved and acknowledged, she was at a loss to say. She just knew that it was—in the same way she knew that she and Mario, sooner or later, would have to carefully reassess the choices they had made.

Linda Wisocki's image came on the television screen, cutting short Felicia's musings on Mario. The request for the interview with Linda had come through Felicia's office and because Felicia knew the reporter to be a compliant and sympathetic soul, she had been happy to set it up.

"Of course I love him," Linda was saying, "but no marriage is perfect. We've had a good many problems. Still, with John, even during the worst of times, I never knew him to be less than a good and very decent man."

"Perfect," Felicia responded, a huge smile on her face. Thanks in no small part to her coaching, Linda was doing very well with her maiden news interview. She had positioned herself nicely—as the loving yet modern wife who, having weathered troubles in her marriage, would stand by her man and make it all work out. If only all reporters were as agreeable as Jennifer Thomas. Felicia reclined further into the sofa and closed her eyes, savoring her small success.

Controlling the press, she was learning, was far from a precise art. Yet, it had to be courted and, to the extent possible, managed. For though its emissaries were often unpleasant—demanding, inaccurate, rude, intrusive, and selfish in the extreme—they could be extremely useful.

Because of her success in her previous high-profile cases, Felicia had considered herself something of an expert on press relations. She now knew that to be nonsense. Since casting her lot with John, she had come to see how meager her experience truly had been. Never before had such huge hordes of reporters been interested in one of her clients. And those reporters demanded a steady diet of quotes. Felicia's tendency was to try to accommodate, even if she had nothing to say. She was realizing, however, that she had to resist that impulse, or risk saying something embarrassing, idiotic, or perhaps even detrimental to her case.

Also new to her was the attitude of her interviewers—of whom the fool on Channel 3 who wanted to "mix it up a bit" was the latest unhappy example. In her previous experience journalists had either been neutral or openly supportive. Now many of them behaved as if she were engaged in something vaguely illicit. Even as they swarmed to her, titillated by the case and the issues she raised, they threw off titters of disapproval. They would offer broadsides in the form of questions. *"Aren't you afraid of offending other people of color with your legal strategy?" "How can a black woman be a conservative?"*

The worst assaults came from the idiots on talk TV. Seduced by the high ratings and a producer's assurances of civility and fairness, Felicia had made the mistake of going on the Jackie James show—

a syndicated wallow into depravity that generally ended with the host smiling and shaking her head as manifestly demented guests lobbed insults and curses at one another. Three minutes into the show, a loud-talking audience member confronted Felicia. Shaking and bobbing her head as if in the grip of some psychedelic drug, the finger-wagging woman, practically foaming at the mouth, had screamed, "You ought to be ashamed of yourself. Don't you have nothin' better to do with your time than defend some racist white man?" In the future, Felicia had resolved, she would pick her TV spots better.

Still, all in all, she wasn't doing too badly. Jake O'Hare's Sunday column, titled "Linda Wisocki Steps Out of the Shadows," had unveiled Linda in an extremely flattering light—thanks in large measure to Felicia's efforts. Not that O'Hare didn't have good material to work with. For as Felicia had quickly realized, Linda's life story was a moving tribute to the American immigration experience.

Initially, Linda had been reluctant to talk about herself. "I'm a technical editor. Who wants to hear about me?" she had asked Felicia when they met for coffee. But Felicia, sensing an interesting story, had deftly drawn her out. And Linda, in a voice barely rising above a whisper, had quickly confirmed Felicia's suspicions.

Her parents had fled to Hong Kong in 1957, "a step ahead of the Great Leap Forward," recalled Linda. "We barely made it to Hong Kong with the shoes on our feet." She was four at the time, too young to understand politics, or even why they had to move, but old enough to sense that for her, for her parents, for her country, it was time to begin again. Linda's odyssey through Hong Kong, Taipei, and Toronto finally brought her to San Francisco, where her father, once a respected jurist, found work in a grocery store. Her mother, a lifelong member of the aristocracy, ended up working in a laundry.

Both parents died in a car crash when Linda was sixteen. "Funny how quickly the steam can go out of teenage rebellion when there's nobody to rebel against," Linda wryly observed. Although she was taken in by an aged woman distantly related by marriage, responsibility for her three younger brothers had fallen largely on Linda's fragile shoulders. She took a full-time job as a waitress. Working weekends and nights, she managed to support herself and her brothers, even as she struggled with her high school studies. Her grades were good enough to get her a scholarship to the University of San Francisco, which she attended while continuing to work full-time, graduating with a joint degree in English and history. Her career as a technical editor and writer of software manuals eventually brought her to New York where she found, in John, an introspective man whom she took, wrongly, to be a kindred soul.

Felicia had been only too glad to help O'Hare gain access to Linda for his column. And in O'Hare's hands, the story of John and Linda became the passionate stuff of a Shakespearean romance. Her favorite part of the column, however, was the end—what O'Hare referred to as the kicker: "I ask the question because it is my journalistic duty. 'How can you know that deep in the depths of his heart John Wisocki is not a raving racist?' Linda fixes me with a steadfast stare and provides an answer eloquent in its simplicity: 'He married me, didn't he?'"

Jake, as usual, had laid it on a bit thick, but his column was having the intended result. It had gotten Linda the television interview, and other requests were pouring in. The attention would humanize Linda and burnish her image. More important, it would cause people—some, at least—to reconsider their take on Wisocki. Would it sway someone like Geneva? Probably not. Geneva's position was simple, straightforward, and apparently inflexible: racial solidarity demanded that Felicia leave Wisocki to the wolves. Geneva had not put it quite so bluntly, but her admonitions and questions over the last few days (*"Don't you feel strange representing him?" "You know, some folks are going to call you a traitor." "Has it ever occurred to you that he might be using you?"*) amounted to the same thing.

Stephanie Kaufman was another matter. A legal aid lawyer before starting up the firm with Felicia, Stephanie was constitutionally incapable of believing that Wisocki, or virtually any other defendant, deserved to be found guilty. "Who are we to judge?" was her mantra. Yet she was extremely uncomfortable with the Wisocki case. Part of the reason had to do with the media frenzy. Although Stephanie understood, intellectually, the value of exposure, she instinctively recoiled from bright lights. She had no desire to see herself on the evening news. Nor was she at all comfortable with Wisocki's politics.

"I went to work for legal aid because I wanted to defend the good guys," she had said. "Naive me. That was before I realized most of the good guys don't need defending. They're not the ones usually accused of rape, armed robbery, or murder. But even when I was representing a rapist or a drug dealer, I could always sleep at night because it was not so much the individuals I was fighting for as it was their right to counsel. I never got into defending their philosophy or their rationalizations for their behavior. I feel the same way about Wisocki. He has a right to the best defense you can give him. And I don't mind picking up some of the slack from your other cases while you provide that—especially since he's already shelled out a sixty-thousand-dollar retainer. But you don't have to defend his beliefs. The fact is, he is accused of murder, not of being a racist."

"He is accused of both," Felicia had shot back, "and the defense needs to take that into account."

It was typical of Stephanie to reduce a matter to its essence—a trait that could be invaluable when grappling with a complicated case. But in this situation, as Felicia tried to explain, the essentials were not enough. The Wisocki case only made sense, for her at least, if she could use it to make some larger points; but it would also enhance Wisocki's chance of winning if she could get the jury—the one inside as well as the one outside the courtroom—to see her client as a complex and sympathetic character, as a principled man with a grudge that made sense, as a victim who had been shattered by misguided corporate policy. In her eyes, the jury outside was just as important as the one actually seated in the jury box. It was the outside jury to which the judge (and just about everyone else in court, including the *real* jurors) would be playing. So she saw this case, she had told Stephanie, as a many-layered affair: criminal at the core, but overlaid with political, psychological, even propagandistic elements.

Stephanie, always the pragmatist, had nodded skeptically and replied, "Sure, Felicia. If you say so. Just don't forget that your client hired you to be a criminal attorney, not a philosopher or a shrink. And his main concern, I'm willing to bet, is not whether you can get his wife on TV, but whether you can save his butt in court."

Stephanie did have an irrefutable point. Unless the legal work was done well, all the rest wouldn't matter. But as Felicia thought ahead to tomorrow's arraignment, she felt confident she could deliver. Tonight she could afford to relax.

As she got up to pour herself a glass of wine, the doorbell rang. It was Frank, she assumed, just in time for a nightcap—and also to tell her that she was every bit as capable as she tried to appear.

Much as Mario tried to tell himself the arraignment was no big deal, he wasn't buying his own reassurances. Although he had done a thousand Supreme Court arraignments, he had never done one under the media floodlights. As he reviewed his paperwork spread out on the kitchen table, he asked himself, for the zillionth time, what he could be forgetting. What stupid mistake was he on the verge of making? What task had he left undone? The Voluntary Disclosure Form—documenting Wisocki's statement to the arresting officer and other relevant evidence against him—had been ready for several days, as had the copy of the indictment. He would hand both over to Felicia tomorrow.

As far as he could determine, she had no real grounds for seeking a change in Wisocki's status. The very fact of the indictment made Mario's argument for continued remand stronger. Since there was now no doubt that Wisocki was facing serious time, his incentive for flight would be stronger. Yet he knew Felicia well enough to be certain that she would make a bail application and an argument—probably an outrageous one—for his release.

Detective O'Rourke, who had spent some time nosing around in—or "canvassing," as he called it—Wisocki's neighborhood, had been able to find out very little about the man. Most of the people simply didn't know him, and those who did knew him only barely. For someone who had been in the same apartment for a decade, he hadn't made much of an impression. In a sense, that was good news; it weakened any argument about Wisocki's deep ties to the community. Still, Mario wished that O'Rourke had been able to come up with more concrete evidence of Wisocki's unworthiness.

Mario gazed across the table at his wife and said, "I wish I knew what was on Felicia's mind. I know she has something up her sleeve. She always does."

María Cristina wrinkled her nose, as if an unpleasant scent had settled in the room. "She may be flashy, but she's not as smart as you think," said María Cristina. "What can she do, for God's sake? Nothing substantial has changed over the past couple of weeks. What argument does she have?"

"That's exactly the problem," said Mario. "I have no idea what she has. I mean, what if Wisocki's confession at the scene wasn't exactly spontaneous? What if Felicia has gotten some dimwitted cop to admit that they interrogated him without Mirandizing him? You know how these cases can go. Everybody's trying to get the defendant to talk. I wouldn't put it past her—"

"Yeah. The 'fruit of the poisoned tree.' Listen to yourself, Mario. I've never heard anything so farfetched in my life. You're imagining your worst nightmares. Do you really believe Felicia has better lines into the department than you do? You're worrying about nothing, honey. What does O'Rourke say?"

"He says everything's cool, and so do the other investigators."

"So what's the problem?" asked María Cristina, her voice rising in frustration. "Felicia will come in with a lot of sound and fury. But she's not likely to have anything substantive. She's just a human being, Mario, not some genius on a pedestal. She's as mortal as the rest of us, just a bit less principled."

"Of course, you're right," said Mario, as he softly, nervously, tapped his finger against the table. "But with her, you just never know. That maudlin profile in the paper on Linda Wisocki, for instance, was clearly her doing. That's the kind of shit Felicia does. So Wisocki has an Asian wife. Big deal!"

"So now you have something against Asian wives?" asked María Cristina, feigning indignation.

"Well, the truth is that there's one Asian wife, or at least one kinda-Asian wife, I think is really cool, but she doesn't happen to be the one profiled in the *Inquirer*. That bullshit profile is obviously Felicia's way of telling the world that Wisocki is not a racist. As if his marriage to a Chinese woman somehow exonerates him of murder. And then there's the matter of the judge. Frankel doesn't have a whole lot of affection for prosecutors. He can be a real bastard."

"But he does have some respect for the law. And the cameras will help to keep him honest. Even Frankel doesn't want to make a fool of himself with a million New Yorkers watching. You should just try to relax."

"Easy enough to say, but Felicia likes surprises."

"So, surprise the witch back."

"Are you saying I should adopt her style?"

"No, I'm saying you can handle her . . . in your own style."

She smiled seductively, rose silently from her chair, and perched astride his lap, staring into his eyes. "I'm also saying you can handle me, in whatever style pleasures you," she murmured, as she kissed him deeply, closing her eyes, her petite frame lazily wriggling atop him. After several moments, she rose to her feet and, flashing an impish grin, quickly undid his trousers, waiting only long enough for him to stand before pulling them off, along with his briefs. She kissed him lightly on his legs and torso, reaching up to undo his shirt as she progressed. As she gently pushed him back into the chair, her nightgown fell open, revealing her slender, sensual body. She repositioned herself astride his legs, and he pulled her tightly to him, his thumbs tracing tiny circles as they inched along her inner thighs. They kissed deeply, their tongues playing with each other as he continued to massage her thighs. She moaned softly as his

thumbs met at the juncture of her legs and, when he felt the damp-
ness of her readiness, an explosive charge shot through his insides
and he moaned in return. She guided him into her as he stared into
her beautiful features and he greedily surrendered to passion. But
even as pleasure enveloped him, and he breathlessly called her
name, he dared not to close his eyes for fear that, looming in the
darkness, he would find Felicia's face.

Normally, Felicia would have cursed the drizzle, if only for its
effects on her hair, especially when combined with the stifling
August heat; but today, she welcomed the cooling sprinkle. It
seemed to lighten the mood, to make things almost festive. Even the
hundreds of demonstrators assembled outside, shouting at the tops
of their lungs in Spanglish, looked to be in a partying frame of
mind. The atmosphere inside the courtroom itself, with the bright
lights and concomitant media horde, was decidedly carnival-like,
excepting the stern demeanor of the judge. Felicia's own mood was
on the verge of giddiness. For reasons she could not quite unravel,
she had awakened in a supremely confident state. She smiled at the
notion that maybe Frank's nocturnal presence was a great deal more
ameliorative than she had thought.

The court officer called the case almost immediately—Judge
Frankel's concession, Felicia surmised, to the swarm of reporters in
the courtroom. Wisocki, wearing a blue business suit Linda had
picked out, was brought out from the pens to the right of the judge.
Felicia and Mario approached the bench as Judge Frankel rifled
through the court file.

"So what do we have here?" the judge uttered to himself, in a
show of studied casualness that Felicia found almost laughable.
*Sure, he has a hundred reporters in his courtroom and is just now get-
ting around to figuring out why.* She said nothing and smiled sweetly
in the judge's direction. "Ah, a renewed application for bail,"
Frankel mumbled, and waved them to their places behind their
respective tables. They went on the record and quickly dispensed
with the formalities—the serving of the indictment and the VDF,

the entrance of a not guilty plea—and then turned to the only matter of interest, with Felicia leading off.

"I am requesting, Your Honor, that the court set minimal bail in the interest of justice. John Wisocki is a man of sterling character, reputation, and habits. He has a long and stable employment record and considerable financial resources, including a co-op apartment, almost fully paid for, valued at roughly four hundred thousand dollars. He has lived in that apartment for ten years and in the same community for most of his life. He has attended the same church since he was a teenager and is deeply devoted to his family. Mr. Wisocki's wife, Linda, and his mother, Sophie, are present in this courtroom today."

Felicia whirled dramatically and motioned in the direction of Linda and Sophie Wisocki, seated together in the second row. Both women beamed in her direction. "Mr. Wisocki has no prior criminal record," Felicia continued. "Indeed, during the course of his life, he has not even collected a moving violation ticket." She drove home the point with a theatrical flourish of her fingers, not bothering to mention that Wisocki had also never owned a car.

"It is true, Your Honor, he has had hard luck of late. He has, through no fault of his own, faced serious problems both at work and at home. And his personal psychiatrist, Dr. Albert Strober, has diagnosed him with major depressive disorder, a malady which can be controlled through counseling and the use of Prozac. My client is now on Prozac and Dr. Strober is eager to resume counseling upon his release."

"Would counsel care to wrap this up?" asked the judge, a hint of irritation in his tone.

"Of course, Your Honor," Felicia replied, knowing full well that with so many reporters present Frankel would let her go on as long as she insisted. She placed a supportive hand on John's shoulder and picked up her narrative. "My client is also the principal support for his mother, who, last week, experienced an unfortunate and potentially serious mishap as a result of improper monitoring of her diabetes medication. Thank God she managed to call nine-one-one.

Because of that medical emergency, she will require even closer monitoring. She relies heavily on my client to transport her to her doctor and medical appointments. Without his presence, particularly in light of the events of last week, her quality of life is substantially diminished, and her life itself is unnecessarily endangered."

Felicia gave Sophie Wisocki a loving but fleeting glance, before returning her attention to the judge. She felt no obligation to tell him that the hospital would gladly send a home-care attendant for Mrs. Wisocki, nor to tell him that Linda and John would be sleeping in separate beds. Her only obligation was to present her client in the best possible light and, if possible, to goad Mario into showing his hand.

She went on for several minutes more. Her client, she asserted, had committed "no crime." And remand, she insisted, was never intended as a form of pretrial punishment. Finally, she concluded: "I realize, Your Honor, that in a high-profile case like this, it can be difficult to do what is just. Nonetheless, I respectfully request that you do what is right and that you correct an earlier injustice done to my client by setting reasonable bail."

Mario, who had been seething, and was barely able to restrain himself while Felicia was speaking, balled his hand into a fist and struck the air for emphasis as he bellowed: *"No crime?* Isabel and Blanca García, the widow and young daughter of Francisco García don't agree that there has been no crime. Blanca García, who is not yet six years old, has lost a father. Nothing will ever make up for that loss. Isabel García, who is present today, has lost a loving husband. I would direct the court's attention to the first row on the left. Mrs. García is seated next to Detective O'Rourke. That counsel can pretend no crime has been committed is indicative of the desperate state of the defendant's case and of the dishonesty which is his only defense.

"No crime? The medical examiner begs to differ. He has ruled Francisco García's death a homicide. The police also beg to differ. They showed up at the scene and literally found the defendant with

a smoking gun—the same defendant, I might add, who showed up late Sunday night in the office of a man he hated. He knew Mr. García would be there to meet him, and therefore to meet his death.

"The fact that the defendant does not have a criminal record does not make him an innocent man. He is an individual who, without provocation, and before killing Francisco García, leveled an automatic weapon at two defenseless men on the street."

Felicia indignantly interjected, "As far as I know, my client is not charged with anything having to do with any so-called defenseless men. There is absolutely no proof of that charge. I demand—"

"The fact of the matter," continued Mario, shouting over Felicia's interruption, "is that the defendant, by his own admission, is unstable. He is also desperate. The fact that he is under suicide watch is clear evidence of that. A desperate, unstable man accused of murder has every reason to flee.

"While the people are not unsympathetic to any problems his family may be facing due to his absence, the defendant should have thought of that before he decided to take another man's life. He should have thought of that before he deprived a little girl of a father, not merely when he is begging to be set free. The supposed fact that he may have a sick mother is irrelevant to the fact that he stands accused of the crimes of murder and criminal possession of a weapon, and is facing substantial jail time if convicted of these charges."

Mario wrapped up with a demand that Wisocki's remand status be continued. Nothing material had changed, he asserted, that would justify setting Wisocki free.

The judge took a sip from the large coffee mug resting on the dais and pronounced his decision in a thundering voice: "Bail will be set in the amount of three hundred thousand dollars, cash or bond." A sudden commotion started up behind them, but Mario and Felicia stood still as stone, their eyes fastened to the judge as he set dates for the filing of the defendant's motion papers and for the people's response. They then exited through the velvet rope, with Felicia in the lead, beaming like a movie star about to greet her adoring fans.

Only after she was out of the courtroom, did Felicia turn and search for Mario's face. She glimpsed him, barely, as he leapt into an elevator and she shrugged and continued on her way. *There would be plenty of time during the next several weeks to gauge his reaction to her in court.* When she reached the sidewalk, Felicia stopped to talk with and romance the reporters trailing in her wake.

Getting free of the press took nearly an hour, partly because Felicia could not help but revel in her victory. Once in the car, she placed a call to the office.

"The phone here has been ringing off the hook," Tracy announced.

"Anything important?"

"I'm not sure. But you got two calls that are kind of interesting."

"Oh?"

"One is from Lester Hawkins."

"The Harlem preacher?"

"One and the same. And the other is from Dick Rogers, the radio guy."

"The Nazi. So what does he want?"

"They both want to meet with you. Hawkins said something about organizing a community campaign for justice. And Rogers, well, he said he wants to help, that he wants to put you in touch with some money people."

"Did he say who?"

"Nope. Want me to call him back?"

"Don't bother. I'll deal with it when I get in. I have a feeling this day is only going to get stranger, and I'd rather be seated behind my own desk when I face it. See you in a few."

7

The task of putting the money together for John's release went smoothly. The equity in the apartment, his investment portfolio, and the money in the bank got him past the $300,000 mark. He was still, however, facing an expensive trial—and had inadequate funds to pay for it. Not that his budget was his first concern upon being released. He was so grateful just to be free that to even mention money would have been mean-spirited. Upon setting eyes on Felicia, he hugged her so tightly that she found it difficult to breathe. With Linda, he was considerably more restrained. He grabbed her hand and held on, like a man grasping a lifeline, staring into her eyes with a bashful smile, silently, fervently, pleading for acceptance. They looked painfully awkward, his body language saying, "Please embrace me," and hers responding, "Don't come too close."

Twenty-four hours later, a certain reality set in. Wisocki, who was something of a numbers whiz, focused on the fact that financial ruin was an imminent possibility.

"No matter how well you try to manage your money, you can never factor in the effect of a catastrophe like this," he said. "My life is over," he glumly told Felicia. "I'm going to have to find a new one."

Felicia did not bother to disagree. Instead, she placed her hand on his and tried to reassure him that, come what may, he would manage to pull through. "You have a lot of support, John, probably more than you have had at any point in your adult life. My mother always used to say that only when things get rough do you find out who your real friends are. I know it sounds trite, but it's true. If you can keep your faith in the people who care about you, and keep your faith in yourself, you'll end up just fine. But you'll have to give those people who want to support you the opportunity to do so."

She did not mention that one of those people might end up being Dick Rogers, the ranting xenophobe of a radio host who had taken up Wisocki's cause. Rogers had called three times in the last two days. After ignoring the first two calls ("The last thing I need is to be accused of is conspiring with a cheerleader for the Third Reich," she had told Tanya), she had finally returned the third, her curiosity peaked by Rogers's insistence that he had a way to help. Given his reputation for arrogance and incivility, she had been prepared to slam the phone down in his ear, but he had been on good behavior, even unctuous in his blandishments. He wanted to set up a meeting between Felicia and a mysterious-sounding, unidentified "friend." Her attempts to get the name out of him had only resulted in stonewalling flatteries, along with brief homilies on the goodness of her cause. Seeing no harm in a simple get-together and eager to learn what Rogers had in mind, she had finally agreed to a meeting, but only if they came to her office alone—meaning without a press entourage. The meeting was scheduled for 4 P.M., following her chat with Lester Hawkins, who, as Tracy had informed her several minutes earlier, was waiting in the reception area.

Felicia neatened the papers on her desk and buzzed Tracy to send him in. Hawkins was tall and thin, about sixty years of age, with a goatee that was nearly totally white. He had a full head of hair, also white and heavily pomaded, and wore an elegant, Italian-cut plaid gray suit that would have fit beautifully had his stomach been a bit flatter. Felicia stepped from behind her desk and he grabbed her hand, pumping it furiously.

"Felicia. My dear Felicia. It's so good to see you again."

"It's good to see you, too, Reverend," said Felicia, a bit surprised by the fervor of his greeting. Their only previous encounter, best as she could recall, was at a huge charity event three years ago at Gracie Mansion. There they had barely exchanged two sentences. "So, how can I help you, Reverend?" she asked, waving him into the most comfortable chair. She positioned herself catercorner from him on the leather sofa.

"Call me Les, dear, please. And . . . Oh, what a beautiful painting," he said, standing up momentarily to admire the ornately framed abstract rendering on her wall.

"An artist friend of mine in Chicago did it," replied Felicia.

Hawkins nodded approvingly. "Beautiful. I like the use of color. And the lustiness of the brushwork. It's so . . . sensual. Ah. You can feel the passion. It reminds me of a piece I have hanging in my bedroom." Turning his gaze back toward Felicia, he added, "How very interesting. Seems we have similar tastes in art."

"Guess so," said Felicia. "At least it seems we share a fondness for the works of Youtha Cromwell-Oliver. She is quite special. If you're interested, I'm sure I can get you a catalog of her stuff."

"That would be extremely nice."

"Great. So what is it we have to discuss, Reverend?"

"Oh, I'm sorry, Felicia. I know you're busy. Let me get to the point. You know, a number of the brother pastors have been trying to decide where to come down on this . . . ah, how shall I say it . . . on this case of yours. You are no doubt familiar with Nelson Flores, one of our Puerto Rican brothers out of Washington Heights. Well, Flores has some very strong feelings concerning your client. In fact, he—"

"As far as I know, Nelson Flores does not know my client."

"That may be, Sister Felicia, but nonetheless, he has approached our little group of ministers in Harlem about forming a coalition. He calls it a 'Coalition for Justice' and wants all the brothers to sign on. He's pretty determined. And he has a great deal of community support."

"Yeah?"

"Well, the brothers haven't really decided yet. One thing is that this fellow who was shot, Mr. García I believe his name is, is from another country. Hell, there are folks in our neighborhood who think Colombia is somewhere in Europe. It would be different if this guy was Puerto Rican, or Jamaican, or from Brooklyn or some such, but he's from all the way down in South America. Also, the details of what happened are a little less—"

"This has something to do with me?" asked Felicia, exasperation breaking through her calm facade.

"Of course, Felicia. This Wisocki fellow is your client. And . . . well let me put it this way. I have a certain amount of influence with the brothers. And I have always admired your . . . ummm . . . many, many fine attributes, and I think we have a great many things in common."

"Reverend Hawkins," she began, more bewildered than ever, "I don't under—"

"Les. Please call me Les. The point, my dear, is that if we, you and I . . . Ahh . . . If we were on the same team, so to speak, the brothers would not be terribly inclined to get involved in this matter—which would certainly be in your interest. I mean, it's not really their affair, if you know what I mean." His eyes turned, again, to the painting on the wall, and he said softly, almost as if speaking to himself, "You must come over and see mine. It's really very similar. Amazing."

Hawkins drew his right hand along the crease of his trousers as a smile flitted across his lips and Felicia, heretofore mystified by his bizarre behavior, suddenly remembered his Don Juan reputation. Even before his wife had died five or six years ago, Hawkins was known as one of the most notorious skirt-chasers in town. At one point, two of his lovers, both faithful parishioners, supposedly had gotten into a fistfight in the middle of 116th Street over his affections. Legend had it that one of the women eventually tossed a Molotov cocktail into the other's car and then threatened to throw another one into her apartment. Since becoming a widower,

Hawkins had been seen with a succession of shapely and much younger women. Still, Felicia found it hard to believe that he had nothing more than sex on his mind, so she pressed for an explanation.

"I'm sure the painting in your bedroom is stunning, Reverend Hawkins. But I still don't understand why you're here."

"I'm suggesting, Felicia, that it might be a good idea for us to get to know each other better." He leaned closer, his breath giving off a faint bouquet of Bourbon. "There are a lot of treacherous cats in the world of politics," he continued, "and, realize it or not, that's where you've landed. It's a vicious, vicious world. It's my world, and I can help you. I can get your back . . . You are a beautiful and brilliant woman, Felicia Fontaine—*I love to say your name*—but you need somebody to watch over you."

"You could do that, for *me*?"

"I would do it for any beloved child of God, but especially for one as lovely, dedicated, and talented as yourself."

"I see. And what is it you would expect from me?"

"Nothing. Your company itself would be reward enough. I won't be overmodest, Felicia. I think you could profit hugely from the guidance of an experienced older man like myself. As I said before, we have much in common—more, I suspect, than you realize. I can take one look at you and see we're cut from the same cloth."

He touched a finger to her knee, as if to accentuate his point, but let it linger, moving smoothly across her stockinged leg. She deftly brushed his hand away and, looking him dead in the eyes, asked, "Are you saying you want to go out with me, Reverend Hawkins?"

"I'm saying we should start with a nice dinner," he said evenly. "We all have hungers that need satisfying, corporeal and spiritual, body and soul."

"Of course we do," she agreed, standing up and reseating herself behind her desk, "but I'm not sure dinner's a good idea. Anyway, I'm on a diet. I don't eat out much these days."

"It can get pretty ugly out there if you're all alone," said Hawkins, smiling smugly as he pulled a bit of lint from his suit jacket. "I believe it's really in your interest to have me on your side."

"I'm sure you're right," she replied. "And that's exactly why I, and my boyfriend Frank, will make a point of stopping by your church service sometime soon. I'm really glad you came by, Reverend Hawkins. Thanks so much for your advice."

Before he could recover, she had waltzed to the door and called out to Tracy to show him the way out. Hawkins left with a slightly dazed look in his eyes, shaking his head all the way to the elevator.

The meeting with Rogers was nearly as bewildering. Rogers was both shorter and trimmer than she had imagined, and he carried himself with considerably more dignity and good cheer than she would have thought possible from the host of such a hideously hateful radio show; but there was still something oily, even sinister, about him. He arrived with Mike Smith, a heavyset man with broad shoulders and a big belly, whom he described as an entrepreneur and funder of conservative candidates and causes. His name, though vaguely familiar, Felicia could not quite place. She seated them on the sofa and plopped into the chair facing them.

"So, gentlemen. Here we are, together, though I must admit I have no real notion why."

"Since it's my idea," said Rogers, "I should probably provide the answer, which is really quite simple. We admire your politics and your honesty. And we particularly admire your willingness to take on the civil rights establishment."

"I appreciate your admiration, Mr. Rogers, but I haven't exactly taken on the civil rights establishment. I'm just a lawyer."

"You're way too humble, Miss Fontaine. By vigorously defending John Wisocki, you have, indeed, taken on the civil rights establishment. That takes real guts. And I admire you for that."

"That's well and good, but, let me be candid, Mr. Rogers," she said, as she looked him dead in the eyes. "I am not anti–civil rights. And for that matter, I am not a big fan of your radio show. It seems, to me, to be a pretty wild and pretty extreme display of intolerance toward virtually everybody."

"That's show business," Rogers said with a smile. "I make no apology for my program. The audience has to be entertained. And I do a very good job of it. My show is the leader in its time slot. I'm very proud of that. But if all you know of me is the side I project on the radio program, you don't know me at all. I would advise you to withhold judgment. I'm a very complex man."

Smith spoke up in his croaking foghorn of a voice. "Miss Fontaine, I agree with Dick that you have taken a courageous stand, and I applaud you for it. More members of your tribe should be so enlightened."

"My tribe?" she exclaimed, casting her eyes heavenward, as if inviting divine intervention.

"Your people, if you prefer. My point is that your case is very important, in part because you're involved with it. And I'm prepared to invest in it, and to suggest to my friends that they do likewise."

Smith's words brought Felicia hurtling back to earth. She looked him over warily and asked, "Invest? What in God's name are you saying? It's not as if I'm offering stock options here."

"What I'm saying is that we are willing to set up a defense fund for John Wisocki, to help cover the costs associated with his trial."

"And why might you be willing to do that?"

"For the reasons I suggested," said Smith. "I believe your defense of Wisocki is important, enough so that I am quite literally willing to put my money where my mouth is."

"As you no doubt know," added Rogers, "I have discussed the case quite a bit on my show, and always get a positive reaction. I suspect many of my listeners would be eager to support a defense fund for Mr. Wisocki."

Felicia sighed and leaned back in her chair, trying to process what they were telling her. Even if they could deliver on their pledges, could she afford to accept their money? Would the ill-will generated by their collaboration cancel out any benefit it might bring? Yet, if Smith and Rogers wanted to champion her and Wisocki, did it make sense to say no? That all depended, she concluded, on the expected quid pro quo; and she was prepared to promise them absolutely nothing. The very thought of being in bed with Rogers, even if only figuratively, filled her with revulsion. Still, there might be a way things could work out.

"That's certainly the most interesting proposition I've heard today," said Felicia. "It is, however, ultimately up to my client to decide how he intends to pay for his defense; just as it is up to you to decide who and what you wish to support. That being said, I must tell you, I find your offer intriguing but problematic. I have no idea how you would propose to administer this fund, but I do know that it would join us at the hip in a way that I would find extremely uncomfortable."

She paused for several seconds, allowing time for her meaning to sink in, and just as Rogers seemed on the verge of breaking the silence, she abruptly continued her thought. "On the other hand, as you may know, my client is a long-standing member of a Lutheran church on East Eighty-ninth Street. Now, it's possible some parishioners there might organize a Friends of Wisocki Fund. If they do, I suspect they would be quite open to accepting funds from whomever wished to donate, at least if the money was given with no strings attached and with the understanding that any excess capital would be earmarked for the church. I personally would not get involved in such a project, but I could certainly let you know if, in fact, it comes together."

They bantered awhile and then she ushered them out, with everyone promising to stay in touch. Those promises, Felicia assumed, were strictly pro forma, since it seemed clear that she and Rogers were not even close to being in sync. But within days, and to her astonishment, her proposal was on the way to becoming a self-fulfilling prophecy.

John seemed fascinated by the very idea that anyone might be willing to support him; but it was his mother, Sophie, who was galvanized to act. If using the church to launder tainted funds would get her son to Sunday service, she was all for it. "He stopped going, in a regular way, about ten years ago and some of the hope went out of him," she told Felicia. "He needs the Lord now more than ever."

Sophie's sometimes impenetrable Eastern European accent, her habit of nodding at virtually whatever was said and then asking that the phrase be repeated, and her practice of murmuring "Praise God from whom all blessings flow" at the oddest times had initially left Felicia with the impression that she was on the road to senility. After a few conversations with her, however, Felicia realized that Sophie's only real problem was a rather marked hearing loss that she was too vain to acknowledge. Otherwise, she was a dynamo, not only of sound mind but of tenacious spirit. It was Sophie who took the first concrete step to bring Felicia's idea to life by corralling her pastor after Sunday service and insisting he meet with John and his lawyer. The pastor, a young, easy-going transplanted Minnesotan, had no choice but to comply.

During the meeting, after Felicia had outlined her scheme, Reverend Berge had spoken at length about the affection the congregants felt for Sophie and about how delighted they would be to do something to help her son. He promised to take the matter up with a committee of the laity but assured Felicia and John that things would work out. "We will gladly take money, even from sinners, to do the Lord's work," he said with a smile.

Once Reverend Berge signed on to the plan, Sophie called Rogers and admitted, apparently sincerely, to being a longtime fan. Rogers began touting the "fund for justice" on air and Jake played it up in a "Streetlife" column. Even Wisocki, who, on Felicia's orders, scrupulously avoided the press, did a short, tightly scripted interview with Channel 3, in which he thanked those people who believed in him and confided, in a moment of faux spontaneity, "I'm an ordinary man with ordinary worries, so it comes as a bit of a surprise to me that anybody cares about my problems."

The one immediate adverse consequence of Smith's visit was the effect it had on her law partner, Stephanie. Shortly after Smith left, Stephanie demanded to know exactly what business Felicia had with him. Once Felicia had explained, Stephanie launched into a lecture. Did she have any idea who Smith was? Didn't she know he was an anti-Semite and patron of Holocaust deniers? Finally, in a frosty tone Felicia had never heard her use before, Stephanie had snapped, "Please, never have that man in this office again. He stinks up the whole place," before storming off. They reconciled almost immediately, but Stephanie had made her point. And over the next several days, Felicia found herself reassuring Stephanie, repeatedly, that she would never get the firm involved in anything even remotely anti-Semitic.

For Felicia, the weeks after the arraignment presented her with an unusual combination of tasks. In addition to reconnecting with some of her temporarily neglected clients and filing assorted motions for discovery of documents and information necessary for the defense, she was coping with countless requests to appear on radio and TV and at public forums. She declined most of the invitations, pleading lack of time, but accepted a good number, both out of a sense of obligation to the firm (free advertising, she constantly reminded herself, was a gift devoutly to be wished) and because something she felt deeply about—affirmative action and its effects on American life—was, largely through her own efforts, a hot issue in New York. So when a nonpartisan group calling itself New Yorkers for a Civil Society asked her to debate affirmative action, she had agreed, after laying down one condition: that her opponent be someone white. Why even risk the possibility, she reasoned, of the discussion degenerating into a silly name-calling contest, in which she was likely to be accused of being an "Auntie Tom." With a white opponent, skin credentials would not be an issue. In addition, as she pointed out to the NYCS, the debate would seem much less conventional and stereotypical with her arguing against affirmative action and a white person arguing for it.

The debate, which was taped for broadcast by public television, took place in a high school gym. The opponent they produced was John Irwin, a law professor from New York University who wore a rumpled, ill-fitting gray suit that made him look like a housewares salesman. The audience was a multicolored mixture that spanned the class divide.

Felicia opened with a story she thought was both pertinent and poignant, about a letter she had received from a white woman who had gone to a black physician for several years but had already decided that any new physician of hers would be white. "Her point was that she could no longer be sure black doctors were qualified. And that is solely because of affirmative action," said Felicia.

"So are we to cater to ignorant assumptions?" asked Irwin, who then went on a rant about corporate fat-cats whom he saw as beneficiaries of affirmative action. "A white male got to be president of Disney because of an unfair preference. His buddy hired him and then booted him out after sixteen months because he proved himself to be unqualified. Yet he got something like one hundred million dollars for his time. Much the same happened at ATT and Sony. Unqualified white males hired and then fired because of incompetence, all given tens of millions of dollars. But nobody says, as a result, that affirmative action has given white males a bad image. Nobody says let's stop hiring white males. Nobody says, 'He's a white male, therefore he must be incompetent.'"

As the back and forth continued, Felicia realized from the audience's increasingly spirited reaction that she and her opponent both had their partisans in the room—many of whom were spoiling to get into the battle. She also noted, without surprise, that Irwin's fans tended to be black and hers tended to be white. As she continued to press her points, however, she felt that she was winning respect, that even those who disagreed with her had to acknowledge that some of what she said was right and also had to see that she was speaking from her heart.

Frank, who had been quietly sitting among the spectators, appeared at the edge of the crowd that gathered around her at the debate's end. Felicia caught his eye and nodded, signaling him to rescue her. He smoothly worked his way through the mass of people and placed his arm around her shoulder as he said, in a loud though cordial voice, "We're going to have to run to make that ten o'clock interview." There was no interview at ten, but the ruse worked well enough to allow them to quickly exit the school.

A taxi immediately pulled up and, as they headed home, he

turned to her and said, "I didn't tell you this earlier because I didn't want to throw your concentration, but I got a call from a friend at the *Partisan* just as I was leaving the office. Apparently they located the second guy who had the encounter with Wisocki and are running a feature in tomorrow's edition. The reporter, a guy named John Britton, is a brother. And he doesn't think too much of your guy. This piece, from what I hear, nails him to the wall." He shrugged and added, "I suppose it was only a matter of time. But I promise not to say, 'I told you so.'"

The next morning, Felicia made a point of getting to the corner newsstand even before drinking her morning coffee. She found the story bannered across the top of the *Partisan*'s third page—CLOSE ENCOUNTER OF THE STRANGE KIND—along with photographs of Wisocki and a man identified as Juan Hernández. She read the article as she walked, pausing only to nod a greeting at the doorman.

The article, as Frank had suggested, was potentially devastating to her client. For if this Juan Hernández was to be believed, John had attacked him and his friend totally without provocation. As Hernández told it: "This guy came out of nowhere, started screaming and shouting. He kept repeating over and over, 'Where's the game? Who won the game?' or something really strange like that. Then he waved that big gun in our faces. Said he would kill us both if we so much as moved a muscle. Man, I ain't never been so scared. I mean, that crazy bastard with that weird look on his face and all. It was like looking into the face of Freddy Krueger or somebody."

"This man's testimony, if it holds up, could be very detrimental to the defense case," the *Partisan* quoted Laura Miranda, some hotshot defense attorney, as saying. The story concluded with: "Calls to Mr. Wisocki for comment were not returned. His lawyer, Felicia Fontaine, was also unavailable for comment."

"Those assholes," Felicia sputtered as she unlocked the door to her apartment. "Like they really called."

"What did you say, dear?" asked Frank, from behind the closed bathroom door.

"Nothing," shouted Felicia. She angrily tossed the newspaper onto the cocktail table and noticed, lying there, the autopsy report she had brought home and set aside the previous evening. She had perused it quickly at the office but had been in too much of a rush— and then too tired—to sort out what it might mean.

She picked it up and began to read: "I hereby certify that I, David K. Miller, M.D., City Medical Examiner-1, have performed an autopsy on the body of Francisco García." His body was "well nourished," his genitalia "normal," and his extremities "unremarkable." His rigor mortis was "strong and symmetric" and his body was cold. There was one gunshot wound to the chest, with "stippling"—caused by the gunpowder residue—and an exit wound in his back. Felicia flipped to the last page and studied the final two items: the cause and the manner of death. Homicide was the finding for manner of death. Cause of death was attributed to "Gunshot wound to chest with perforation of lung," followed by a notation indicating "ventricular fibrillation." She stared at the words for several seconds and softly read them aloud as a smile slowly made its way across her face.

8

Once upon a time the *Partisan* had been a fairly decent paper, back in the era of long hair and revolution when it was the certified voice of the counter-culture and regularly showcased some of the best writing in New York. But its glory days were long gone. And accuracy had never been its strength. Still, Mario was intrigued by the story on Juan Hernández, so much so that he invited him down for a chat. On the phone, Hernández seemed eager to come, but missed the first and then the second meeting. Only when Mario sent a police officer to retrieve him, did he manage to show up.

He was a big man, at least six feet, well over two hundred pounds, and built like a weight lifter. His clothes were bright-colored and fashionably baggy. His hair was styled in a hip-hop fade. And he had a gold chain, with a molded "Juan" at its center, hanging from his neck. His manner, which Mario could easily imagine as threatening, was congenial but annoyingly cavalier.

"Sorry about yesterday, man. I forgot we had set something up," Hernández said with a grin. He sailed into Mario's office and sprawled across a chair, his ankle resting over his knee. Mario grumbled, in what he intended to be a gesture of forgiveness, and started off the interview with not-quite-idle chitchat, getting Hernández to talk about his family and his childhood. Hernández claimed he had grown up between Aguadilla and East Harlem—between small-town, largely rural Puerto Rico and New York City. "P.R. was always nice to go back to, you know, but New York is home. When I was little, I couldn't wait to get back here. It wasn't just that all my homies were here, but there wasn't shit to do in Aguadilla."

He had known his father only as a ghost, a lumbering bull of a man who would infrequently appear, generally late at night, bearing trinkets and gifts, and mysteriously vanish at dawn. His sister, thirteen years younger than himself, was fathered by another man who, though accepting partial responsibility for her support, had never become part of their family. "You know, that's just whacked, man. My kids aren't going to come up like that. A *real* man raises his own kids. You know what I mean? But I've got to get my act together first. Right now, though, I ain't doing so bad. I got me a little job helping a man fix up things in the 'hood. Got a little money in my pocket. I ain't never been arrested, or nothing like that. And I'm getting my school thing together. A couple of years, homes, I get that degree—"

"Talking about that degree," Mario interrupted. "I subpoenaed your City College records."

"Say what?"

"I subpoenaed your records from CCNY."

"You can do that?" he said, a look of amazement on his face.

"Yep. I can do that."

"You just ask for my personal shit and they give it to you?"

"Yep. And, according to them, you only enrolled for two courses and dropped one without finishing it. What's up with that?"

"You must have got the wrong records, man."

"That's possible. Could be another Juan Hernández enrolled there," said Mario, skeptically scrunching his eyebrows. "I guess I must have gotten the wrong rap sheet too."

"What do you mean?"

Mario picked up a computer printout from his desk and flipped through it as he spoke. "According to the State of New York,

Division of Criminal Justice Services, you've been arrested several times for crack dealing, convicted once. You've got a couple of arrests for assault, no convictions. A lot of little stuff, including turnstile jumping, before that."

"That's bullshit, man. You know how cops are. I was being hassled. They got all that shit in the computer, huh?" he asked, in a voice brimming with disgust.

"You pled guilty and served six months because you were being hassled?"

"Yeah. They got me a lawyer who didn't know shit. If you ain't got money, you get fucked. You got money, you walk. That's the way it is. You don't see no rich folks at Rikers Island. Anyway, that was a long time ago. I was nothing but a kid, then."

"That may be," said Mario. "But you've got to understand that if I'm going to put you on the stand, I have to think about your credibility as a witness. And if you're lying to me about your school and jail record—"

"I ain't lied about shit. And I ain't asking to be no witness," yelled Juan. "Ain't nothin' for me in that."

"Chill, man," Mario commanded, fighting the impulse to wring Juan's neck. "What's in it for you is not the point here. But if that man actually did what you say he did, if he really called you a spick and menaced you with a gun, it might be good to have that on the court record. And that's my decision, not yours. Not anymore anyway. You made yourself a potential witness the minute you and Nelson Flores went to the press. Given that, I need to know whether you're being straight with me."

"What happened, happened, man. And that's a fact," said Juan, who seemed wounded Mario would dare doubt his word. "You see that movie with Michael Douglas? The one where he goes crazy in L.A. and starts shooting up all the minorities? Took off after the Koreans and then after the *mejicanos*. That's what that man was like. He went nuts. Called us all kinds of names. Thought I was going to die, man."

"What about your buddy? What happened to him?"

"Wish I knew. I ain't seen Angel since that night."

Over the course of the next two hours, as Mario continued to quiz Juan on his story, his life history, and his relationship with Angel, he felt himself growing increasingly uneasy. It would be great to have someone place Wisocki on the street with a gun, and all the better if they could testify to his use of anti-Latino epithets; but he was not sure that that someone should be Juan—who was clearly something other than what he said he was: an upstanding, hard-working college student who doted over his mother and sister and aspired only to a life of service to humanity. Juan was a convicted felon with a cocky attitude and putty for brains who lied apparently by force of habit. The jury would hate him, and Felicia would tear him apart. Still, as Juan said, "what happened, happened," and one did not get to pick one's witnesses purely on the basis of their innocence, intellect, and public appeal. In the end, the equation was rather simple: Would Juan do the case more harm than good? Not that there was any guarantee the judge would allow Juan's testimony at any rate. Rather than sort out the matter immediately, Mario decided to put some feelers out on the street and see what, if anything, came back.

Over the next several weeks, there was little news on Hernández, or on much of anything else associated with the case. Mario's time was increasingly devoted to his other, less sensational litigation, in addition to reviewing police reports and lab analyses and responding to motions on the Wisocki prosecution. As Wisocki all but vanished from the front pages, Mario recovered some semblance of his former life. Though he continued to call Isabel García and Blanca—it was crucial, he felt, to maintain an emotional connection to the murder victim's family—he was also going to the gym, getting sleep, and every so often visiting his parents, who had accused him, not totally in jest, of forgetting that they existed.

During one visit to their East Harlem apartment, his mother turned to him, over a dinner of rice, beans, and codfish and said, "I don't know that it's so nice to use language about kicking people's *nalgas*." His father and brother broke into chuckles. Apparently, she had been fretting for days over just how to express her concern. It seemed that her friends at church, who had seen Mario's profile in *La Nueva Prensa*, were astounded that such words as "kick this guy's ass" could come out of her son's mouth. "*Que malo muchacho*," she added with a snicker.

Despite Mario's protest that he had never said any such thing, his family refused to let him off the hook. His father praised him for being such a tough guy: "*Mi'jo, el peleador para la gente*." And his younger brother, Manolo, chimed in, "I'm just sorry you weren't such a warrior in the old days. I could have used you to kick a few guys' asses back in school." Later, in the kitchen and out of earshot of the rest of the family, Manolo, who lived in Vineland, New Jersey, but had come in to the city for the day, confided that he had broken up with the woman he had been dating for the past five years. He had met someone new who he said, with a faraway look in his eyes, just might be "it." "After all these years," said Manolo, "I realized that I didn't feel much of anything for Miriam. I was just there, going through the motions, pretending to love her. Funny how things end up in life, how the one you think is the right one sometimes isn't. Look at you, for instance. I always figured you would end up with Felicia. She's a lot of woman, bro. But things don't always work out. And now, you and her doing battle with the whole world watching. Funny how things work out."

Felicia took advantage of the lull in activity to spend a relaxing weekend in Washington. There she reconnected with Larry Roberts, a black defense attorney and friend of the family, on whom she had had a crush as a teen.

As a child, she had thought him to be something akin to a god. A tall, trim man with wire-rimmed glasses and gold and diamonds—or so it seemed at the time—encircling his fingers, Roberts spoke in sentences full of ornate words that rolled off his tongue like gentle thunder, and he walked with the grace of a dancer. His suits, always with matching pocket square, seemed lifted from the pages of a fancy magazine. No wrinkle—either on clothing or skin—

dared to mar his physical perfection. Felicia suspected he knew that she worshiped him, and part of his cool was that he managed not to show it or to belittle her infatuation; even while maintaining a respectful but affectionate distance, he refused to treat her as a child.

It was Uncle Larry, a graduate of Princeton and Howard Law School, who had insisted that she go to Harvard. And it was he who, before Felicia went for her interview, contacted an old friend in the DA's office to make sure she would not be overlooked.

They met for brunch at an outdoor café in Northwest Washington. And as they waited for their orders to arrive, Felicia assessed the impact of the passing years. His hair was thinning, his shoulders slightly stooped, slender fissures ran along his face, but he still had the carriage and aura of a star.

"I read your piece in the *Herald* today and I found it very well done," said Roberts. "Can't say I agree with it, but it was excellently argued. No wonder you're such a good advocate."

"So what part of it don't you agree with?"

"You're not going to draw me into that, Felicia," he said, smiling. "Suffice it to say that I'm quite a bit older than you, which means my memory is a good deal longer. I remember what it was like before affirmative action. Hell, I remember what it was like during Jim Crow. And if I pushed my poor, tired brain cells enough, I might even be able to remember slavery—which, I gather, you think was rather a good thing."

Felicia laughed. "I didn't exactly say that, Larry. What I said is that I had benefited from it, in that if it had not existed I would never have been born. And my point was that the simple fact you have benefited from something is not a reason to support it."

They bantered through brunch and well into the afternoon, and when Felicia left it was with a deep sense of reluctance, for she so enjoyed the serenity that had settled over her, the kind of tranquillity that comes only from being tightly wrapped in love.

She returned to New York refreshed, but reluctant to give up the relaxing pace of her Washington weekend. For even though it was the seat of government, Washington was also a rather sleepy town, with greenery, a Southern pace, and comfortable, human proportions. New York was a farrago of towering buildings, bustle, and never-ending noise, a place full of rude reminders that childhood innocence had no place, that one must constantly be on guard. It was also a place where, in the last few weeks, she had become almost famous.

She took a number of media calls her first morning back. A Washington bureau reporter for Australian television wanted to line her up for a special Sunday morning broadcast the following week. A producer from a network magazine show was seeking someone to debate an aging icon of the civil rights movement. Felicia passed on the Australian show, promised to get back to the network producer, and did a series of short phone interviews with an array of radio and newspaper reporters. Celebrity, she was discovering, could be time-consuming—especially when she still had all the responsibilities of a full-time lawyer.

In addition to making time for the media, Felicia also had to interview a psychiatrist she was considering using in the Wisocki case; and later that afternoon she was scheduled to be in court to argue for the suppression of evidence uncovered during an illegal search.

Two minutes into the interview with the psychiatrist, she decided he was probably what she was looking for. A young, nice-looking guy with an M.D. from (and faculty appointment at) Columbia University, he had a relaxed, easy-going yet authoritative manner that she knew a jury would like. He also was capable of throwing in just enough jargon to appear knowledgeable ("In this particular case, I wouldn't necessarily diagnose dysthymic disorder. From what you've described, Mr. Wisocki hasn't been among the walking wounded long enough. At least two years is required to diagnose that. He does, however, seem to have some Axis One disorders. Major depressive disorder, for instance ...") without becoming hopelessly confusing.

The suppression hearing, later that afternoon, was one of those obligatory lawyerly tasks that made her wonder about her choice of profession. Her client, who was on probation for armed robbery, had been stopped by police for "driving funny" and "looking suspicious"—which translated, she presumed, into being a garishly dressed black man driving a Lexus. Instead of meekly accepting being hassled, he had taken offense at a cop's remark and challenged the officer's manhood. Predictably, the police had ordered the man and his companion out of the car and roughed them up, but they had not stopped there.

They claimed to have spotted drugs on the backseat of the car, leading them—or so they said—to demand the keys to the trunk. Inside the trunk, they found a locked case, which they opened. There they had discovered and seized eight semiautomatic weapons along with a small quantity of cocaine. That her client's companion was a convicted drug dealer made matters even worse.

Nonetheless, the hearing was relatively routine. Once she established there was no evidence that any drugs had been found on the backseat, it was clear to everyone involved that the cops were lying. After that, the prosecutor put up only token opposition. For it was equally obvious that the only reason for the lie was that the cops lacked a legal reason for the stop, the arrest, and the subsequent search. That her client was in violation of parole for consorting with a criminal was irrelevant, as far as the court was concerned. Though Felicia prevailed, she walked out of court somewhat depressed, feeling slightly unclean. What kind of victory was it, she wondered, that resulted in freedom for a homicidal gun merchant? And why should she even care about the rights of a man who recognized no one else's rights, who would as easily kill a man as talk to him, who, she assumed, had already killed several, and whose most memorable comment, after the hearing, was, "Is there any way I can get my guns back?" She generally tried not to think about such irksome moral questions too deeply; but today, she could not easily put them out of her mind.

No longer in a mood for work, Felicia decided to have a glass of wine. She stopped by Jason's on Baxter Street, a few minutes' walk from the criminal courts. Though not as crowded or as noisy as Forlini's, it drew some of the same courtroom crowd. The decor, heavy on mirrors, brass, and wood, had not changed in more than a decade. There was something comforting in its stability. It was a place she and Mario had often come to together, and today it put her in a nostalgic frame of mind.

It did not take Mario long to turn up. He came in perhaps fifteen minutes after Felicia. The moment he entered, Felicia realized that she had been watching the door, hoping, for reasons she could not understand, that he would appear. That he did was not at all unusual, given that he often stopped at Jason's at the end of the day—at least that had been his pattern when they were dating; and it pleased her, in some unacknowledged corner of her heart, to know that had not changed. It also delighted her to see that the wife, the woman with daggers in her eyes, was nowhere to be seen.

"Want to buy a lady a drink?" Felicia asked, rising from her booth. "Better yet," she added, motioning him over, "why not let a lady buy you a drink? It's the least I can do for a hardworking public servant."

Mario slid into the booth across from her, a wary look in his eyes. "Hello, Felicia," he said evenly. "So you're socializing with us poor folks today?"

"Getting back in touch with my roots," she replied, beckoning the bartender over. "Stoli on ice?" she asked, glancing at Mario.

"Sure."

"And I'll have another wine," Felicia told the barman.

"I always liked this place," she said, turning again to Mario. "It's like a little island of serenity."

"I never quite thought of it that way," he replied. "So, what brings you to the neighborhood? Are you on trial down here?"

"Just a suppression hearing. Nothing complicated."

"Which judge?"

"Kougasian."

"I like him. He cuts through the bullshit."

"He sure does. And there's so much of it. I sometimes think that without the bullshit there would be no need for lawyers."

"Speak for yourself, lady," he said, flashing a smile.

"No need to get nasty. Well, at least I got a smile out of you. Remind me to mark that in my calendar," said Felicia.

The drinks came and Felicia hastily drained the remaining drops in her glass and handed it to the bartender. She lifted the fresh drink and said, "A toast. To complicated entanglements."

Mario touched his glass to hers and replied, "For sure. *Salud*."

"You know, it's funny how much this place reminds me of you," said Felicia. "I associate it with a very particular point in my life. You know we did have something pretty hot."

He winced, as his mind flashed back to the kiss in her apartment and to how difficult it had been to walk away. "I certainly can't deny that," he said.

She grinned, knowingly. "No. I don't think you can. Don't you ever wonder how we could have been, what we would have become if we had stayed together?"

He looked at the ceiling, a thoughtful expression on his face, but said nothing. She thought at first that he was ignoring the question, and realized that she couldn't blame him if he were. It was not he who had left her, after all. It was she who had decided to move on. If anyone bore responsibility for the way things had turned out, it was she. Still, ever since they had reconnected, albeit as adversaries, she had been wondering whether, in looking elsewhere, she had made a horrible mistake. So she was dying to hear his answer. And after an eternity, he gave it.

"I guess I used to think about that," said Mario, whose gaze had settled on her eyes. "I used to think about it a lot, but that was a long time ago. As you must know, I'm basically a pragmatist, always have been. The fact is, it wouldn't have worked out. And the even greater fact is it doesn't matter. You can never go back in life."

His speech was as much for himself as for her. And he suspected that she knew it. For though he believed what his words implied, that they would never have truly meshed, he also knew that, had she been willing, he would probably have made her his wife. And as he faced her across the table, he realized, as he had in her apartment, that he was far from being free of her spell.

"For all the shit we put each other through, we had something special," said Felicia.

He shrugged. "Everything is special in some way, I suppose."

"Yeah," she said, regret blanketing her face. "I suppose it's not too late to be friends," she added, a question mark in her voice.

"You have very interesting timing," said Mario, trying to sound flip.

"We all need friends, Mario."

"That may be true, but we don't have to find them at the table of opposing counsel."

"So it's war?"

"Why be so melodramatic?" he asked, shifting uneasily in his seat. "No. It's not war; it's a murder case."

"I wasn't just talking about the case," she said.

"Well, for some reason, I have a hard time getting it out of my mind," he said.

She sighed. "You're going to lose, you know."

"The Wisocki case? I don't think so."

"Believe me. You can't win. It's no reflection on you, Mario. But the fact is, you don't have a case."

"I guess we'll see," he said, sensing that her mood had changed. Something hard had come into her eyes, which he took as a sign of recognition that flirting served no purpose, and which he also took as a reminder of how unpredictable, ruthless, and infuriating Felicia could be.

"In the end," Mario continued, "this case will not be up to either one of us to decide, whatever tricks you may think you have up your sleeve. And I think I've probably seen most of them at this point."

"Which means?"

"That I know you."

"That goes both ways," she replied.

"But what we know about each other is different. And I know enough about you not to trust you. I know exactly what you're capable of. I remember Carl Murphy, for one thing. Still, I expect you to play fair. In fact, I will insist on it, even if that means embarrassing both of us."

"Are you threatening me, Mario?" she asked.

"Think of it as explaining the rules of engagement. Anyway, I'm sure you're a better person than you used to be."

He finished his drink, thanked her, and quietly walked away, leaving her with an inexplicable sense of sadness, with a feeling that, in a way she could not appreciate when it was happening, something precious had been lost, perhaps forever.

As Mario rode the subway home, he replayed the conversation with Felicia. He was certain she had been up to something, but was not at all clear as to what. If she had been fishing for information, she had done a remarkably inept job. And if she had been looking for romance, she had picked an awfully odd time—though, despite his best effort to hate her, Mario was grateful they had met in a public place, that she'd had no opportunity to test him again; for, as he was sure she knew, and had demonstrated in her apartment, the powerful passion he'd once felt for her was not far beneath the surface. It was hard to believe, however, that she was seriously trying to seduce him. Maybe she was just trying to unsettle him, to shake his confidence. Or maybe she wasn't playing mind games at all but was just screwed up. Indeed, maybe "all the shit we put each other through," her use of the phrase as well as the reality, had simply been a manifestation of her continuing confusion—of her inability to decide what she wanted, to recognize it when she saw it, or to accept its loss when it was gone. "Sometimes what seems to be clever is merely crazy," María Cristina had once said when talking about Felicia. And perhaps she had a point.

Felicia's reaction to his mention of Carl Murphy was intriguing. Yet Mario himself was uncertain whether he meant what he had insinuated. Going to the authorities, or even the newspapers, several years after the fact would seem a bit odd. Also, he was not really the whistle-blower type. And then there was the inconvenient fact that, in some measure, he was involved.

Murphy was a big-time uptown drug dealer Felicia had been prosecuting for murder, and Mario, who was new to murder cases at the time, had been second-seating her. The office considered the case particularly important since Murphy had managed to literally get away with double murder the year before—or so believed the police—by killing a romantic rival and later killing the only witness. Felicia's theory concerning the most recent murder, as she had spelled out in her opening statement and throughout the case, was that Murphy had killed an associate over stolen drugs. They had fought about something an hour or so before the victim's death. Several witnesses had sworn to that. Murphy was the last person to be seen with him, and was known to have threatened him in the past. And when the police had searched the dead man's mother's house, they had found a huge quantity of cocaine. The murder weapon had never been recovered, but the bullets had been fired from a gun of the type Murphy was known to own. Murphy had insisted, when picked up by the police, that the drugs did not belong to him, and that he had no reason to kill the man. Their argument, he had claimed, had not been an argument at all, but their way of joking with each other. The jury did not seem to be buying his story, and neither, for sure, was Felicia, who was so intent on getting the guy behind bars that she would have put Satan himself on the witness stand to attest to the man's depravity.

Felicia, to the delight of the DA and the media, had won the conviction. And Mario, proud of her work and proud of her—and elated to have her on his arm—had basked in her reflected glory. Murphy, later sentenced to twenty-five years to life, was dragged out of the courtroom proclaiming his innocence and threatening death to those who had "lied against me."

The problem, as Felicia spelled out over drinks with him eight or nine months later, was that Murphy had a valid complaint. The night before closing arguments, a snitch had backed up a portion of his story. According to the confidential informant, the drugs belonged to a rival drug dealer, whom the victim and Murphy, working together, had ripped off. If the snitch's story was true—

and the detective claimed he was reliable—the rival drug dealer had a much stronger motive for murder than Murphy.

Felicia had proceeded as if the information did not exist, and apparently advised the detective to keep quiet about what he knew. In burying that exculpatory information—so-called Brady material, named for a 1963 Supreme Court case—Felicia had committed a cardinal sin, one which entitled Murphy to a new trial. For Mario to reveal that at this late point would certainly create a major headache for Felicia, perhaps even get her disbarred; but it would also raise a number of uncomfortable questions about himself. It was a potential weapon he had no idea what to do with, other than to remind Felicia that he had it. If nothing else, it had given her something to worry about. And given Felicia's own penchant for mind games, Mario figured that was not at all a bad thing.

9

A colleague of Mario's was fond of comparing a high-profile trial to a championship prizefight. At the arraignment, as at the announcement of the boxing match, there was a flurry of media activity. Then press interest tapered off as the adversaries withdrew to prepare and to contemplate each other's weaknesses. Finally, as the day of the contest approached, anticipation mounted, and the world, once again mindful of the combatants, began to scream for blood. The analogy was far from perfect, but it seemed to Mario to be a fair description of the dynamics in the Wisocki case. Certainly, as the trial date approached, interest had resurged.

He could track the public's emotional engagement by the size of the protest demonstrations, which, in a stubborn show of resolve, the Reverend Flores continued to hold—though sporadically—throughout the fall and early winter. Flores broadened his rhetorical focus beyond Wisocki to the justice system in general—to its treatment of defendants of color and to the dearth of Latino prosecutors and judges; but as the temperature dropped and press coverage died down, he had a progressively harder time drawing a crowd.

Nonetheless, Flores persevered, even on days when so few people showed up that his assemblage looked more like a discussion group than a protest rally. But as the trial approached and the media presence increased, so did the size of Flores's flock. And today, the first day of jury selection—with Wisocki again on the evening news and with the tabloids running banner headlines pegged to the case—Flores's followers had come out in numbers. He no longer, however, had the stage to himself. Several black preachers and protest leaders had joined the parade and would take turns, along with Flores, leading the protesters in rhythmical chants.

Also, a group of counterprotesters had sprung up. They were, for the most part, rather shabbily dressed and virtually all were white. Marching under the banner of something calling itself Citizens for Equality in Society, they shouted slogans against welfare, affirmative action, and big government when they weren't chanting "John Wisocki, innocent!"

Mario tried, as best he could, to ignore the circus outside. His job, he repeatedly reminded himself, was to focus on the show inside: on the elements of the case he could actually influence or control. Still, his mind wandered. He found himself wishing that it were colder. In his imagination, the spring-like January warmth that encouraged crowds and stirred emotions was swept away by a raging snowstorm that left everything frozen and pure. When he glanced outside the courtroom window, however, the sun beamed bright as a billion beacons. The possibility of a snowstorm was about as remote as the possibility of a visit from Zeus.

Mario drew comfort from the fact that he had won the last pre-trial skirmish with Felicia. It was a sign, he believed, that, in the end, this case would not turn on technicalities but on the facts of the crime. The dispute concerned a search warrant that had been executed at Wisocki's home for files from his company-furnished computer. Felicia had argued that the personal diary found among those files—a diary which contained comments sharply critical of García—was not within the scope of the warrant. The judge, however, had sided with Mario, which meant Mario would be free to use the diary to demonstrate Wisocki's dislike of García. Along with Hernández's testimony and that of Wisocki's coworkers, the computer files would allow Mario to sketch a precise and convincing portrait of Wisocki as a resentful, Hispanic-hating bundle of rage fully capable of taking a life.

Mario remained uncertain whether he would risk putting Juan Hernández on the stand. Although in the last several months no new negative information on Hernández had come to light, the guy was as likely to alienate the jury as to persuade them. Still, it would be nice—but hardly essential to documenting his theory of the crime—to have the jury see Wisocki as Hernández described him: a crazed, gun-toting caricature of Dirty Harry shouting anti-Latino slurs.

Mario glanced at the defense table. Felicia was busily taking notes during the judge's initial questioning of the prospective jurors panel, and Mario wondered whether she had a specific image of the type of juror she was seeking. She presumably was not simply looking for those willing to believe García's death was an accident, but who were also willing to accept the idea that Infotect and its diversity program were somehow responsible. It would be the rare juror, it seemed to Mario, prepared to accept all of that. Still, Felicia was a rare woman. Who could say what nonsense she was capable of selling?—even to him, if he let down his guard.

Over the past several months, as they had jousted in and out of court, their relationship had settled, if not exactly into amicability, into a professionalism with edge. The flirtatious persona he'd glimpsed that evening at Jason's had not surfaced again, but he was not sure he preferred the replacement: a woman who, when he caught her eye, often looked straight through him. At the moment, as she stared at the jurors, she seemed friendlier and more vulnerable than she had seemed in weeks. It was, he assumed, a pose, her way of turning on the charm not only for the panel, but for the courtroom crowd.

The judge, Keith Campbell, was in his early forties and vaguely resembled Mel Gibson, though Campbell was taller and flabbier. His name was often in the newspapers, principally because of the social prominence of his wife, who worked in public relations for a huge manufacturing company that was controlled and largely owned by her family.

Though considered a decent enough judge, Campbell seemed to have no genuine love for the law. He was often mentioned as a possible candidate for senator—maybe even governor—of New York. He clearly liked the cameras and also believed in giving lawyers a great deal of leeway, which, from Mario's perspective, were less than ideal attributes for a judge in a case when television cameras were present and the defense attorney was an assertive showboat.

Campbell had nearly completed his initial questioning of the first group of sixteen—or so Mario assumed, from the shift in the tone of his voice. The panel comprised a typical ethnic mix for Manhattan juries. There were two blacks, two Latinos, one Asian, and the rest were white. Usually Mario didn't mind such proportions, but today he envied his counterparts in the Bronx. There jury panels were significantly darker and of a mind-set certain to be more sympathetic to García than to Wisocki.

Campbell had begun the session with a little spiel to panel members about how the court worked and about their responsibilities as citizens and jurors. He had then proceeded to interrogate them, individually and collectively, on a series of matters, ranging from their professional and personal responsibilities to their ability to be fair, their willingness to convict, and their amenability to sequestration during deliberations. By the time he yielded the floor to Mario, the majority of general questions had already been asked. Mario focused on a few areas of special concern: their willingness to listen to witnesses (he had Hernández in mind) they did not personally like, their sentiments on gun ownership, and their ability to shut out the news media. He also emphasized, and got them to talk about, the importance of separating whatever feelings of sympathy they might have for a defendant from their responsibility to decide that defendant's guilt.

Felicia's questions ranged over more eclectic terrain—probing the panel's feelings on psychiatry, corporate downsizing, and expert testimony. One panelist, an executive for a large insurance company, acknowledged having been involved in the layoffs of several hundred employees. "It was hell," he said. "You're being second-guessed by everybody. You're worrying about lawsuits. I have a great deal more sympathy now for those folks who have to make the difficult calls." One woman revealed that her husband had killed himself nearly a decade ago. "I should have recognized the signs," she whispered. "I should have seen that he was suffering. To this day I think I could have done something." A political science graduate student was among the most outspoken. "Most expert witnesses are whores," he declared. "There is just no other word for it."

Though Felicia did not directly ask about race, she did explore their feelings about corporate diversity programs. She also seemed to be arguing bits and pieces of her case. *Do you agree depression can cause people to do idiotic things?* Mario objected. *Isn't it a shame so many New Yorkers don't feel safe without guns?* Another objection. *Can you recognize the clear difference between murder and accidental death?* Objection, again. The judge, though sustaining Mario's objections, seemed not particularly annoyed with Felicia's questions. And as Mario reflected on Felicia's possible motivation, his aggravation abated. That she would ask questions that were so clearly improper seemed to be an implicit admission that she lacked confidence in the integrity of her case. Why else would she be trying so hard so early to win the jurors to her side?

By the end of the first day, they had settled on eight jurors—and excluded many more. A psychiatrist who specialized in trauma was among the first to go, along with the political science graduate student. They had also eliminated the insurance executive who had overseen layoffs, the woman whose husband had committed suicide, another woman who had been in treatment for clinical depression, and a freelance journalist who hoped to get a book deal. Several panelists had been so influenced by news coverage as to make impartiality impossible. Others simply seemed hostile to either the defense or prosecution view of the case, or had expectations of high drama—stemming from watching Perry Mason and O. J. Simpson—that no real trial could deliver. ("Frankly, I'm looking for a little excitement in my life," a retired receptionist had confided.) The easiest call, for Mario at least, was a middle-aged machinist who pumped his head in seeming agreement whenever Felicia spoke and, when asked his view of corporate layoffs, replied, "I think it's about time they started sending some of those CEO bastards to jail. They're ruining the country and have just about destroyed the workingman."

Mario could see no real pattern to Felicia's peremptory challenges other than her rejection of those who were strong supporters of corporate diversity initiatives or who hadn't paid much attention when she spoke. He was confident, given the progress they had already made, that they would have the jury and alternates in place sometime the following day.

Felicia also felt good after the first day of jury selection, and figured several of those chosen would be good for her side. In particular, she liked the older black man who had recently sold his small grocery store in Lower Manhattan. In that line of business he had enough run-ins with stickup men and other real criminals that he was likely to be sympathetic to a workingman like Wisocki. She also was pleased with the choice of the middle-aged white man who, after several months of idleness following an amicable corporate buyout, had recently found work as a travel agent. Though he was doing just fine with his new career, many of his old colleagues were in desperate circumstances. He would surely be sympathetic to Wisocki's situation on the job.

Felicia had been somewhat surprised at how John's and her opinions had converged. He had, for the most part, followed her lead, voicing approval of those she had selected. With the exception of a recently naturalized woman born in Korea who worked in a flower shop on the East Side, they had had no major difference of opinion. John had wanted to keep the woman and Felicia had wanted to bounce her. Finally Felicia had given in, conceding that perhaps she was operating out of defense-lawyer bias, out of an unproved assumption that Asians, stereotypically considered law and order zealots, love to convict regardless of the facts of the case.

"That's nonsense," John had insisted, with more passion and indignation than she had ever previously seen him express.

"Probably so," Felicia had agreed.

Following the voir dire, John and Felicia ducked into a chauffeured town car and headed north in the direction of her office.

"What did you think of that schoolteacher?" John asked.

"A little spacey, but basically good for us. She's a sweet lady, and she doesn't have the heart to convict anyone for murder."

John winced at the word, which Felicia had used intentionally. For the next several weeks he was going to be called a murderer not only by Mario but by strangers and commentators all over town; he might as well get used to it.

Felicia got out of the car at the Carlyle Hotel and John continued home. Jake O'Hare was waiting inside at the Bemelmans Bar, nursing a drink and looking bored. He brightened up immediately upon spotting her.

"Am I late?" she asked.

"No. I got here early," Jake replied. He rose to greet her, kissing her on either cheek. "Good to see you, as always," he said. "How goes the voir dire?"

Felicia laughed. "You know, Jake, the enduring legacy of the O. J. trial is that it taught all America legal jargon. Voir dire, indeed. Anyway, it's going great. We'll have a jury tomorrow. Then we put on a show."

"Which I presume will be worth the price of admission."

"I guess we'll see," said Felicia, as she slid into a chair next to Jake. The waiter came over and she ordered a wine spritzer, raising her voice to be heard above the ballad the pianist had just begun playing. Another hour or so and the singer would start up; but she planned to be gone long before that. She examined Jake more closely, taking in his nicely tailored gray suit and monogrammed silvery white shirt.

"Nice threads," she said. "They must be paying you well at the *Inquirer*."

"I believe they get their money's worth. Talking of which," he said, in a conspiratorial whisper, "what can you give me?"

"Not sure," she said, affecting a come-hither smirk. "Maybe something."

"Don't be a tease."

"It's my nature, Jake."

"So what do you have?" he asked. "Other than a pretty smile."

"Something I think you'll really like, which I'll gladly give you, but there's a condition."

"I'll bite," he said, perking up.

"You will have to call me so we can talk things over before—and if—you run with it," she said, staring into his eyes, enunciating each word clearly and precisely.

He nodded. "Okay. That sounds fair. So what have you got?"

"Not so quick, love." She took a sip of the spritzer and placed the glass back on the table, then turned her attention back to Jake. He looked like a well-behaved child waiting to be offered a piece of candy; though it was hard to imagine a juvenile Jake as anything other than a brat.

"You remember my investigator, Hector González?" she asked.

"The former cop?"

"That's the one."

"Sure I do," said Jake, his eyes widening in anticipation.

"Do you still have his numbers?"

"I believe so."

"Call him tonight. And call me later, at home."

"Will do," he said, raising his right hand in a salute. "Want to tell me what this is about?"

"I think I'll let Hector surprise you," she said, grinning.

"Tell me this is something worthy of the best and most widely read columnist in New York," he pleaded.

"Have I disappointed you yet?" she asked, with a wink.

"Only if romantic rejection constitutes disappointment. But I still have my hopes," he said, facetiously.

"I'm suitably flattered," she said, in a wry, world-weary tone. "But isn't it unethical for you to get involved with your sources?"

"Hell, Felicia. In this town, I think it's unethical not to."

She smiled demurely and gulped down the spritzer. "Got to go, sweetheart. Thanks for the drink."

"So I'm buying?"

"Of course you are," she said, getting up from the table.

"All right. Later," he said, and gave her a peck on the right cheek.

"Only one cheek this time?" she asked, putting on a good-natured pout.

"I don't want to spoil you," he replied.

The hotel doorman instantly got her a taxi and within minutes she was in her office. Stephanie had not yet left, and judging by all the papers spread out on her desk and by the glum expression on her face, she planned to be there for quite some time.

"Obviously a late night for you," said Felicia. "What are you working on?"

"Mostly moving paper from one side of my desk to the other," she replied with a grimace. "I've got a pretrial conference tomorrow morning on the Jim Williamson case. Wanted to make sure I have everything sorted out."

"That's the guy with the gun, right?"

"Yeah, the one who's suing the manufacturer because the gun failed to function when he tried to shoot the clown who broke into his house. Ended up clunking the guy in the head with the butt of the pistol. Sent the would-be burglar to the hospital. In a sense, the gun worked after all. Poor Jim just never thought he would have to use it as a club."

"Are they going to settle?" asked Felicia.

"They say not, but they're not saying it too loudly. I think they will."

"Great. Good luck."

"Thanks," said Stephanie, casting a weary look at the papers spread before her. "So you're working on your opening for the Wisocki case, I presume."

"Exactly," said Felicia, easing into the chair facing Stephanie. "And I have a question for you. You said Judge Campbell was pretty good, but I was wondering."

"Yes."

"About how best to handle him. I'm going to be trying to get some stuff in that I suspect he might have problems with. Any pointers you can give me would be useful. I've only had one trial before him, and it was over in a day. So I don't have a real good sense of the man. What do you think of him as a human being?"

Stephanie let out a long, sorrowful sigh. "A lot and not much. What can I say? Ultimately we're all somewhat the same—frail, vain, and insecure. He just happens to be more of all of those things than your normal individual. Freud himself wouldn't know where to begin."

"You're getting a bit heavy on me, Stef," said Felicia.

"You asked," she replied with a shrug.

"All right. Let me rephrase the question. What can you tell me about Campbell that I don't already know that might be useful?"

Stephanie laughed. "That's easy. Wear a mini-skirt."

"You mean—"

"He likes women."

"Oh. Any particular type?"

Stephanie grinned sardonically. "Mostly the female type, preferably breathing. He can be quite a charmer when he wants to. He can also be a class-A jerk. But don't worry. I'm sure he'll like you. And he'll give you plenty of running room."

"I'm not sure I want to know the answer to this, Stef," Felicia began warily, "but, do tell, just how well do you know Judge Campbell?"

"Let me put it this way, Felicia: a whole lot better than I should."

"Oh!"

Through much of that Friday—the second, and final, day of voir dire—Felicia found her mind conjuring up images of Campbell and Stephanie in bed. The bed was huge and covered by a canopy and the two of them were locked in an endless orgasm, slamming more and more furiously into each other, shaking the bed, screaming their lungs out in ecstasy. The picture so dominated her thoughts that several times when she glanced at Campbell staring sternly from the bench, a huge smile broke out on her face. When she tried to order up a more somber mien, not wanting the judge to think she was flirting, the grin only grew larger.

Despite the distraction, she managed to conduct her questioning of the panel as efficiently as ever. By mid-afternoon they had seated a jury, whereupon the judge adjourned the proceedings until next Monday morning, leaving Mario and Felicia the weekend over which to ponder their opening statements.

For Mario, who would be addressing the jury first and had been working on his opening, off and on, for weeks, the seating of the jurors meant the trial had finally begun. That thought filled him with both apprehension and joy. As he had anticipated, the racial mix of the jury was not especially to his liking—ten whites, one black, and one Asian, with one black, one Latino, and two white alternates.

That Felicia had used two of her peremptory challenges to knock Latino prospectives off was a source of aggravation. He doubted, however, he could prove she had used racial discrimination as the basis and so, reluctantly, he had let her get away with it. But even though the jury was largely white, the jurors all seemed to be solid. He was confident he could persuade them to accept his theory of the case.

When Mario left the courtroom later that afternoon, Flores and his protesters were still out in force. "No justice, No peace!" they chanted, along with their familiar unity refrain: "*¡Un pueblo unido jamás será vencido!*" The demonstrators no longer either embarrassed or annoyed him. Indeed, in the past several weeks, he had come to look forward to their presence, considering them, quite literally, cheerleaders for "the people" he was proud to represent.

As he stood watching Flores's boisterous parade, Mario felt a hand on his shoulder and knew, without turning, that it was María Cristina. Their plan was to have dinner at the Thai restaurant on Baxter Street and then perhaps take in a movie. As María Cristina had pointed out earlier in the day, he had the entire weekend to polish his opening act. "You owe it to yourself to take one night off," she had said.

"How do you feel?" she asked, after kissing him on the lips.

"A bit nervous, but good. I've run the arguments through my mind a million times. As always, there's this nagging feeling that I'm missing something, but I think I have it under control. Just need to do a bit more work on the opening."

She beamed, looking radiant in her white double-breasted trenchcoat, which nicely highlighted her dark tan skin. "If it's the same opening statement I read last night, it's already brilliant."

"Then I'll try to make it more brilliant. I also want to tinker with the closing."

"You'll be tinkering with that for the next couple of weeks. I'm not so sure it should be your priority this weekend."

"It won't be."

María Cristina grabbed his hand, squeezing it tightly, and kissed him again. "You've been living with this case for so long," she said. "It's hard to believe it's finally going to go."

"Well, believe it, beautiful. You know, research shows that most jurors make up their minds during opening arguments. So the way I see it, Monday I walk into that courtroom and either win or lose this case. High noon, so to speak. What do you think?"

"I think you have one hell of a pistol," she said, with a smirk. "So if it's a shootout, you can't lose. What can I say, baby? You know damn well my money's on you, no questions asked."

"It had better be," he said, smiling broadly, as they headed toward Baxter Street. The smile faded when he spotted Felicia heading directly toward them and was replaced with something closer to a scowl, which vanished as quickly as it had appeared when he realized that the woman was actually someone else.

The fax arrived at the office shortly after 9 P.M., the top sheet bearing the distinct logo of the *Inquirer*. Felicia, who had been waiting by the machine since Jake's call a few minutes ago, pulled out the pages as they arrived and began reading.

She smiled as she skimmed the text of Jake's forthcoming Sunday column, certain that Mario would be shocked. "Not a bad way to begin a trial," she said to herself.

Taking the information supplied by Hector, Jake had put together an article that would destroy Juan Hernández's credibility—and thereby his utility to Mario and the prosecution. Evido Gómez, a Harlem bodega owner interviewed by Jake, had fingered Hernández as the robber who had ripped off his store.

As Jake summed it up: "Gómez couldn't help noticing that the thief wore a name on a chain around his neck. That name—surprise—is Juan. 'I've never seen a robber with his name on his neck,' said Gómez. 'I thought it was really strange. I guess he must have forgotten to take the damn thing off.'

"It seems to me we have two possibilities here. Juan is either the stupidest criminal in creation, or the robber appropriated the name tag as part of a clever disguise, a nefarious plot to shift the blame to some innocent chap who was no doubt baby-sitting and studying at the time."

The call came late Saturday night from Barry Frommer, the public relations man at the DA's office. "Have you seen Sunday's *Inquirer*?" he asked in a voice a half octave higher than normal.

"Of course not," Mario replied. "Why?"

"One of your witnesses is in it," said Frommer, and began reading O'Hare's front-page column out loud.

As he listened, Mario's anger mounted by the second. By the time Frommer had finished, Mario was trembling with rage. The story had obviously been planted by Felicia. If she was going to play hardball, so could he. "Give me your number, Barry. I'll call you back," Mario said.

He hung up, forced himself to take several deep breaths, and then pulled out his phone book. He found the Reverend Flores's home number, lifted the receiver, and dialed. Upon hearing the minister's voice, Mario identified himself and said brusquely, "First of all, I never called you. Understand?"

"What?"

"This call never took place. Do you understand?"

"Sure."

"Good, 'cause I'm going to tell you a story you might find interesting. Remember a man named Carl Murphy, a drug dealer who used to operate in your neighborhood?"

"Yeah, got sent up for murder. Sure. I know him."

"Well this story is about him and it's also about Felicia Fontaine. And at this point, it's without an ending. So relax while I tell it."

10

The moment the conversation with Flores ended, Mario felt a heart-stopping wave of apprehension. He knew he had overreacted, and briefly considered calling Flores back. He could tell him, in effect, to forget they had spoken. To do that, however, would be to look like a fool and a coward; and, on reflection, he decided there would be no point. Even assuming Flores stirred up enough public interest to generate an investigation, Mario figured he had relatively little to hide. He had been ignorant of the Brady violation at the time it occurred, and had never seen any hard evidence that it had actually taken place. Until the night, nearly a year after the event, when Felicia had experienced her fit of candor, he had assumed everything was precisely as it should be. He had not spoken up because he had not been sure—given Felicia's sometimes weird sense of humor—whether to take her confession seriously. At least that was what he had once told himself. The real reason, he realized, was that he had loved her too much to willingly play a role in her fall from grace.

If Flores managed to get the story out now, speculation about Mario's own possible involvement might be embarrassing, but his behavior was eminently explainable. So he reassured himself, forcefully enough so that by the time he arrived in court Monday morning, his focus, once again, was primarily on his opening statement.

The scene around the courtroom verged on chaos. News cameras were whirling, protesters were screaming, and scores of people were waiting to get into the building. Mario flashed his ID and waltzed pass security, bypassing the metal detectors and a wait with the crowd. He only lingered in his office long enough to compose himself and to call for help with his evidence cart before proceeding to the courtroom. "It's going to be one hell of a day," he forewarned the officer pressed into duty as his evidence assistant.

Mario pushed through the crush of people outside the courtroom and quickly made his way to the prosecutor's table, careful, as he had learned to be during the past several weeks, not to pay particular attention to the swarm of reporters. María Cristina was seated right up front, and Linda and Sophie Wisocki were on the other side of the room, two rows behind the defense table. The courtroom was bathed in lights, and there was an audible buzz emanating from the audience, but Mario tried to shut it all out and focus only on the matter at hand.

Judge Campbell disposed of the pretrial preliminaries and then spoke directly to the jurors, lecturing them on their role and responsibilities. Finally, he nodded at Mario and said, "We will now turn to assistant district attorney Santiago to make an opening statement."

Mario cleared his throat and moved to the lectern facing the jurors. He reminded himself to control his hands, to keep them, despite his nervousness, from playing with his face. His upper body was tense and his heart beat furiously, but his gaze was steady and his voice clear as a trumpet as he gazed at the jury and spoke.

"Thank you, Your Honor. May it please the court, Ms. Fontaine, ladies and gentleman of the jury. My name is Mario Santiago. As the assistant district attorney responsible for prosecuting this case, it is my duty under law, but also my honor, to address you at this point on behalf of the people of the State of New York."

Mario's body began to relax as his voice echoed through the courtroom. He felt secure enough to remove his hands from the lectern and let them move naturally as he spoke.

"In the next few minutes I will outline how I propose to prove to you that on August twenty-fourth of last year John Wisocki, the defendant, murdered Francisco García. The evidence will show that the defendant committed that murder by intentionally shooting Mr. García in the chest with a nine-millimeter semiautomatic pistol—and that he did so out of a combination of professional jealousy, hatred, and rage. You will learn that, in an effort to cover up this monstrous crime, the defendant concocted a phony suicide note that is tantamount to an admission of murder. You will also learn that this murder was made possible by the defendant's illegal use and possession of a handgun—a handgun that was obtained with no conceivable legal purpose, a handgun whose only function was to kill an innocent man and fulfill a murderous fantasy."

Mario declaimed determinedly, passionately, loudly, and at length, detailing the specific witnesses and evidence he would present. After several minutes of disparagement directed at Wisocki, he suspended his narrative just long enough to glower at his target before returning his gaze to the jury and spitting out his next point.

"There will be times during this trial when you may ask, 'How could such a meek man commit such an evil deed? How could he take an innocent life in such brutal fashion?' And I will ask of you, during such moments, only one thing: that you look to the evidence."

Mario, conscious his rhetoric was pushing the bounds of permissibility, stole a glance at the judge, who seemed content to let him continue. Felicia, he figured, would save her objections for later. Nonetheless, Mario paused dramatically, giving his words time to sink in. He felt the last smidgen of nervousness sweep away, replaced by a sense of indignation and anger.

"In the course of this trial, you will also learn that the man the defendant killed was an exemplary human being and a dedicated worker, that he put himself through graduate school at night while raising a family, that his professional success, in short, had come precisely as a result of the kind of hard work that brought him to the office that Sunday evening where he met his death. You will learn, as well, that Mr. García was a dutiful husband and father, that he left behind a grief-stricken wife and a five-year-old daughter—now six—who will never again feel the touch of her father's embrace, who spent her sixth birthday only a few weeks ago crying inconsolably because of his death, mourning her incomprehensible loss."

He addressed the subject of the suicide note, calling it a sham; and he underscored the fact that the evidence would prove both murder and criminal possession of a weapon. He paused, as if gathering his thoughts, and looking directly at the jury, he leaned forward and made his final points:

"I will address you at the conclusion of this case and I will ask you to remember what I promised to prove today. I will ask you to remember that no crime—*no crime*—is worse than murder, and that no petty jealousy can excuse it. I will ask you to hold the defendant accountable for that crime. At a time when many people quite literally want to get away with murder, when many people try to blame their problems on anyone but themselves and refuse to take responsibility, I will ask you to hold responsible the man who committed this horrible act. I will ask you to listen closely to the testimony that will be given, to critically size up the witnesses, and to trust your judgment. I will ask you to follow your hearts, and yet that you not be blinded by appeals to your emotions. Most of all, I will ask you to look to the evidence. I will ask that you, in the name of the people of the State of New York and in the interest of justice, find the defendant guilty of murder and of criminal possession of a weapon. Thank you for your courtesy and your attention."

He sat down, feeling both triumphant and relieved, confident he had accomplished his objectives. He had kept the statement relatively short, while outlining and supporting his theory of the case, and he had made it difficult for Felicia to bury the evidence under a blanket of obfuscating rhetoric. Still, there was no predicting what nonsense she might inject, so he tensed up as she began to speak.

"May it please the court, the people, and you, ladies and gentlemen of the jury. My name is Felicia Fontaine and as counsel for the defense

I have no obligation to present an opening statement. Indeed, we have no obligation to prove anything since my client must, by law, be presumed innocent. Nonetheless, I could not let go unchallenged the assertions you have heard this morning, assertions which, contrary to Mr. Santiago's representation, have no basis in fact.

"At this moment it would be understandable if you were a bit confused," she said, wearing a look of mild bemusement and concern. "The people, in the person of Mr. Santiago, have just accused my client, John Wisocki, of a horrible murder. And worse, they have painted him as a man with evil motives, as a wicked villain waiting in the night. What you have just heard, however," she continued, her voice rising, "is a fable, a fabrication built upon a tissue-thin framework of unsubstantiated speculation that cannot withstand the piercing light of truth."

Felicia knew she was going overboard, but she reckoned she and Mario had entered into an unspoken pact: *I don't object to your bullshit during opening, you won't object to mine.*

"Mr. Santiago asked you to look to the evidence," said Felicia, as she stepped out from behind the lectern and approached the jury. "I beg you to do the same. For the evidence will show a very different story from the one you have heard. It will show that my client, wrongfully dismissed and lied to by his employer, plunged into a dreadful depression that resulted in his trying to take his life. The evidence will show that when he went to his office, late Sunday night, after drinking in an attempt to escape his pain, it was only with the intent of killing himself and with absolutely no expectation that anyone else would be present. It will show that that evening, at the very moment at which he intended to kill himself, Mr. García appeared and tried to wrestle the gun away. And it will show that the result of that intervention was a horrible accident that resulted in Mr. García's death.

"The evidence will show, in short, that there was no intent to kill Mr. García. And, unless the people can prove intent *beyond a reasonable doubt*," she said, stressing each word for emphasis, "my client must be set free."

"Objection," interjected Mario.

"Sustained," said the judge, with a nod. Glancing in the direction of the jury, he softly added, "I will instruct you on the law."

Felicia shrugged. *So Mario was going to be a bastard. Two could play at that.* She continued: "My client, the accused, John Wisocki, will take the stand. He will face you and he will face his accusers and he will tell you precisely what occurred that night, as opposed to the fable presented by the people.

"You will learn, in the course of this trial, that Mr. Wisocki has never previously been accused of a crime, that he has never previously harmed a soul, that he is a loving husband and a caring and supportive son. You will learn, in short, that he is not the monster that the prosecution has portrayed him to be."

She described the witnesses who would support various parts of Wisocki's story, and summed up Wisocki's life as "a parable, a *Christian* parable, of service and selflessness."

She hesitated, briefly glancing upward, as if appealing to God for guidance. When she again found her voice, it resounded through the courtroom, a musical mixture of reasonableness and outrage. "Look to the evidence, Mr. Santiago said. On that, we agree. But I also ask you to look at the man, that you peer into his soul. And I implore you, above all, to look to the law."

She paused only briefly before leaping again onto the judge's turf, betting that he would not stop her and that Mario would not bother to object again, that he would rather have her make her point than have the jury think he was trying to silence her.

"For if you have even a shred of reasonable doubt, you must resolve that doubt in favor of my client."

Felicia briefly closed her eyes as she stood quietly, reverently, before the jury. A beatific smile was on her face when her eyelids lifted, and she added, in hushed tones:

"You and only you are in possession of both the power, the wisdom, and the goodness to give this very dark fable, this nightmare, the happy ending that it deserves."

Felicia slowly drew in her breath and turned toward Wisocki, bestowing upon him a look of concern and affection. Turning back to the jurors, she concluded: "At the end of this trial, I too will come before you and I will ask that you search your conscience. And I will urge you and I will expect you, on the basis of the facts, to return a verdict of not guilty.

"I am grateful for your kind attention, and I thank you."

Felicia leaned forward in a partial bow to the jury before returning to her seat. The judge declared a short recess and, following a brief conference on exhibits and the order of witnesses, Mario began presenting his case.

His first witness was Jack Kelly, one of the cops who had arrested Wisocki at the scene. Mario quickly led him through a series of questions designed to re-create the events of the night of the murder and to establish that Wisocki had admitted to pulling the trigger. He also used Kelly's answers to enter the recovered gun, bullets, and suicide note into evidence. The questioning went smoothly and without any objections from Felicia, who, during her cross-examination of Kelly seemed primarily interested in establishing that Wisocki had cooperated with the cops and had insisted from the beginning that the shooting was accidental. Having established that, Felicia tried to make yet another point.

"Did Mr. Wisocki make any threatening gestures whatsoever?" she asked.

"Not that I can recall," replied Kelly.

"So he did not exactly look like a raging murderer?" she exclaimed, a slight but triumphant smile on her face.

Mario immediately objected and Judge Campbell sustained him, as Mario mumbled, too quietly for anyone to hear, "Up to her old tricks."

Dave Strachan, Kelly's partner, corroborated Kelly's version of events. And Gene Sahadi, an artist from the DA's engineering department, was the morning's final witness. With his testimony, Mario entered the diagram of the crime scene into evidence and the judge recessed for lunch.

Several voice-mail messages awaited Mario when he returned to his office, including one from Scott Wagner, his detective friend from the 23rd Precinct. "I know you're busy with the trial," said Wagner, "but I figured you would want to know that the Hernández situation is looking very strange. Call me. Or you can catch me at McGuire's after work."

"What now?" muttered Mario, as he dialed Wagner's beeper number. The last thing he needed was another Hernández headache.

First up that afternoon was Milton Morris, the guard who had been on duty at Computertronics. He testified to Wisocki's arrival and to being surprised at his showing up. "I can't recall the last time Mr. Wisocki worked on a Sunday," he volunteered. Mario produced a large stack of sign-in sheets for the building.

"These documents have been previously marked as People's Exhibit Number Fourteen for identification," said Mario, and asked the judge's permission to show them to the guard. Judge Campbell consented and Mario walked Morris through a series of identifying questions necessary to enter them into evidence. Mario then showed the papers to Felicia, who nodded noncommittally.

"Your Honor, I offer into evidence People's Exhibit Number Fourteen for identification," he said.

Felicia did not object, and Judge Campbell consented.

Turning his attention back to Morris, Mario asked, "Are those sign-in sheets marked with specific days and dates?"

"Yes," said Morris, as he leafed through them. "They all appear to be for Sundays, going back a year or so."

"There are certain times, you indicated, when tenants have to sign in. When are those times?"

"Only on Saturdays, Sundays, and after business hours."

"Are *all* tenants required to sign in during Saturdays, Sundays, and nonbusiness hours?"

"Yes, sir."

"Does that include all employees of Computertronics?"

"Yes it does."

Mario nodded meaningfully at the jury before turning his attention back to Morris: "Can you determine, by examining those documents, when was the last time Mr. Wisocki worked on a Sunday prior to the date the shooting occurred." Mario paused and added, "Take your time."

"Yes," Morris said, as he carefully perused the papers. "The last Sunday that Mr. Wisocki worked was in January of last year, January nineteenth."

"*Really*," mumbled Mario, raising his eyebrows as if surprised. To ensure that the information sank in, he added, "Are you sure?"

"Yes."

He then called, in succession, two cleaning ladies who testified to hearing two shots—one or two seconds apart, they thought. On cross-examination, however, Felicia forced them to concede that they really had no idea how far apart the shots were fired, or even if they were certain the sounds they had heard were gunshots.

Mario's final witness for the day was Patricia Gattling, the police department's ballistics expert. She was a tall, stern woman who would have been very attractive had her body language been a tad less off-putting. For his present purpose, her aura of control and authority was perfect. In Mario's eyes, she had two functions: to establish that Wisocki's gun had in fact fired the shots and to confirm that they could not have been fired by accident. He began with basic questions about her duties and training, allowing Detective Gattling to attest that she had been with the ballistics unit for five years, and had received specialized training in weapons and forensic science in the Army and with the FBI. He concluded the so-called pedigree questions by asking the judge to accept her as an expert in her field. He then had her talk about the tests she had performed.

The "filter paper test," she explained, entailed firing slugs into filter paper at various distances and examining the marks made by the bullets and powder. By comparing those to the marks made on the victim and his clothes, it was possible to determine how far the shooter had been from the victim. García, she added, had been shot from roughly six inches away. Another bullet from the same gun, she noted, had gone into a wall, without striking any other target.

Mario next established that the recovered gun was similar to the standard firearm issued by the New York Police Department. And he questioned Gattling on the amount of pressure required to make it discharge.

"In reference to the Glock Model Seventeen, are you familiar with the factory specifications for trigger pull?" asked Mario.

"Yes. The Glock Model Seventeen, according to factory specifications, has a trigger pull of five and a half pounds."

"And did you perform a trigger pull test on People's Exhibit Number Three, the gun recovered from the scene?"

"Yes, I did."

"And what was the trigger pull of this gun?" asked Mario, holding the weapon aloft in a plastic bag.

"The trigger pull for the recovered weapon is set at factory specifications—five and a half pounds."

"Are you familiar with the term hair trigger?"

"Yes, that's a layman's term used to describe a weapon that fires with the application of just a small amount of pressure on the trigger."

"Does the Glock Model Seventeen have a hair trigger?"

"The term is subjective in that there is no precise definition for one. It could probably be applied most meaningfully to some specially made weapons, such as target pistols, that are intentionally designed to be easy to fire. The Glock is not such a weapon. It is designed to require a real effort to pull the trigger."

Mario paused momentarily to stare at the jury before asking the crucial question. "In your opinion," he said, raising his voice, "could the trigger be pulled accidentally?"

"Objection," yelled Felicia. "The question is extremely speculative."

"I will allow it," said the judge.

"To repeat the question," said Mario, nearly shouting and punching the air for emphasis. "In your *expert* opinion, could the trigger of this Glock Model Seventeen be pulled accidentally?"

"No. Not under normal circumstances," she replied calmly. "The gun is designed to require an intentional squeeze, not simply a light touch. It's difficult to imagine a scenario when the gun, properly working, would discharge without the shooter intending to fire."

"Is it safe therefore to assume that, under normal circumstances, two shots could not be discharged accidentally from this weapon?" Mario asked, again brandishing the gun before the jury.

"I would consider that a safe assumption."

"I have no further questions. Thank you, Detective," Mario said, with a self-assured, satisfied smile.

Felicia leapt from her chair as if on fire, and positioned herself directly in front of Detective Gattling. "Detective, what did you say was the trigger pull of the Glock Seventeen admitted into evidence?" she asked.

"Five and a half pounds."

"Could you put that into perspective? To pull the trigger takes relatively little weight, does it not? A fraction of the weight of the defendant? About as much energy as it takes to pick up a hardcover book. Correct?"

"Objection, Judge," said Mario. "Argumentative. Also, the question assumes facts not in evidence."

"Sustained."

"Let me rephrase," said Felicia. "To pull the trigger requires less than one thirtieth the weight of an average man of one hundred and eighty pounds. Is—"

"Objection. Irrelevant," screamed Mario. "May I approach?"

The judge motioned for Mario and Felicia to come nearer, which they did, the court reporter in tow.

Mario began, "The weight of an average man has nothing—"

"It is not an irrelevant question at all," replied Felicia, shooting Mario a dirty look. "The question of how much force it takes to pull the trigger goes directly to the defense theory of the case."

"Asked and answered," interjected Mario, meeting Felicia's gaze and matching her look of irritation with one of his own.

"Please move on, Ms. Fontaine," said the judge, and waved them both back into the arena.

Felicia again faced the detective and, after pursing her lips into a thoughtful frown, asked, "How would you compare the pressure required to pull the trigger on a Glock to the pressure applied by two men struggling, two men whose combined weight is over three hundred pounds?"

"Objection!"

"Sustained."

Felicia glanced at the jury and shrugged as if to say: *I'm really trying to get this answer for you, folks.*

"Do you have anything else, Ms. Fontaine?" the judge asked, his tone suddenly stern.

"Yes, Judge."

"I suggest you get to it."

"You have great experience with the Glock Model Seventeen, you say. Is that correct, Detective?"

"Yes."

"How much of that vast experience consists of trying to hold onto your gun when someone is aggressively trying to take it from you?"

"None."

"Oh, I see," she said, gazing expressively into the jury box. "Detective Gattling. Are you familiar with the concept of a stress reaction?"

"Objection. Beyond the scope of the direct," shouted Mario.

"Sustained."

"Nothing else, Your Honor," said Felicia, and returned to her table, satisfied with the questions she had raised about the relevance of Gattling's expertise.

On redirect, Mario limited himself to one question: "Is it conceivable, under any scenario, that a Glock Model Seventeen, in working order, would accidentally discharge twice?"

Felicia objected: "Repetitive, Your Honor."

"I will allow it," declared Judge Campbell.

"Detective, is it conceivable that a Glock Model Seventeen, in working order, would accidentally discharge two separate times?"

"Conceivable? Maybe," she said, after a second's reflection, "but it's not very likely."

"Thank you, Detective Gattling," said Mario.

The judge recessed the court until morning and Mario grinned, feeling exultant, almost lighthearted. He had done real damage to Felicia's case and she was smart enough to know it. Finally he could relax. While in front of the judge, he had tried to pretend the crowd did not exist, that the world stopped at the velvet gate marking off the court's inner sanctum. Now he could acknowledge the universe beyond. He turned and gazed out at the audience, spotting several of his colleagues, who had come down to watch his performance and provide emotional support.

On his way out, Mario embraced Isabel García. She held him tightly, as if she had not seen him for years. "*Por fin,*" she whispered. "Finally."

Mario solemnly nodded in agreement. He left the courtroom squeezing María Cristina's hand, trying to ignore the flashing lights, and he whispered to her, with a smile, "I think the first day goes to the good guys."

"I couldn't agree more," she replied.

When Mario got to his office, he found another message from Detective Wagner, who had apparently responded to his beeper message shortly after Mario had left for court. Rather than try to get him on the phone, Mario turned to María Cristina and asked, "Feel like stopping by McGuire's?"

In the heavy evening traffic, the ride uptown took nearly half an hour, which Mario and María Cristina largely spent discussing the next day's testimony and Felicia's annoying penchant for trying to bend the rules.

"She's intentionally trying to get under your skin," said María Cristina. "Since she doesn't have much of a case, she figures her best hope is to cause you to lose your concentration."

"If that's her game," said Mario sanguinely, "she's not even close."

McGuire's Pub was on Second Avenue, a few blocks south of East

Harlem, and it reeked of beer and sawdust. It also had what Mario called "testosterone vibes," the feeling, so common in bars frequented by cops, that a brawl could break out at any minute.

They spotted Scott Wagner seated at the bar and Mario tapped him on the shoulder and motioned toward a table near the back. Wagner, a large, solidly built man with a round face and a perpetually cheerful manner, had worked on several homicide cases with Mario, and they had developed what amounted to a working friendship. Two or three times a year they would get together socially, and generally ended up spending most of the night getting near-drunk at a blue-collar pub like McGuire's.

Mario and María Cristina both ordered beers and, after an exchange of pleasantries, Mario turned to Wagner and asked, "So what's so strange about the Hernández situation?"

"A lot," Wagner replied, gulping his beer. "I pulled the original robbery report on that bodega owned by Evido Gómez. When he first filed the report, Gómez didn't say dick about a chain with Juan on it. He said the perp had a chain, all right, but he didn't say shit about it having a name on it. Also, his description. He said the robber was about five foot ten and maybe one hundred and sixty pounds. Juan's a big guy. Not very likely anybody would peg his weight at one-sixty. Also, we talked to Juan. And he has a pretty good alibi for when this thing went down."

"Are you saying he didn't do it?" asked Mario.

"That's exactly what I'm saying. Don't get me wrong. Juan is no angel, but this job, he didn't do. Plus it ain't his thing, sticking up bodegas."

"Do you have the original report?"

Wagner smiled expansively. "Thought you might want it. I just happened to bring along a copy."

"I owe you," said Mario.

"Damn straight. What you owe me is another drink."

Mario nodded and shouted for the bartender, his mind racing as it contemplated how best to circulate the information that had just fallen into his hands.

* * *

Tonight was no time to be going out for a fancy, leisurely dinner, but the date had been planned weeks earlier, long before Felicia had realized she would be up to her elbows dealing with the trial. And busy as she was, she was not prepared to disappoint her young protégée by canceling or rescheduling their get-together. Having made such a point of dependability with Muriel, she was not about to squander her own credibility by becoming undependable herself, especially given that the teenager finally seemed to be taking heed.

The ostensible reason for getting together was to celebrate Muriel's three consecutive A's on English papers. But an additional reason was Felicia's determination to provide Muriel, and a classmate of her choice, with a glimpse of a life far beyond her Washington Heights neighborhood. Muriel had selected Jackie, her best friend since the third grade. And Felicia had called upon Geneva to complete the foursome.

Geneva initially had been reluctant to give up the evening. "You seem to forget, Felicia, I have kids of my own. I sure as hell don't need to be adopting nobody else's," she had protested.

Felicia kept at her. "These girls need to learn that successful black women exist, that people like you and me are part of the natural order of the world," she exhorted. "And if we don't show them, who will?"

It had not taken long to wear Geneva down. For Geneva, as Felicia well knew, had the soul of a missionary, and was ever ready to save willing, young souls from the damnation of unenlightenment.

The girls came to Felicia's apartment together. Muriel, in a simple tan pantsuit, looked more elegant than Felicia had ever seen her. Jackie, in a clingy white dress and a ton of makeup, looked as if she were decked out for a prom. *She may not know how to dress, but she's certainly making an effort*, Felicia thought as she ushered the girls in. "My God, you both look so beautiful," she raved, in what she hoped was a sincere tone of voice. "Do you want a soda or something before we head out?"

Neither answered. Instead, they stared, speechless, at the living room walls adorned with artwork and books, and at the huge dining room adjoining it. "You live in this big place all by yourself?" Jackie blurted out. "God. You must pay a lot of rent."

Felicia smiled. "Actually I don't pay any rent."

"Your man pay for this?" asked Jackie, grinning, clearly impressed.

"Nope. I don't pay rent because I *own* it. But you're right. It's not cheap. I bought it because it gives me a comfortable place to come home to. This apartment is my gift to myself for all the years I spent in school and at work getting to the point where I could afford a place like this."

"You really bought this *yourself?*" asked Jackie, astonishment blanketing her face.

"Yes, I did," said Felicia. "It's not that hard, you know. You could get an apartment like this, someday, if you stay focused on what's important."

Jackie nodded. "I know. I'm thinking about being a model. I hear they make a lot of money. And when I get tired of that, I can always find a man who'll get me whatever I want."

"Maybe so," said Felicia, "but I'm not so sure I would count on either of those. Modeling is a very fickle field, and men can be even more so."

"I sing pretty good too."

"Well, that might work out. You never know."

Muriel, wandering around the living room, stopped in front of a large bookcase and gingerly ran her fingers over several volumes. "I should have known you would have a lot of books," she said, almost in a whisper. "Have you read all of them?"

Felicia grinned. "I've at least looked at most of them. Some of those are law books, reference books. They're not the kinds of things you sit down and read, no more than you would sit down and read a dictionary. But I have lots of other books that are just for pleasure, especially in this bookcase over here."

She motioned to Muriel's left, causing Muriel to turn slightly.

"Yeah, right there," said Felicia. "You see these four shelves have books just by black authors, everybody from Frederick Douglass, to Toni Morrison to Terry McMillan. Sometimes when I read one of those, I have the feeling they were writing just for me. When I don't feel like being bothered by the nonsense in the world, I come to this part of the room and enter a nice, safe place far away from anywhere else. I also have a shelf of poets. Have you ever read Derek Walcott?"

Muriel shook her head.

"I'll get you a copy of his collected poems if you promise to share it with Jackie," said Felicia. "We can discuss them later."

Felicia glanced at her watch and added, "Well, ladies, you've blown your chance for a soda. Time to go. Geneva is probably already at the restaurant."

The taxi ride to Romero's took only five minutes and Geneva was indeed waiting when they arrived. She was leafing through some papers, which she immediately stuffed into her briefcase upon spotting the three figures heading toward her.

"Just looking through some résumés," Geneva explained, as Felicia and her guests settled into their seats.

Though both girls tried to play the role of sophisticate, Felicia knew that neither had been in such a fancy restaurant before. They followed Felicia's lead in ordering mineral water, and also in declining an aperitif. When confronted with an appetizer of salmon rubbed with herbs and baked in a flaky pastry shell, Muriel stared at it for several seconds before cutting off a tiny portion and delicately popping it into her mouth. Her smile radiated something close to bliss as she gushed, "This is good stuff!" She greeted the angel hair pasta with shrimp and lobster with the same dainty gusto.

As Felicia watched the girls wallow in the waiters' attention, she reflected that being fussed over was not their usual experience in the world, and she was gratified that they were enjoying themselves.

"Maybe you should tell them what a marketing director does," she said, glancing at Geneva.

"That's easy," said Geneva. "I help think up ways to convince people to spend money on stuff they don't need. And I get them to buy our food products instead of some other company's."

"How do you do that?" asked Jackie.

"I spend a lot of time thinking about packaging and about how food is presented. I also have to think about advertising and how we go about showing consumers that our products are different from those made by everybody else. Sometimes, when the difference is not all that great it can be harder than it sounds."

"Do you get paid a lot of money for that?" asked Jackie.

"More than enough to live on."

"So do you have an apartment as big as Ms. Fontaine's?"

"Not exactly. I have a house, so it's bigger. A family takes a bit more space than one person, even when that person requires as much space and has as many clothes as Felicia."

"So your man pays for it, then," said Jackie.

Geneva laughed. "Hah. I wish. My ex-husband's not what you would call the generous sort. He's also always short on funds. Actually, he doesn't contribute that much."

"How did you get your job?" asked Muriel.

"The company called me. Or rather their head hunter called me. He asked if I was interested. And one thing led to another."

"A lot of people work for you?"

"Yes, Muriel. About thirty people report to me."

"White people, too?"

"Mostly white people."

Muriel shook her head in astonishment. "I didn't think white folks gave most blacks a chance to do much of anything. I guess you was lucky."

"It's a lot more than luck," interjected Felicia. "Geneva's got a good job because she proved she could do the work, and she showed that she was a valuable employee to have around. Your assumption may have been right thirty years ago, but the world has changed a lot. Just about anything you want in this world, you can have, if you're willing to prepare yourself to get it."

"Anything?"

"*Within reason*, Muriel. The point is that we're all responsible for ourselves. It's our decision what we do with our lives, and luck or racism doesn't have much to do with it. It's easy to make excuses, but excuses never get anyone anywhere. If we can't take responsibility for what happens to us, we might as well just sit down and die."

"What about things you have no control over?" pressed Muriel.

"If you're truly helpless in the face of events, all you can do is accept them. And sometimes that is the situation. But in my book, there is precious little you have absolutely no control over. If bad things happen to you, it's usually because you allow them to happen. But I think it's better to focus on good things. Don't you?"

Muriel nodded as she pushed a fork into her mouth.

"Anyway," added Felicia. "We're not talking about what *most folks*, black or white, get a chance to do, we're talking about what's possible if you're really smart and determined. And, for you, for either of you, I don't see any limits."

She beamed at Muriel, noting the teenager's reverential expression, and found herself fantasizing about motherhood, and concluded she might make a pretty good parent—if only she had the right man.

11

During the hour or so he and María Cristina sat chatting with Wagner, one question was uppermost in Mario's mind: Was it possible to salvage enough of Hernández's reputation to render him useful as a witness? By the time he arrived home, Mario had come up with something of an answer—or at least with the name of a person he presumed would have one. Marci Adler, an assistant district attorney in Brooklyn had, over the past few years, become a hot legal commentator on local TV. She even occasionally appeared on major national shows to deliver thirty-second takes on the trial of the moment. Her long blond hair, willowy figure, and pretty, angular face made her a natural for producers looking for a lawyer to put on camera. And she was smart enough and quick-witted enough that a case could be made that she was not getting the attention on looks alone.

Mario had discovered years ago, when they were dating, that Marci was constitutionally incapable of less than total involvement. Her interests—whether personal or professional—invariably became preoccupations. Having dipped a toe into the media's world, she no doubt had become obsessed with it—meaning, he hoped, that she had learned to manipulate it, that she would know how to get the *Inquirer* to retract O'Hare's column on Juan. He dialed her number from memory and was delighted to find it had not changed.

"I didn't really expect to catch you at home, Marci. But I'm glad I did."

"Mario?" she said, her astonishment obvious in her voice.

"Yep. It's me," he said, trying to mask his nervousness. Calling out of the blue after being out of touch for so long, he had no idea what to expect.

"I'll be damned. It's been quite some time, stranger."

"I guess so," he said, relieved that she sounded pleased. "I see you've become quite the TV star."

"Look who's talking. I can't pick up the paper these days without coming across your name."

"To my eternal consternation. In fact, well, that's sort of why I'm calling. I need to pick your brain for a second or two about this case I've got."

"The case that's getting all the press?"

"Yeah, *that* case," said Mario. "Does the name Juan Hernández mean anything to you? Jake O'Hare did a column on him the other day. Claimed he had robbed a bodega in East Harlem."

"Um huh. I remember. The guy who claimed to be a choirboy."

"Well, he's no choirboy, but he's also not an armed robber. The *Inquirer* story was flat-out wrong. And since I was thinking of using the guy as a witness, I'd like to see his reputation rehabilitated a bit before I do. It would be great if we could get the *Inquirer* to run a retraction, but our press office, as you know, is so chickenshit that there's no point in even talking to them about it. Ergo, my call to you."

"Never happen," she said, in a tone so emphatic that it momentarily struck Mario dumb.

Finally he managed to mumble, "What'll never happen?"

"The *Inquirer*, as far as I know, never retracts anything. And since Jake O'Hare is writing an opinion column instead of news, the odds are even greater against them running a retraction. And if they did, by some miracle, run an admission of error—because they feared a libel suit, for instance—it would be so tiny and buried so far back in the paper that no one would ever read it. You'd be much better off not even thinking about the *Inquirer* but trying to get somebody else to do an entirely new piece."

"Someone like *who*?" he asked.

"One of the TV stations, or, more likely, the *Daily Journal*." She laughed suddenly and added, "You know, I just got an idea. Quentin Varner, the *Journal* page-three columnist, can't stand O'Hare. He and O'Hare have been feuding for years. Varner would love a chance to take a righteous poke at him in print."

"Well, like I said, our press folks are bullshit. So how do I make it happen?"

"Why don't you start at the beginning, Mario, and tell me exactly what we're dealing with here? Maybe I can help."

Thirty minutes later, when Mario hung up the phone, his mood had brightened immensely. Marci had agreed to meet him for breakfast and to do what she could to get the corrected Hernández story into print. She had also reminded him that ultimately the jury's verdict was all that mattered, and that the verdict hinged much less on what the press printed than on what he said in court. It was not a reminder that he needed, but it underscored, for Mario, how easily, in a big press case, the route to justice could become lost in a fog of media smoke.

The breakfast with Marci was pleasant but rushed; Mario was too preoccupied with his case to dawdle over small talk. He was pleased to see that she was still unaffected and lovely, and apparently bore him no ill-will, but once he had given her a copy of the police report and filled her in on the relevant facts, his attention shifted to his first witness. Marci, too perceptive to mistake his monosyllables and grunts for attention, graciously relieved him of any obligation to entertain by pretending to be rushing off to a pressing appointment. Only afterward did Mario recognize her white lie for what it was— when he recalled, as he reviewed his case files later that morning, that she had confided during the phone conversation the previous evening that she was planning to take the whole day off "just to veg." He made a mental note to apologize for his lack of sociability, gathered up his materials, and headed for court.

The scene in the courtroom was much as it had been the previous day, with every available seat taken and an overflow crowd queued up in the corridor. The level of tension, however, was noticeably lower—largely, Mario conjectured, because both sides, having survived the initial flurry of exchanges, were now settling down to the hard—and relatively mundane—work of the trial.

He spent the morning filling in many of the details he had sketched the day before. He introduced Wisocki's 911 call, re-created the drama and particulars of the police response, and walked detectives, item by item, through the photographs taken and the evidence collected at the scene. During the afternoon, he took testimony from the emergency medical service crew, from the pathologist who had called for the wagon to pick up García's body, and from several officers subsequently assigned to the investigation.

Felicia, for the most part, was content to listen. She objected infrequently and her cross-examinations were brief, and mostly had the effect of forcing investigators to concede that none of the evidence eliminated the possibility that García had been wounded accidentally or that there had been a struggle over the gun. The only real excitement of the day occurred not in the courtroom, but in the streets—just after court adjourned.

Felicia, accompanied by Stephanie and the Wisocki family, emerged from the courtroom and plunged into the crowd of reporters just as a procession of protesters passed by. Spotting Felicia amid the horde of journalists, a small band of agitators broke off from the larger group and started walking in her direction. The leader, a young black man wearing a green skull cap, stopped about five yards in front of her and screamed in a booming baritone that startled the reporters into silence, "Hey, you. I got some words for you, Miss Hollywood."

Felicia ignored him and started talking to Wisocki. The man took a step forward and shouted even louder, "I'm talking to you, Miss Hollywood." His six comrades, also in green skull caps, fell into formation behind him, scowling, with their hands crossed over their chests. "It's flunkies like you who are holding us back," he proclaimed. "You need to get yourself together, sister. You need to get your head together. You need to stop warring on your own people. You need to get real, Miss Hollywood."

Felicia glared at him for two or three seconds and then shook her head and sighed as if to ask, *What asylum did you just check out of?* The gesture provoked another outburst. "What are you looking at, Hollywood?" When she turned, as if to leave, he yelled louder, his voice as piercing and hard as a knife, "Don't walk away from me, house-nigger bitch. You don't walk away from me." At that moment, he drew back his hand, in which he held a brightly colored object. Someone shrieked, "Watch out." Suddenly it seemed as if a thousand voices were screaming in unison.

Felicia stood paralyzed as she watched his arm moving in apparent slow motion; but when she sensed, more than saw, the glossy object hurtling toward her, she spun out of the way. She stumbled into John Wisocki's arms, which prevented her from falling to the ground; and as they clung to each other, terrified, the missile landed behind them with a splash, releasing a yellowish liquid on the ground.

"It's only a balloon," sang out a man somewhere in the crowd in a voice cracking with evident relief.

The cops, who heretofore had been strangely passive, abruptly came to life. Two rushed the man who had tossed the balloon and wrestled him to the ground. Several others surrounded his green-capped associates and herded them toward the curb. A court officer materialized at Felicia's side and demanded to know, "Are you okay, ma'am?"

She could not answer. Instead, she stood shaking, holding onto Wisocki. Linda and Sophie seemed equally shell-shocked. Competing cameras whirled around their heads. Stephanie, who alone had kept her wits, grabbed Felicia's free hand and towed her toward the waiting town car. The Wisocki family and the court officer followed as the reporters closed in.

"Did you expect emotions to get out of hand like this?" asked a TV reporter whose face she vaguely recognized.

Felicia paused at the car door and steadied herself, giving her voice time to find its proper pitch. "No, I didn't expect this particular kind of madness, but I have always known that there are people who disagree with what they believe I represent. And I have long known that there are people who would prefer that I go away, or just shut up. But I can't do that. It's not my nature. It never has been."

She shook her head as other reporters began to call out questions and she stepped into the car. The Wisocki family followed and Stephanie walked off with the officer. As the car pulled away, Felicia let loose a breath, releasing the tension in her chest. "Thanks for catching me," she told John.

Later, Felicia and Frank watched the balloon attack replayed on the nightly newscasts. Two of the stations led with it and all of them prominently featured it. Channel 3 framed Wisocki in such a way that he looked absolutely heroic holding her up as she fell back, a stunned expression on her face. The mysterious green-capped man, according to the reports, called himself Adam Two. Apparently, he saw himself as the patriarch of a regenerated Garden of Eden and as the founder of a new black nation. "I am the word and the way," he shouted on a Channel 3 file clip.

The Reverend Flores appeared on one of the broadcasts insisting that Adam Two was acting on his own. "I don't know what Mr. Two is protesting," said Flores, "but it has nothing to do with us or our grievances. We remain concerned about the murder of an innocent man, Francisco García, who was killed for no good reason. We are here demanding justice. We will not leave until justice is done."

When the broadcasts finally ended, Frank turned to her and said, "I don't like this case one bit. It's not only insane, it's dangerous. And all this press. I'm not crazy about that either. You've been fairly fortunate so far. I mean, you haven't been hurt. What if that fool had had a bomb instead of a balloon filled with God knows what? And you really haven't been trashed by the press. But you have to understand, it won't last. Reporters are capricious, and they're vicious. It's only a matter of time before they turn on you. And the community will be right behind them."

The next morning, as Felicia stared at the *Daily Journal* on her way to court, she recalled Frank's words and wondered whether his prophecy was already coming true. The paper carried two long stories on Juan Hernández. One was a fairly straight news story— played on the front page—by crime reporter Diane Rogers. According to Rogers, the police had checked out Hernández's alibi and cleared him of any involvement in the Gómez robbery. The bodega owner, Evido Gómez, had conceded that he might have been mistaken in his identification: "Sometimes you're not at your best regarding exact details when a man has a gun to your head. Also, the robber had that rag over his mouth, so I can't be absolutely sure it was his face, but it sure looked like him to me," the article quoted Gómez as saying.

The column, on page three, by Quentin Varner was an unabashed hatchet job on Jake O'Hare, suggesting he was a "second-rate talent" who manufactured "phony facts."

Brenda Noel, the *Journal*'s star gossip columnist, dropped the other shoe. "What well-known criminal attorney may soon be the subject of an investigation for an unethical act she allegedly committed as a prosecutor. This beautiful, black rising star of the bar is suspected of burying information that might have cleared an innocent man convicted of murder. Though she is riding high at the moment, she may be in for a horrible fall, according to sources in a position to know."

Bad as the stories on Hernández were, it was the gossip column item that rankled. The Hernández situation, after all, was fair game for comment. Hernández had injected himself into a very public trial, and O'Hare had called his bluff. Now Varner had done the same with O'Hare. And who could say where the actual truth lay? She knew better than to question Hector González too closely on the information he turned up while investigating her cases. As a former cop with scores of friends in borderline neighborhoods throughout the city, and with thousands of outstanding IOUs, he operated in a world of relative morality; there was no telling how a crony or informant might twist the truth to make it into what González wanted to hear. If the information on Hernández turned out to be flawed, no one was done any real harm—least of all Hernández, whose reputation was worth less than a damn at any rate. And certainly not O'Hare, who seemed to take it as his mission to print outrageous, and often erroneous, disclosures.

But the gossip item was a different matter altogether. It was not only a breach of confidence, but a breach of etiquette. It was intensely personal in a particularly ugly way. It was an invitation, in short, to a street fight. And if that was the way Mario wanted to play it—for the information, she was certain, could only have come from Mario—she had some street moves of her own.

Felicia pulled out her cell phone and dialed the home number of Eleanor Lamont, the public relations consultant she had retained in anticipation of the trial's special demands.

"Elli, Felicia Fontaine. Glad I caught you at home."

"Good morning, Felicia. You must be psychic, I was just getting ready to call you."

"I guess you read the *Journal*," said Felicia, her irritation manifestly apparent.

"Yeah. And I'm sure your back is hurting, given that's where Brenda plunged her knife. But I think we can work with this."

"What do you mean?" asked Felicia, surprised at Eleanor's equanimity.

"Just what I said. This may actually work to your advantage. But only if we take the initiative, starting with a press briefing later today and also an appearance on WBLK."

"Exactly what's on your mind, Elli?"

"For starters, making you the aggressor instead of the victim," said Eleanor. "And whatever it takes from there."

Although the jurors had been instructed to ignore the press coverage, no one expected them to actually obey. So Felicia was not surprised that Mario took advantage of the opening provided by the *Journal* to call Hernández as a witness; for the story had not only removed the taint of the armed robbery accusation, but had made Hernández an object of potential sympathy as the victim of a slanderous attack by the press.

Mario, wisely in Felicia's view, made no attempt to portray Hernández as a wronged innocent. Such an approach would have been so lacking in credibility as to risk insulting the jury. It also would have made Hernández into a sitting duck for a hostile cross examination that dredged up his criminal history. Instead, Mario, with a sympathetic manner and pointed questions, got Hernández to talk about his conviction for crack dealing and to acknowledge other transgressions of his past. Hernández also admitted he had no full-time work, but did odd jobs, lived at home, and was partially supported by his mother while he tried to earn a degree, though he was taking the current semester off. Finally, Mario got to the meat of the testimony, and the only reason Hernández was on the stand.

"Where were you the evening of August twenty-fourth of last year?"

"I had been at home, baby-sitting my little sister, but around eight o'clock or so, I left. I had promised to meet my friend Angel Martínez. He was interested in getting off the street, getting into school, and I was going to tell him about City College. You see—"

"Did you in fact meet Mr. Martínez?" Mario cut him off with the question, trying to signal Hernández, by the sharp tone of his voice, to keep his answers focused and short.

"Yeah. We met around eight-thirty, I think, at this little deli on Ninety-seventh and Second. We each had a cup of coffee and then decided to take a walk."

"Did either of you have anything other than coffee?"

"No, just coffee."

"Where did you walk?"

"We headed no place in particular, a few blocks south, just walking and talking."

"Did anything unusual happen during your walk?"

"Yeah, you could say that. We had crossed Ninety-fifth Street, or maybe Ninety-fourth, when this man comes up and—"

"What did the man look like?"

"He was kind of short, maybe about fifty."

"Do you remember what he was wearing?"

"He had on a suit, I think it was gray, and a light shirt, open at the collar and no tie. He also had one of those pouches you wear around your waist to keep money and stuff. I don't remember what color."

"The man you saw on the street that evening, do you see him in the courtroom today?"

"Yeah," said Hernández, purposefully nodding his head.

"Could you point him out and describe what he is wearing?"

"He's right over there, with the black suit," said Hernández, pointing to Wisocki.

"Your Honor, may the record reflect that the witness has identified the defendant," said Mario.

"The record will so reflect," intoned the judge.

"What happened that evening after you saw this man?" asked Mario.

"Like I was saying, he comes up and then all kinds of weird sh . . . stuff began to go down. He just went crazy."

"Can you be more specific, Mr. Hernández? What happened at the point when you encountered the defendant? What exactly did he do or say?"

"He was talking strange. He said something about not needing any money, and then he starts throwing change at us, pennies. Like, he just reached into his pocket and started throwing the coins hard as he could, hit both me and Angel in the face with it."

"What happened after that?"

"More strange sh . . . stuff. He acted like he had lost his mind. He started screaming something about a game. I really don't remember all what he was saying about that, but it was something about a game. And then he said, 'Go to hell.'"

"Were those his exact words?"

"Yeah, man," said Hernández, his tone indignant. "I remember 'cause we was both in shock. And then he said, 'I ain't got to respect you. I ain't got to respect no damn spicks. Get out of my face, you damn spicks.'"

"Do you have any doubt that that is what he said?" asked Mario, looking his witness directly in the eyes.

"None at all. At that point, I was getting mad. So I was listening real hard. Then he said it again, 'You damn spicks.' And I—"

"Did he say anything else at that point?"

"Yeah. He said we were going to die," said Hernández, looking appropriately horrified.

"What happened next?"

"He pulled a gun out of that pouch he had around his waist and said, 'You are going to die.'"

"What happened at that point?"

Hernández tittered nervously and answered, "We ran, man. We just got the hell . . . I mean, we ran."

"Your Honor, I have no further questions," said Mario, as he returned to his seat at the prosecutor's table.

Felicia approached the witness stand timidly, as if unsure of how to proceed. She stared at Hernández for several seconds before finally asking in a voice virtually devoid of inflection: "So, you are a student, Mr. Hernández?"

"Yes, ma'am."

"But you are not attending CCNY right now?"

"That's right."

"So how in the world are you a student?"

"Objection. Asked and answered," shouted Mario.

"I'll allow it," said the judge.

"So how are you a student if you're not taking classes?" asked Felicia.

"I'm a student, but I'm taking the semester off."

"I see. And so far you've completed how many courses?"

"Objection. Irrelevant," interjected Mario.

Mario, who noticed the judge was hesitating, was immediately on his feet. "May we approach, Your Honor?"

At the judge's nod, Mario and Felicia rushed to the front.

Mario exploded: "Judge, this is going nowhere. The number of courses he has completed has absolutely nothing to do with any issue before the court."

Felicia, who sensed that Judge Campbell was as interested in hearing the answer as she was, whether it was relevant or not, was determined to give him a pretext for overruling the objection. "Your Honor, the question goes directly to the witness's credibility. If allowed to pursue this line of questioning, we will establish that he has never really been a college student in any meaningful sense of the word, despite his prior testimony to that fact."

"All right. I will allow it," replied Campbell.

Felicia, her back to the judge, smirked at Mario before turning again to Hernández: "How many courses did you say you've completed?"

"I don't remember exactly."

"Okay, well inexactly. How many would you guess? Twenty, thirty?"

"Objection."

"Overruled."

"How many would you guess?"

"I'm not sure exactly, like I said."

"Well, is it a very high number?"

"I don't remember."

"Yes, I suppose it must be difficult to remember that you've only completed one course. Just one. Extremely hard for you to recall, isn't it?"

"Objection. Argumentative."

"Sustained. Move on, Ms. Fontaine," ordered Campbell.

Felicia smiled grimly and glanced at the jury, shaking her head as if bewildered, momentarily making eye contact with the flower shop lady and the travel agent before pushing on. "So since you are not a student, what exactly do you do with your time?"

"Objection. Irrelevant."

"Sustained."

"You testified that you don't really work, didn't you, Mr. Hernández? That is, that you don't have a job?"

"I do odd jobs."

"Is one of those odd jobs selling drugs?"

"No. I do repairs and fix stuff. It's not a regular job, but I do things around people's houses. I work with my hands."

"Do you report the income from your repair work?"

A perplexed look appeared on Hernández's face as he replied, "Well . . . uh . . . I haven't done my taxes yet, but, uh . . . But I'm sure I will when I do. Anyway, José, the guy I work with, keeps the records."

"So this José would have canceled checks documenting your employment."

"He might. But, you know, he prefers dealing in cash."

"So, at this point, as far as you know, there is no documentation of this work that you claim to do?"

"Maybe not."

"How many drinks had you had that night?"

"None. I mean, a cup of coffee."

"So if anyone said, under oath, that they served you a drink of alcohol that night, that person would be lying. Right?"

Mario objected, but was overruled, while Hernández sat silent, staring at Felicia with obvious disdain.

Felicia frowned, as if deep in thought. "Please answer the question, Mr. Hernández. Are you saying that anyone who says you had a drink that night is lying?"

"Jesus, I'm not really sure. Maybe one drink. Yeah, just one drink, a rum and Coke."

"And what about your companion, Mr. Martínez?"

"I don't understand."

"Was he drinking alcohol that night?"

"I don't know."

"But you do know he was a crack dealer, right?"

"Objection. Beyond the—"

"He used to be," Hernández sputtered, talking over Mario's objection, "but he had gotten out of that. It's been a long time . . . "

"Objection," Mario called, louder.

"Sustained."

"Your Honor," said Mario, "may we have the answer stricken and the jury instructed to disregard the improper answer."

"The answer is stricken. The jury will disregard the answer," said the judge.

Felicia continued. "Did you know Martínez had two convictions for crack dealing and there was an outstanding warrant on him for armed assault?"

"Objection," screamed Mario, but Hernández insisted on answering.

"Those convictions were bogus," said Hernández. "And the cops, they look for lots of people. A lot of folks in the neighborhood ain't too down with the police. That's just the way it is."

"Oh. Now I think I understand. Despite his problems with the police, you were with him because you planned to put him on the proper path, the same path you were on, the path to unreported income and a phantom education?" Felicia again looked at the jury, grimaced, and shook her head.

"Objection."

"Sustained."

"You have no doubt that it was my client who attacked you?" asked Felicia.

"It was him, all right."

"Answer me this," she demanded. "You're a big tough guy. Why, when a man half your size insulted you verbally and assaulted you physically, did you do nothing? Why did you just stand there like a punk?"

"He had a gun," Hernández screamed. "What was I supposed to do?"

"According to your own testimony, you weren't aware of the gun until well after the time of the insults. So why did you take them? Were you afraid of him?"

"Of *him*? Why would—ah . . . Hell, the way things are out there these days, anybody could be dangerous."

"Could it be that you didn't respond to the insults because they were never made?" said Felicia, leaning in close to his face to make her point. "Could it be you felt no fear, because he never attacked you, but that, in fact, it was you who attacked him?"

"Objection."

The judge sustained it, but Hernández rambled on: "We thought the man was crazy. You—"

"Mr. Hernández," bellowed Campbell. "You don't answer the question when I sustain an objection. Never. Never again. *Is that understood?*"

"Yes, sir."

Judge Campbell ordered the answer stricken and turned to Felicia. "Miss Fontaine, you're getting very close to being held in contempt."

"Sorry, Judge," she mumbled, with a sheepish, almost coquettish smile, which immediately turned into a scowl when she faced Hernández.

"Didn't the police question you for beating up an old man just—"

"Objection."

"Sustained."

"Do you really expect us to believe that you, a convicted felon with a violent record and an even more violent temper, would stand by while some little pipsqueak called you a spick?"

"Objection."

"Sustained."

"No further questions, Your Honor."

Felicia whirled around and returned to her seat, content with the job she had done, certain the jury would see Hernández's testimony for the garbage that it was. There was no point in continuing to batter him; better to save her energy—and the jury's forbearance—for witnesses who were more of a threat.

Mario was not exactly thrilled with Hernández's performance, and he was incensed at Judge Campbell's indulgence of Felicia, but he was not altogether displeased. Hernández had made a fool of himself, pretty much as expected, despite Mario's efforts to keep him on track, but he had also put racially offensive words in Wisocki's mouth and a gun in his hand. Even if the jurors discounted much of what Hernández had said, his assertions would linger in their minds—particularly in light of the allegations Wisocki's colleagues were prepared to make.

The testimony of those colleagues consumed the remainder of the day. Although none had heard Wisocki use racial or ethnic slurs, several had heard him call García a "Hispanic quota hire" or observe that García was "trading on his accent and his Spanish name." Others noted that the relationship between the two men, which once had been amicable, deteriorated once García was promoted to an equivalent level. "It was like he resented the fact that Francisco was moving up faster than he was," said the final witness for the day.

As Felicia waited for the reporters to assemble, she reviewed the testimony of the past several hours. Hernández was clearly a fool and a liar. And without him, all Mario had was a bunch of people saying that Wisocki didn't care for the company's favoritism toward García—a sentiment with which most of the jurors could easily sympathize, especially when it was put into context. As she saw it, Mario was batting around zero in the courtroom. And if the press conference went as she expected, he would end up doing just as poorly in the court of public opinion.

Felicia considered herself lucky that Geneva had pointed her in the direction of Eleanor Lamont. Although Eleanor, who headed her own small black firm, was not a big name, she was clearly a player in the world of the media. She seemed to know every important journalist in town. And she was in partnership, as she called it, with Myers and Clark, one of the biggest public relations firms in the industry. As a result of the alliance, she had access to M&C's resources, including its posh auditorium, which is where she and Felicia had scheduled their first press conference.

That Eleanor had taken a seat onstage and was no longer pacing behind the podium seemed a sign that the briefing was about to begin. Felicia, who had been watching from the wings, took the seat beside her.

"Good timing," said Eleanor. "I was just about to come get you. All set?"

"I think so," Felicia replied.

"Let's do it then."

Eleanor took a few moments to thank the reporters for coming and to sing Felicia's praises—"the most brilliant and innovative lawyer in New York"—before turning the microphone over to her star, who got right to the point.

"Many of you I know and some of you I don't," said Felicia, gazing into the ocean of faces, "but whether I am personally acquainted with you or not, I know you all are dedicated to the pursuit of truth. So allow me to be frank.

"This morning the *Daily Journal* ran a gossip item, an item alleging unethical conduct. From the description of the alleged perpetrator in the paper, I can only conclude that the article was directed at me. That item is, in a word, libelous. And when I have time, I will consider the appropriate legal remedies. As you know, I am rather busy at the moment. I cannot, however, allow such a serious charge to go unanswered even for a moment. That is the main reason I have asked you here today.

"If the *Journal* has any proof of unethical behavior, I challenge them to produce it, *immediately*. But I can tell you in advance, the *Journal* will not do so. The reason is simple. There is no proof to produce. The charges, I can only assume, were planted by parties who, for reasons of their own, wish to drag my good name through the mud. I will not be a silent victim to such tactics. Nor do I feel any fair-minded community will sanction it.

"I will now try to answer any questions you may have."

The sparring session with reporters took nearly an hour, but Felicia felt certain she had made her point. She had put the gossip columnist in league with racist conspirators, a notorious drug lord, and other enemies of "the community." Later that evening she continued the offensive, with a lengthy personal interview with the

Daily Defender, a black newspaper that circulated throughout the city, and with an appearance on WBLK, one of New York's most popular black-oriented radio talk stations. If the outraged listeners who called the station were at all representative, her message of a racist plot was winning support even in quarters where her politics were suspect. Her denunciation of Carl Murphy was equally well received. "The opportunists who are now this drug dealer's champions obviously have no personal experience with crime," she railed on air, "nor are they at all interested in our communities. I will not be destroyed by their lies. And I refuse to apologize for putting Carl Murphy away. My only regret is that I couldn't do it sooner—before another mother was forced to bury a son."

If her fiery words skirted the morally messy issues raised by the gossip column item, so much the better. Mario, after all, was hardly in a position to argue the point. For even assuming he had the guts to try, he had no facts on the record to back him up. And if he didn't care for her tactics, he had only himself to blame.

12

Only when she was almost upon them did Felicia realize the demonstrators were screaming her name. "Felicia Fontaine! We're with you, Felicia!" The shouts emanated from a group of regulars she had come to recognize. Marching under the banner of Citizens for Equality in Society, they generally declaimed on the evils of affirmative action. Across the street was a lone, tall bushy-haired man with a sandwich board reading FIGHT CHARACTER ASSASSINATION, SUPPORT FELICIA FONTAINE. He was talking to another man, who was handing out leaflets and shouting something about "Fighting Felicia Fontaine T-shirts."

Flores's followers were also in evidence. They had assembled about a block away and were chanting in Spanish and English. In front of the courts building stood a familiar neighborhood character, a beggar with a sign reading TRYING TO RAISE ONE MILLION DOLLARS FOR WINE RESEARCH. Of all those assembled, he was, in one sense, the most stable: he had been there before the trial and would be there afterward. It said something scary about the nature of the crowd, Felicia figured, that in such company a wino was a symbol of stability.

The crowd seemed considerably larger than it had been the first few days of the trial. Also, there seemed to be more energy—or maybe just more lunacy—in the air. Apostles of all kinds of causes, from spiritualism to pyramidism, had materialized around the building. All we need now, Felicia thought, is extraterrestrials for John Wisocki.

The commotion and the crush of humanity outside the court had created an atmosphere not unlike that of a rock concert. There was a sense of gaiety and also of anticipation. There was a spirit of communion that loosened inhibitions and that magnified the meaning of the shared experience.

Felicia waved at the people from Citizens for Equality, zipped into the building, and made her way to the courtroom. When she sat down, Mario did not acknowledge her presence; instead he brooded in silence. And she reminded herself, as she had previously, that he had brought her reaction on himself; if he hadn't gone to the press, she would not have had to respond, and his attempt at psychological blackmail would not have blown up in his face.

Today's testimony, she had assumed from the witness lineup, would go into Wisocki's relationship with García. And sure enough, Mario called one co-worker after another who swore to the envy and bitterness felt by her client. Mario also entered into evidence diary entries from Wisocki's home and office computers that documented his growing obsession with García. One that was written a week and a half before García's death read:

"I feel that Francisco García has taken the most precious thing in the world from me. He has robbed me of my livelihood, which, in the order of things, is even worse than stealing a man's wife. This all would be easier to take if he truly were the better man, but that is not the way things work these days, especially around Computertronics. All that matters is that he has a Spanish surname and I do not. That is what this country has come to, a place that rewards foreigners for not being American.

"It is as if all my life, all that I thought I was counts for nothing in this world. That fills me with an emptiness I cannot begin to describe."

Mario entered into evidence several similar entries—forlorn, rambling confessionals Wisocki had written, apparently as a way of working through his distress. Some of them ranted against Infotect or Computertronics and did not mention García at all. Others made García out to be all but a demon from hell.

"Lately I have this recurring daydream about Francisco," read one. "I see him hanging from a tree in the middle of the desert as bugs and buzzards devour his body."

In another memo, Wisocki wrote, "I find his very presence irritating. There is something superior in his manner, something that says he believes he has a perfect right to whatever he wants. Maybe it's typical of Latin men to see themselves as holy objects of worship instead of as mediocre human beings."

He confessed in yet another entry, "If I could find another place to work, perhaps I could let this thing go. As it is, I think much about killing, and much about my own death, my real death, as opposed to this living death."

Several co-workers described Wisocki as a loner who had withdrawn even more once the layoffs were announced. "He generally kept to himself," testified a software trainer who reported to Wisocki, "but I did hear him say once that he was fed up, and that he didn't understand the new corporate priorities. He made it pretty clear he thought García was taking advantage, and was getting special treatment he didn't deserve."

"Do you recall exactly when that conversation took place?" asked Mario.

"Yes. It was in the morning, two days after the announcement about the layoffs. I stopped by Mr. Wisocki's office to talk about the takeover and he began talking about Mr. García."

"What exactly did the defendant say?"

"As I recall, he said something like, 'Francisco's going to do okay. He's a real self-promoter, plus he's a minority.'"

"Did he say anything else?"

"Yes. He said that Francisco was not to be trusted."

"Do you recall the defendant's exact words?"

"Yes. He said, 'I don't trust Francisco.'"

A fellow training supervisor, with whom Wisocki sometimes lunched, recalled even uglier comments Wisocki had made as they had commiserated over their mutual firing: "I remember him saying, 'García is a leech. He's living off our blood.' And then he added, 'That really bothers me. Why should that bastard have it so good.'"

Other witnesses testified as to why they believed that Wisocki knew that García worked on Sundays. A secretary claimed that Wisocki had interrogated her about García after she had mentioned, in idle conversation, that García had worked the previous Sunday.

"He asked me whether Mr. García worked every Sunday," she testified.

"What was your answer?" asked Mario.

"I told him that as long as there is air-conditioning, Mr. García will work, that he always seems to have a lot of catching up to do. In retrospect, maybe it's not something I should have mentioned, but he asked and I didn't see any harm in answering."

On several occasions, as his hard-drive diary was read in court, Felicia stole glances at John. At times he seemed so choked up that she feared he would burst into tears. She finally became so concerned about his emotional state, that she placed a comforting arm around his shoulder. Even Linda seemed affected. Though Linda customarily kept her feelings to herself, Felicia twice noticed her weeping quietly in court, and she could only imagine what the reading of the diary entries had forced Linda to relive.

Throughout the testimony, Judge Campbell and the jury listened attentively, swept up in the tale of a lonely, defeated man pouring his anxieties and resentments into his computer. Even the audience seemed less restive than usual, perhaps, Felicia conjectured, out of embarrassment at sipping from the cup of Wisocki's private pain.

She conceded the day to Mario and surmised, from the looks on their faces, that the judge and jury saw it as his day as well. All in all that wasn't so bad. No jury liked to see a totally one-sided case; there was neither fun nor mystery in that. But one good day would not be enough to repair the holes in Mario's theory of the case. And as Felicia assessed the evidence, one good day was all that Mario got.

On the way home, Felicia reread O'Hare's column, which she'd only had time to skim that morning. Jake had advised her not to miss it when she had called him yesterday and tried to clear up the confusion concerning Hernández. She was still convinced that the original story about the bodega robbery was right, she had told him, but the bodega owner was so afraid of Hernández that he had backed away from his identification. That made sense to O'Hare, who was not as upset as she had imagined he might be at being called a hack by Varner.

"He's so threatened by me," O'Hare had explained, "every few months he finds an excuse to try to sock it to me. Don't worry about it. I'll fix his wagon. Make sure you read tomorrow's paper. You'll get a kick out of it." Sure enough, O'Hare had devoted part of today's column to his counterattack, denouncing Varner as an illiterate dupe and the *Journal* as a McCarthyite rag, which had unfairly targeted Felicia for abuse.

The local TV news stations that evening also had a couple of reports related to the trial. The one that most intrigued her was Channel 3's interview with several black ministers who had joined Flores in what seemed to be an uneasy alliance. One tried to square his previous unremitting criticism of the justice system with his support of the prosecution of Wisocki. "What I've said in the past," pointed out the minister, "is that the system sends too many *black* men to jail. I never said I had anything against the system locking up *white* men like John Wisocki." The Reverend Lester Hawkins was also on the show.

When Felicia had told Geneva the story of Hawkins's visit to her office, Geneva had guffawed. "You could do worse," she had said. "He's got money and he probably won't last that much longer. You got to think about your future, girlfriend. Hell, those white girls marry rich old men all the time just to inherit their money. You'd be following in the great tradition of Jackie O." Now the mere mention of Hawkins's name sent Geneva into hysterics.

Felicia had not heard from Hawkins since he had come by that day, but when the reporter asked about the allegations made against her, he did not hesitate to answer: "We will be no part of an attempt to bring down a strong, young black woman. Some of us may have some problems with Ms. Fontaine's choice of politics and clients, but she is one of ours. And we will not sit by and see her character assassinated by our enemies in the press. If we let them come for her today, they may come for us tomorrow." Felicia smiled as she switched off the TV, tickled at the thought that Hawkins was still auditioning for the role of her protector. It wouldn't be a bad idea, she thought, to drop him a note, thanking him for his words of support.

She spent much of the night speculating on the rest of Mario's case. With only one witness—the medical examiner—left to go, he was virtually certain to rest his case tomorrow, and he would no doubt like to do it with something of a bang. His problem, as she saw it, was that there was nothing really explosive to present, so he would be forced to make much ado about essentially insignificant facts. Her job was to keep him from getting away with that. And to accomplish that, she would have to take control of his witness—David K. Miller, M.D., City Medical Examiner—who had already spoken to her not only with his autopsy report but by phone, briefly, when she had called him to clarify his work.

The next morning as Miller was sworn in, Felicia sized him up. He didn't fit any stereotype of a coroner with which she was familiar; he didn't even look like a doctor. He was far too young and a bit too well put together. He wore a pin-striped gray suit that was extremely well tailored, and had dark, medium-length brown hair that looked to be expensively cut. He was not exactly handsome, but he seemed quite well tended. Although she knew better, she still was prone to think of medical examiners as wizened old men with puffs of gray hair. With his deep winter tan and athlete's physique, Miller looked more like an aerobics instructor, or maybe a rather vain plainclothes cop. *But a medical examiner?* She listened closely as he spoke.

Miller was answering Mario's pedigree questions—name, occupation, length and place of employment—in a calm, low-pitched voice. He had been trained at the University of Chicago and done further work at Yale. He was certified in forensic pathology by the American Board of Pathology and had been employed by the Office of the Chief Medical Examiner in New York City for just over seven years. He had been qualified as an expert in forensic pathology in numerous courts and performed scores of autopsies a year.

After asking that Miller be qualified as an expert in forensic pathology and placing the autopsy report into evidence, Mario proceeded to the specifics of the case—first establishing that Miller had been assigned to perform the autopsy on García's body, then carefully laying the groundwork for questions about the autopsy results.

"What injuries did you observe during your external examination of the body?"

"There was a single gunshot wound, an entrance wound to the chest, with a powder burn at the perforation. There was also stippling on the chest. And there was a single exit wound in the back."

"What is stippling?"

"Stippling is the pattern of tiny bruises caused by the powder and other particulate matter expelled along with the bullet when a gun is fired. It can help us determine how far away the weapon was."

"Do you have an opinion based on a reasonable degree of medical certainty as to the cause of the wounds on the body?"

"They appear to have been caused by a bullet of medium caliber from a pistol."

"Based on your examination and the stippling pattern, do you have an estimate of how far the gun was from the body?"

"Yes. It was six to ten inches."

"Were skin scrapings found beneath Mr. García's fingernails?"

"No."

"Based on your examination, can you say with a reasonable degree of medical certainty whether the victim engaged in a struggle with his assailant?"

"I cannot eliminate the possibility of a struggle, although often, when there is a struggle, skin scrapings are found. As I noted, none were found in this case."

Mario led the witness through a series of interrogatories during which Miller described, in detail, precisely how the autopsy had been conducted. Then Mario got to the question which was the number-one reason for having Miller on the stand.

"Can you say with a reasonable degree of medical certainty what the cause of death is in this case?"

"Yes, I can. It was a gunshot wound to the chest. The gunshot passed through the chest, causing a perforation of the lung parenchyma. After injuring other internal tissue, the bullet exited through the back. It also precipitated ventricular fibrillation."

Mario looked at the audience and found Isabel García, who had buried her face in her hands. He stared at her for several seconds, sending her a silent prayer of solace, before asking the next question.

"Did the lung collapse?"

"No. The bullet penetrated peripheral tissues, but it did not cause the lung to collapse. Nor did it lacerate any of the important blood vessels in the hilar portion of the lung."

"With that type of wound, is incapacitation generally instant?"

"No. It is not. In order to instantly incapacitate someone, the bullet would have to pass through the brain or the spinal cord."

"Can you say with a reasonable degree of medical certainty whether it was possible for Mr. García to struggle after receiving the wound you have described?"

"Yes. Definitely. He could certainly have continued to move or struggle."

"Could you explain the meaning of ventricular fibrillation, Dr. Miller?"

"It is a form, a very serious form of arrhythmia—or abnormal heart rhythm. It occurs when the electrical impulses that control the heartbeat go haywire. Instead of pumping blood, the heart twitches or convulses chaotically. Unless there is immediate medical intervention, death is generally the result."

"Is ventricular fibrillation the same as a heart attack?"

"Laymen often call it a heart attack. Physicians commonly dif-

ferentiate. When a physician says heart attack, we are usually referring to a myocardial infarct, or myocardial infarction, which literally means that part of the heart muscle dies. Ventricular fibrillation
is something a bit different than that. It comes about because the
heart is no longer working effectively as a pump and therefore is no
longer sending blood to the brain. It is not synonymous with the
kind of heart attack that results in the death of a segment of the
heart muscle. That type of injury, or infarct, is precipitated by a
blood clot in an artery narrowed by plaque which cuts off the blood
flow to the heart."

Mario asked the next question reluctantly. Yet knowing how
Felicia's mind worked, he had to ask. She would undoubtedly make
a big deal of García's heart attack. So he preempted the question
which, if Felicia asked it, would inevitably lead to a highly dramatic
attempt at obfuscation.

"Why did you list a contributing cause of death on the autopsy
report, Dr. Miller?"

"There was less than one pint of blood in the chest cavity, which
meant Mr. García could not have died just from the blood loss
caused by the bullet alone. So it was necessary to consider other eti-
ologies or causes, additional factors that could explain why he died."

"Can you say with a reasonable degree of medical certainty
whether it was possible for Mr. García to struggle after the onset of
ventricular fibrillation?"

"Yes. It was quite possible. He would have had at least ten to fifteen seconds of consciousness following the V-F, and perhaps considerably more."

"What was the manner of Mr. García's death?" asked Mario, signaling, by the seriousness of his tone and clarity of his diction, that
the answer was important.

"His death was a homicide."

"Are you absolutely certain of that?" asked Mario, looking point-
edly at the jury.

"Yes. Definitely."

"In listing a contributing factor among the causes of death, are you in any way implying that the bullet did not kill Mr. García?"

"No. Not at all. The bullet, in my opinion, was the cause of death—partly because of the damage it did directly and partly because of the arrhythmia it precipitated."

Mario spent much of the next two hours going over fine points of Miller's testimony, trying to establish, beyond a doubt, that Wisocki's gunshot had caused García's death, and trying to forestall, to the extent possible, what he knew would follow—an attempt by Felicia to portray the cause of death as a simple heart attack. Several times during his questioning he paused to look at Isabel García, long enough to ensure that the jury followed his gaze; and often, when he caught her eye, she would solemnly nod in encouragement. It was Mario's way of reminding the jury—some of whose members seemed unnerved during the more gruesome parts of Miller's testimony—that Wisocki's act had destroyed not just one life but an entire family, and that the medical testimony he was dragging them through was an indispensable part of establishing his guilt.

Felicia's turn to cross-examine followed the lunch break. As she stood up, she attempted to conceal her eagerness. The words "ventricular fibrillation" on the autopsy report had been a glorious gift, and she could hardly wait to let the jury in on the good news. She patted Wisocki on the shoulder and slowly, deliberately, approached the witness box, asking her first question in a calm, measured voice.

"You testified that somewhat less than one pint of blood was found in the chest cavity. Isn't that right, Dr. Miller?"

"Yes."

"But that is not enough blood loss to kill someone?" she asked, looking puzzled.

"Not a normal person. People donate a pint of blood at the blood bank, for instance, and experience no adverse consequences because of that. It would take significantly more blood loss to cause death."

She paused and glanced at the floor, as if pondering his meaning. Still looking slightly puzzled, she pressed on. "So, as to how he died—is it correct to say, Doctor, that the mechanism of death in this case was ventricular fibrillation resulting in heart failure—

what a layman might call a sudden-death heart attack?"

"Yes, a layman might describe it that way."

She nodded, a look of comprehension forming on her face.

"You obviously felt it was important to specify the arrhythmia in your report," she said. "Why is that?"

"Because the direct injury itself was not sufficient to cause death. If it had been, there would have been no need to specify a contributing factor."

"Is there any medical consensus on what precipitates ventricular fibrillation?"

"Not precisely. It does not always stem from the same cause. There is a term, idiopathic ventricular fibrillation, to describe those instances in which there is no apparent structural heart disease, and no other known cause."

"Is that to say that structural heart disease is generally a factor?"

"It seems to be in many cases, though a substantial percentage of sudden-death victims have no visible coronary atherosclerosis. Caffeine, alcohol, cigarettes, cocaine, and other substances have been known to provoke arrhythmias. They can be brought about by stress or other environmental factors."

"In cases where there is no underlying heart disease, do arrhythmias generally lead to death?"

"Objection."

"Sustained."

"Did your examination of Mr. García's body find evidence of heart disease?"

"Yes. There was considerable narrowing of his arteries, meaning there was a decreased blood supply to his heart."

Felicia paused, giving the jury time to take in the information. She glanced at Wisocki, who was leaning forward in his chair, his face a study in concentration, then she again turned her attention to Miller.

"You testified during direct examination that Mr. García was shot, and that he also had a fatal arrhythmia. Given that, can you say with certainty that the gunshot wound killed him?"

"I can say with a very high degree of confidence that the gunshot wound was the cause of death."

"But not with total certainty?"

"Very few things are absolutely certain in medicine."

"Indeed," said Felicia, with such force that the word sounded like an accusation. "When a forensic pathologist uses the term homicide, is that equivalent to the term murder?" she asked in a softer tone.

"No. Murder is not a term a forensic pathologist would use."

"In fact, don't you use the term homicide to mean any violent death?" she asked.

"Essentially, yes."

"So even a clearly accidental death, in your terminology, would be classified as a homicide?"

"Yes, it could. That is correct."

She clasped her hands together and gazed briefly at the jurors, taking their engrossed expressions as a sign that they were following along and understood exactly what she was telling them.

"Can you say with medical certainty, Dr. Miller, that Mr. García would not have had heart failure had he not been shot?"

"Objection. Speculative."

"Sustained."

"You did testify, Doctor, that Mr. García's body showed signs of serious heart disease?"

"Yes."

"And that disease would have increased his risk of heart failure. Correct?"

"Yes, it would."

"No further questions, Your Honor."

As Felicia returned to her seat, she noticed a sudden flurry of activity in the front row and picked up a buzz of excited conversation—the lovely sound of reporters rearranging their leads in light of the information. By tomorrow, she was confident, many New Yorkers would wonder why in the world anyone was on trial since García had clearly died of a heart attack.

Mario confined his redirect to two questions.

"In terms of your finding of homicide, does it matter whether Mr. García technically was killed by the bullet or by events set in motion by the bullet?"

"No. It makes no difference. In either case, the finding would be homicide."

"In your expert opinion, is there any reasonable medical explanation, other than homicide, for Mr. García's death?"

"No. There is no other explanation that makes sense."

"No further questions, Your Honor. The people rest."

At home that evening, after dissecting the day's testimony, Mario and María Cristina's conversation naturally turned to the subject of Felicia.

"She's good. I'll give her that much," said Mario, placing his fork and knife on the plate that held the remains of his leftover Chinese takeout.

"A snake and a sneak is what she is," countered María Cristina. "You saw all that irrelevant stuff she was trying to bring in."

"Oh yeah," he said ruefully, "I saw it real well. I just wish Campbell had seen it half as well. He's giving her way too much rope."

"Too bad it's not the kind of rope she can strangle herself with," replied María Cristina, pushing away her moo shu vegetables, which lay essentially untouched. "Do you think the jury will buy any of this nonsense about a heart attack?"

Mario shook his head. "Doubt it. But that sure won't keep her from pushing. She believes that if you confuse the jury enough, the defense invariably comes out ahead."

Mario glanced at the rather glum expression on María Cristina's face, trying to gauge her mood. "Is something bothering you?" he asked.

"Not really," she said. "I was just thinking about the case and that bitch. She seems to have all kinds of screwy theories."

"That's true," said Mario. "But she does get results for her clients."

"So do hit men, for God's sake," said María Cristina, looking thoroughly annoyed. "You know, I never could figure out what you saw in her. I admit, she's pretty, but how in the world could you ever trust a woman like that?"

"You can't. But . . ." His words trailed off as he decided it was a subject better left alone.

"But what?" demanded María Cristina, the fire in her eyes making it clear he was not to get off so easily.

"Nothing," he said softly.

"Mario."

"Yes?"

"Do you still feel anything for her?" María Cristina asked, her voice suddenly timid.

The question had no acceptable answer. So Mario hesitated before replying. To say yes would be to reap María Cristina's anger. To say no would be to tell a lie, which she would recognize as such. He tried to finesse it.

"It's impossible not to feel *something* for somebody with whom you at one point tried to build a life. But if you're asking if I still love her, the answer's no. I haven't for a long time. In fact, I think the whole relationship was a mistake. But obviously I learned a thing or two. I did end up with you."

"Yes, but am I the consolation prize?" she asked, attempting a smile, though her tone was deadly serious.

"Jesus, honey. Of course not," said Mario. "I love you. I have since I met you."

He crossed over to her side of the table and tried to take her in his arms, but she pulled away and asked, "So how come you sometimes get that look when you talk about Felicia?"

Mario, bewildered, groped for an answer. "Look? What look? Baby, I don't know what you're—"

"You know, the 'I wish I had her' look," said María Cristina, seemingly getting more worked up by the second.

Mario gently took both of her hands. Looking directly into her eyes, he spoke as tenderly as he knew how. "I don't know exactly what's bothering you, but I do know my own heart. And I can tell that it belongs entirely to you. It has from the beginning. You believe me, don't you?" he asked, as he kissed her on the forehead.

She hesitated before answering. "I guess so," she said finally, even as her expression said, "I'm not sure."

13

The commentators didn't know quite what to make of the latest twist in the case, except that it heightened public interest in a trial that was already the talk of the town. And Monday morning, as Felicia prepared to call her first witness, she felt the pressure of the press's—and of her own—expectations. She also felt the reassurance of having Stephanie at her side. Having noticed that whenever Stephanie was in court, Judge Campbell seemed to be a bit more lenient, Felicia had cajoled Stephanie into rearranging her schedule, so she could be present for most of the week.

That Wisocki would take the stand had never been in doubt. Without personally accounting for what had happened in that office, he simply had no defense; but before he testified, Felicia felt it was essential to lay the groundwork, to provide a context for understanding his anger and frustration.

Her lead-off witness was Dwight Edwards, the former Computertronics vice president for personnel who now held a similar position with Infotect. Calling an Infotect executive was a calculated gamble. His primary interest would be in putting the corporation's best foot forward, not in helping her client. But she had advised Edwards that it was in his own best interest to simply tell the truth. Otherwise, she was fully prepared to have him declared a hostile witness—which would give her license to batter him and Infotect mercilessly.

Edwards testified that he had developed a reasonably close relationship with Wisocki. So during the time when Infotect was in the process of acquiring Computertronics, Wisocki had often turned to him for information. It was Edwards who had broken the news to Wisocki that there would be no place for him at Infotect.

"As Infotect prepared to acquire Computertronics, was any process put in place to evaluate the workers currently at Computertronics?" asked Felicia.

"Yes, there was. I was asked to coordinate a review of all of our professional people with the various division directors."

"As regards people at the director level in the software training area, how did the evaluation process work?"

"We reviewed all the managers' past performance evaluations. We also asked their supervisors, in this case the division heads, to reassess their performance and potential. Finally, we reevaluated all their professional and educational credentials. We then came up with a numerical score representing our best estimate of their value to Infotect."

"Was this a public process?"

"Not really. There was undoubtedly some general knowledge that an assessment was going on, but we did not advertise the particulars of the process."

Felicia entered into evidence several completed performance appraisal forms for Wisocki, as well as the assessment forms developed for Infotect. As she did so, she glanced at John, who seemed frozen in place, a grim expression on his face, and she offered what she hoped he would read as a nod of encouragement. John offered a weak smile in return and Felicia returned to her interrogation.

"Can you describe how Mr. Wisocki was rated during this assessment process?"

"Yes. He was rated very highly on technical skills and rated adequate on his ability to interact with coworkers, build a team, and motivate a staff. The top possible combined score was one hundred. We rated Mr. Wisocki at seventy-five."

"Did Mr. García receive a comparable score?"

"Objection. Irrelevant."

"I will allow the question."

"Mr. García received a ninety."

"Can you explain what accounts for the difference?"

"Many factors contributed—Mr. García's superior education, his superior people skills, his exceptional initiative. When looked at simultaneously, they put him far ahead not only of Mr. Wisocki but of the other training managers as well."

"Was it as a result of this evaluation process that Mr. García was retained and Mr. Wisocki was let go?"

"Precisely. Those who scored most highly were retained and the rest were let go."

"Did you personally deliver the news to Mr. Wisocki?"

"Yes, I did, in a private meeting in my office."

"How did Mr. Wisocki respond to the news?"

"He was surprised and, understandably, angry. He inquired about Mr. García, and got even angrier when I told him that Mr. García was being kept on. He said it was unfair, and that the company had no right to terminate him."

"Did you respond to Mr. Wisocki's statements?"

"Yes, I tried to sympathize with him. I told him that he was right, that it was unfair, but that I was simply the messenger, that corporate policy determined who was kept and who was not, and there was nothing I could do."

"Did you in fact believe the defendant's dismissal was unfair?"

Edwards, looking acutely uncomfortable, responded in a less self-assured tone: "Not in light of the process that was put in place and the priorities established by Infotect. But I felt I had to say something to show him that I was concerned about his feelings and his welfare."

"Mr. Edwards, your conversation with Mr. Wisocki occurred on what date?"

"July seventh of last year."

"What time of the day was that meeting?"

"Approximately ten A.M."

"Do you remember the reason you gave Mr. Wisocki as to why Mr. García was retained and he was not?"

"Not verbatim," said Edwards, eyes nervously darting about, refusing to meet her gaze.

"But you do remember the essence, do you not?"

"Yes," he said, lowering his voice a bit.

"What was that reason?"

"I told him that Infotect was especially interested in diversity."

"Did you tell him, in effect, Mr. Edwards, that he was out because he was a white male and that Mr. García was in because he was Hispanic?—that it was only because of affirmative action that he was being let go?"

"Objection. Leading question, Your Honor."

"Sustained."

"During your conversation with Mr. Wisocki, did you refer at all to Infotect's affirmative action program?"

"I told him they had one."

"As an explanation for his being let go?"

"I mentioned it, yes."

"Why?"

"I wanted to spare his feelings. I thought it would be easier that way."

"Was it the policy of Computertronics to lie to white males who were being laid off by telling them that affirmative action was to blame?"

"No. There was no such policy."

"Was it your personal policy, then, Mr. Edwards?"

"I guess, sometimes," he said, looking down at his tightly clasped hands. "It made things easier."

"So, in order to make things easier for yourself, you lied to Mr. Wisocki, and led him to believe that Mr. García had unfairly won a position at his expense?"

"Objection. Argumentative, Your Honor."

"Overruled."

"So, you lied to Mr. Wisocki and led him to believe that Mr. García had unfairly won a job at his expense?"

"Yes, I guess I did," he conceded reluctantly.

"Do you believe, in light of the reasons given to him for his dismissal, that Mr. Wisocki's anger at Infotect was justified, Mr. Edwards?"

"Objection, Your Honor. The question calls for a conclusion."

"Sustained."

After Edwards, Felicia called a succession of former colleagues, most also "downsized," who testified to the atmosphere of paranoia at Computertronics as the acquisition proceeded. Several also testified that they had been told that their race was the primary reason they were being let go. The bitterness Wisocki felt and expressed was endemic during that period, they said; for that reason, none of them thought his anger was even remotely threatening to García.

By the time the trial recessed for the day, Felicia was in an upbeat mood. Whatever else the jurors might think of Wisocki, she was confident that they would find it easy to agree that he had been grievously wronged.

Rather than cancel her weekly tutoring session, Felicia had asked Muriel to come down to her office after court recessed. They would review Muriel's assignment, grab a quick bite in the neighborhood, and Felicia would return to work. That way Felicia would be able to stay on top of the case while also giving Muriel a look at a lawyer's life, perhaps inspiring her to strive for a similar life for herself.

In the last few months, the two had grown progressively closer. More and more Felicia was coming to see Muriel as the younger sister she had never had, or as the daughter she might one day raise. And clearly Muriel was responding to the attention. She had taken to imitating Felicia's style of speaking, which Felicia—though tickled by it—pretended not to notice. And she was not only completing all her assigned reading but seeking guidance on books to read on her own. Most remarkably, in Felicia's mind at least, Muriel was virtually never late. She clearly had taken Felicia's admonitions to heart, which made her tardiness tonight all the more surprising.

When the phone rang at eight-thirty—forty-five minutes past their scheduled meeting time—Felicia assumed it was Muriel calling with an explanation. Instead, it was Jackie, Muriel's friend. Felicia knew immediately from the shakiness of Jackie's voice that something was horribly wrong.

"What is it, Jackie?"

"It's, uhh, I . . . Muriel."

"Yeah. What about Muriel?"

"She . . . She can't come today. She wanted me to call you."

"She couldn't call herself?"

"No. I mean, she could, but she asked me to. She's not feeling that well."

"What's wrong with her?"

"Well, it's kind of hard to say. I mean—"

"What, child?" Felicia barked impatiently. "Has she been hurt?"

"Sort of . . . I mean, yes . . . She . . . Miss Fontaine . . . She was raped last Saturday."

Felicia slumped forward, nearly dropping the phone. Forcing herself to sound calm, "Where is she?"

"She's at home."

"Is anybody with her?"

"Her mom, I think."

"Thanks for calling," she said softly as she hung up the receiver.

Felicia sat immobile for several seconds, staring at the phone, her heart imploding. And as she held her forehead in her hands, she suddenly began to cry. She wept quietly for perhaps a minute, then willing herself into action, Felicia wiped her face with a tissue from her purse, fished out her address book, raced out of the office, and hailed a taxi.

She had not previously been to Muriel's home, but the apartment, in Washington Heights, off 163rd Street, was easy to find. As she pushed open the outer door, she was assailed by the sounds of Latin music issuing from a boom box on the dirty lobby floor. The apparent owner, a tough-looking Latino guy in a shiny warm-up suit, eyed her curiously as she headed for the elevator. Felicia nodded at him as she crossed his path, affecting a pose of amicable preoccupation. She imagined being trapped alone with him and cringed, praying that he would not follow, as she pushed for the elevator.

The elevator arrived, discharging a woman with two children and a shopping cart. Felicia stepped in quickly, noting, with relief, that the music man did not move. She rode alone to the fourth floor.

She stepped lightly onto the worn green carpet of the hallway and found the apartment straightaway. A thin woman in her thirties, wearing a pale blue apron, answered at the second knock.

"Looks like I interrupted your cooking," said Felicia, trying to manage a casual smile. The woman nodded, without saying a word, her face devoid of expression as her eyes examined Felicia's face.

"I'm sorry. I meant to introduce myself," Felicia continued. "I'm . . . I'm Felicia Fontaine. I've been helping Muriel with her English schoolwork."

The woman's icy mask vanished immediately, replaced with a flash of recognition and a warm, welcoming smile. "Oh. You're the one. Yeah, Muriel's told me all about you. I've seen you on TV. Come on in. I'm glad to finally meet you. Muriel talks about you all the time." She hesitated and added, "You know, Muriel's not feeling so good today."

"I know, Mrs. Johnson. But if it's possible, I would like to see her."

Mrs. Johnson nodded and showed Felicia into a tiny living room whose walls were filled with pictures, most illustrating biblical scenes. The largest, in the center of the room, just above the television, was of the Last Supper—set against a red velvet background in a bright gold-colored frame.

The woman excused herself and vanished. Moments later, Muriel appeared, wearing blue jeans and a bashful expression.

"I'm sorry I couldn't make it today. But I asked Jackie to call you."

"She did," replied Felicia. "But I wanted to see you. Is there someplace we can go to talk?"

"Yeah. There's a Chinese place down the street. I go there sometimes for dinner."

They walked to the restaurant in silence, which was broken only when they sat down and Felicia asked for tea. The pot and two cups arrived almost immediately. Felicia filled Muriel's cup and then poured one for herself, still wondering where to begin. Finally, she blurted out.

"Jackie told me you were attacked."

Muriel recoiled, but said nothing.

"Is it true, Muriel?"

"I guess so," she said softly.

"*Good Jesus!* You don't know how sorry I am," said Felicia as she took both of Muriel's hands in hers. "How are you feeling?"

"All right, I guess."

"Have you been to the hospital?"

"No."

"Have you told anyone?"

"I told Jackie."

"Anybody else?"

"I didn't feel like talking about it."

"Why don't you tell me what happened," Felicia said, calmly, caringly. "Was it somebody you know?"

"Yeah."

"Who?"

"It was this guy. They call him Coolbreeze. His name is Glen. We go out together, sometimes. I mean, we used to."

During the next half hour, over egg rolls and tea, Felicia coaxed the story out of her. Glen, a neighborhood tough guy and would-be basketball star, had invited her to a party nearby. When they got to the building where the party was being held, he had taken her to the top floor and raped her in the stairwell. He had then taken her to the party as if nothing had happened and threatened to kill her if she told anyone. Felicia, already angry, was visibly seething by the time Muriel finished.

"Do you know where this boy lives?"

Muriel nodded.

"Good," Felicia said. "I'll have him picked up. Who in the hell—"

"Please don't. I don't want to, Miss Fontaine. I want to just forget about it."

"That's not possible, Muriel. *It's just not possible.* He committed a crime. He lied and took advantage of you. He's threatened you. He belongs in jail. We can have a warrant issued for his arrest tonight. I need you to come to the precinct with me."

"Can we do that without my mama having to know?"

"I don't think so, Muriel. But . . . I . . . You haven't talked to your mother about it yet?"

She shook her head. "Mama doesn't even know I was seeing him. She told me not to a long time ago. I was kind of seeing him on the sly. I told Mama the night that it happened that I was going out with Jackie."

"Don't you think you should tell her?"

"She never liked Glen no way. If I tell her now, she'll probably blame it on me."

"I can't believe she would do that."

"She would. And, in a way, it was my fault. I mean, I remember you saying how we're responsible for what happens to us; how, if bad things happen, we're probably to blame. And . . . Well, you see, I didn't have to go there with him. I could have—"

"Muriel, listen to me," pleaded Felicia. "When I said that stuff, I wasn't talking about getting raped. *This is not your fault.* You didn't ask him to assault you. You didn't ask to get threatened. This guy belongs in jail. You say he lives down the street?"

"Yeah."

"And his name is Glen *what*?"

"Glen Thompson."

"Does he have a record?"

"I don't think so."

"Are you willing to come down to the precinct with me and swear out a complaint?"

"I don't think so, Miss Fontaine. I can't."

"Yes, you can, Muriel."

"Please, no. I can't. I really can't."

They wrestled for another twenty or thirty minutes, but Muriel would not be persuaded. Nor would she let go of the idea that she was partly to blame. Finally Felicia walked her home, gave her a hug, and headed back to the office. Once there, she found it nearly impossible to refocus on the case. She kept picturing Muriel, terrified, trapped in the stairwell, as a faceless fiend abused her.

Unable to concentrate on the trial transcript before her, Felicia eventually set it aside and retrieved her address book from her purse. She found the name of a psychiatric social worker she had used as an expert witness on a rape case and dialed the woman's home number. When she answered, Felicia identified herself and said, "I'm glad I got you, Alyssa. A friend of mine was raped over the weekend. I was wondering whether you could make some time to see her this week. She really needs to talk to somebody—the sooner the better."

"Of course."

"Great."

Next she telephoned her favorite investigator.

"Hector, honey," she said. "I need a favor."

Tuesday, Felicia called Wisocki to the stand. For months, she had prepared him for that moment. Nevertheless, beads of sweat coated his forehead. He sat stiffly, staring dead ahead, holding on to his thighs as if he feared they would walk away. Felicia smiled, trying to lend him reassurance—though her own mind was not totally on the case.

After talking to Hector last night, she finally had managed to focus—enough, at any rate, to give Wisocki's testimony a final run-through. And as she faced Wisocki, she ordered herself not to let Muriel's misfortune distract her from the business at hand.

She began with easy general questions—about his education, family, age, work history—trying to get him to relax. John beamed with pride as he discussed his early days at Computertronics and his progression through the ranks. He became almost ebullient as he talked about his promotion to manager and described the praise his work had consistently won. Then, without warning, Infotect appeared on the horizon and his life began to fall apart.

"Did you have any idea you were likely to be laid off?"

"None at all. My performance ratings had consistently been excellent in all areas. I had been promoted to training director of the division. Everything seemed to be going along fine."

"Did there come a point during which you concluded that things were not going along fine?"

"Yes," he said, his expression suddenly glum, "when Dwight Edwards told me I was losing my job."

"How did you respond to that news?"

"I told Dwight that I thought it was very unfair. My language actually was quite a big stronger than that," he said, showing mild embarrassment. "I pointed out that I had trained Francisco and had done the job longer than he had. I felt that I deserved the job more than he did. But Dwight told me that he was only following company policy, and that there was nothing I or he could do to change that."

"Can you describe your feelings at that time?"

"Yes, I believe I can. I was angry, very angry, and I was also shocked. I felt helpless, afraid, and worthless. It was as if everything I had done for the company suddenly didn't matter," John spat out, bitterness manifestly evident in his voice. "It was as if my entire life didn't matter, as far as they were concerned. I felt—I guess betrayed is the word. And the more Dwight talked, the angrier and more depressed I became. He was supposed to be my friend," Wisocki sputtered.

"Was it just Mr. Edwards with whom you were angry?"

"Not just with him, but with Infotect, with the . . . It was a kind of a general anger. I was even angry with myself, for not having foreseen what could happen, for not being better prepared, for not being able to do anything to stop what was happening."

Though Felicia's manner was gentle, her questions were relentless, pushing Wisocki to describe his emotions and his perceptions in painstaking detail. At several points as he described his growing disillusionment, Wisocki looked as if he would burst into tears, but he always managed to regain control.

"I had taken the job for granted," said Wisocki. "And all of a sudden, I was out of work. It was sobering to realize that at the age of fifty-four, a lot of people considered me washed up. It was frightening, especially when I discovered that even those people who were hiring weren't offering anything at all comparable to what I had done."

"How much did you earn a year at Computertronics, Mr. Wisocki?"

"I had a base salary of just under seventy-five thousand. With the bonus I could get up to almost ninety."

"Did you generally receive a bonus?"

"Yes. The bonus was determined on the basis of achieving your goals, your M-B-O, and I always got the maximum."

"When facing the loss of your job, did you share your anxieties and frustrations with anyone?"

"Yes. I talked about them with my wife, Linda, and also to some of the fellas at work, those who were also being laid off. And I wrote a lot of notes to myself. It's something that I do," he said, momentarily burying his face in his hands. "Several years ago, when I sort of got into computers, I got into the practice of writing memos and notes to myself. It helps me to work things out in my head."

Felicia had him identify several printouts of different portions of his computer diary and had them introduced into evidence. She then handed him one dated July 18 and asked him to read it aloud—which he did, in a subdued and quivering voice: "I must find a way to recover my optimism. But how do I do that without a job? Maybe death is preferable to confronting one's own obsolescence."

She then had Wisocki read another cybermessage: "I went to bed early again last night and spent hours staring at the ceiling. Finally, around daybreak, I lost consciousness, but only briefly. I arose more weary than when I went to bed and I tried to eat breakfast, but couldn't. I must either find a way to shake out of this or find the courage to end it. Death is surely better than living in fear of the future."

"Do you remember July twenty-first of last year?" she asked, giving him a tender look of support.

He nodded, pain coloring his features, and spoke in a strained and whispery voice: "Linda, my wife, left that day. She said she didn't know how to help me, and that she couldn't just stand by and watch me mope all the time. She thought maybe I could work out my problems better alone, that it was probably a good time for us to separate for a while. I tried to talk her out of leaving, but she said there was just no point in her staying, and that it would probably be good for us to take what she called 'a mental health break.'"

Suddenly John's self-control evaporated, and tears poured down his face. Felicia, her eyes filled with compassion, asked, "Do you think you can continue?"

He shrugged.

"Would you like a brief break? A glass of water?"

"Maybe some water."

She signaled to a court officer, who brought over a pitcher of water, and she poured Wisocki a glass. He quickly drained the glass, wiped his face, and whispered, "I can go on."

"What happened after your wife left?"

He grimaced. "After that, I just lost it for a while. There was no point in going home after work. So, many days, I began to go out for drinks, hoping that it would make things easier. All the drinking seemed to do was make me more depressed. And I still wasn't sleeping. Every night, I would just lie in bed, imagining a knife cutting into my chest or a bullet smashing into my brain. I was utterly paralyzed when it came to moving ahead with my life."

On that note, Felicia concluded the morning's questioning, confident that her client's suicidal image would linger in the jurors' memories over lunch.

That afternoon, John returned to the stand. He wore the look of a haunted man as he continued his tale.

Though his anger and anxieties heightened as the layoff date approached, said John, "I didn't blame Francisco. I did resent him getting the break I thought I deserved." The week before the shooting, John had finally gone to a psychiatrist. "Nothing else seemed to be working, and I was desperate to get some help." The psychiatrist prescribed Prozac and scheduled a return visit for the next week. John never got around to filling the prescription.

John testified that he had never owned a weapon until roughly two years before the shooting. He had gotten it after being accosted on the street by a gang of thugs. They had taken his wallet and beat him so badly that he had spent two days in the hospital suffering from broken ribs, a concussion, and countless contusions. For months, he had relived the beating in his nightmares, and would tremble with fear whenever passing a group of young men at night. Finally, a friend at work took pity on him. "This guy named Paul Delaney told me that I needed a gun, that it would make me feel safer. He strongly suggested that I get one."

Lacking the nerve to buy a gun himself, John eventually gave Delaney several hundred dollars to get a gun for him. For a time, John carried the gun with him whenever he went out alone at night. Eventually his anxiety died down and he locked the gun in a small safe in the house and left it there until the night of August 24, when he had retrieved it with half-formed thoughts of suicide on his mind.

Finally Felicia led him through the events leading up to García's death. John had gone to the office in a state of intense agitation. His rage at not being kept on burned like embers in his gut. "I wanted to die and I also wanted to make a statement. I felt that if I killed myself in Francisco's office, it would force them to think about what they had done. It would make them see how they had ruined my life for no good reason."

"Did you expect to find Mr. García in his office?"

"No, I did not. I knew he sometimes worked on Sundays, but he always left early. You see, during the summer the building turns off the air conditioning at about three o'clock on Saturdays and

Sundays. It's to conserve energy. But once the air is off, you can hardly breathe in there. You can't open the windows in the building, so it really gets hot. People who work on the weekends know that. I had heard that even though Francisco worked weekends, he always left before the building heated up."

Felicia paused, aware that virtually everyone in the room was leaning forward. She shot John a look of encouragement and continued her questioning.

"What did you do when you arrived at your office?"

"When I first got there, I just paced around for a while, trying to get things worked out in my head. Then I went into Francisco's office, which, well, you can see on the diagram, there's a common area separating the offices. And I sat at his desk and wrote the note. I wrote it to Stan Rothstein, chairman of the board of Infotect, because I wanted it to go to somebody at the highest level, somebody with the authority to change things."

He acknowledged that the note already entered into evidence by Mario was the one he had written that night and he continued, with Felicia's prodding, to relate his version of events.

"I was a bit soused from all the alcohol I was drinking, but I kept drinking anyway, as a way of getting my courage up. I was sitting there, in Francisco's chair, at his desk, with the gun, trying to work up the nerve to do it. To kill myself. Then I started thinking about Linda, and how I had screwed things up, and there was this feeling of just total misery. Finally, I put the gun in my mouth and was trying to get myself to pull the trigger."

"Do you remember what happened after that?"

"I don't remember how long I sat there. But as I held the gun, telling myself to get it over with, Francisco came into the office. He, Francisco, asked me what I was doing, and I hollered at him. I told him to get out, to leave me alone."

"What happened next?"

"Instead of going away, he started moving closer. And he was talking to me. He was asking what was wrong. And I kept telling him to leave, but he kept coming closer. And then, he came around the side of the desk and was right in front of me. And he told me to give him the gun."

"What did you do?"

"I told him I couldn't, and that he had better leave, but instead of leaving, instead of backing away . . . He . . . He grabbed . . ." John choked on the words and took several seconds to compose himself before picking up the story again. "He grabbed my hand, my right hand, the one with the gun, and he kept saying, 'Give it to me. Give it to me.' And I was holding on to it and we were kind of tussling and then he jerked my arm. I mean, it was more like he was holding my hand, when he suddenly slouched, and his grip weakened, like he had suddenly lost all his energy, or like the life had gone out of him."

There was a sudden commotion near the front of the courtroom, but neither Felicia nor John acknowledged the growing murmurs, as he pressed on with his testimony.

"Then the gun went off. There was this loud noise and this force sort of knocking me back, but his hand was still somehow holding onto mine, though no longer very tightly. I pulled the gun free at the same time I felt I was falling backward. And I tried to grab on to something with my left hand, to steady myself, and suddenly the gun went off again."

"Did you see where the bullets went?"

"Not really. The first one I think just sort of went into the air. The second . . ."

Wisocki paused, visibly struggling to gain control.

"The second," he continued, "must have hit Francisco."

"What hand was the gun in?"

"The gun was in my right. But when it went off . . . It all happened so quickly. I dropped the gun and screamed something like, 'Oh, God.' And I forced myself to sort of calm down and I grabbed the phone and dialed nine-one-one."

Those last words seemed to take all the effort out of John, who was trembling and sobbing uncontrollably. Felicia waited for several seconds, until the weeping ran its course; then she nodded at

John appreciatively, and turning to the jury, gravely bowed her head, as she emphatically announced, "I have no further questions, Your Honor."

Mario was out of his seat even before Felicia formally concluded her examination. Wisocki's testimony reeked of bullshit, and he had no intention of treating him gingerly or with undue respect. He wanted the jurors—and whoever else was looking in—to know that Wisocki was a murderer and a liar. He retraced much of the ground covered by Felicia—but in a decidedly hostile manner.

"It is your contention, Mr. Wisocki, that you had the gun with you that evening solely because you intended to use it to commit suicide?"

"Yes."

"But you managed to point that gun at plenty of people other than yourself that night. Isn't that so?" asked Mario.

"Objection, Your Honor. The question assumes facts not in evidence."

"Sustained."

"Did you point your gun at Mr. Juan Hernández?—one of the two men you apparently met on the street."

"I didn't *meet* him," John said indignantly. "He *attacked* me."

"Let's not quibble over semantics," said Mario, in an annoyed tone of voice. "The question is, did you point a weapon at him?"

"Only after he attacked me."

"Oh. Did he hold a gun on you?"

"No."

Mario moved closer to Wisocki with each succeeding question. "Did he pull a knife?"

"No."

"Did he display any weapon?"

"Not exactly."

"Did he grab you?"

"No."

"So how did he attack you? With his handkerchief?" Mario asked, now only inches from Wisocki, sarcasm dripping from his voice.

"He threatened me, I meant to say."

"Were you prepared to shoot Mr. Hernández even though he had no weapon?"

"Objection."

"Sustained. Mr. Santiago, you do understand this is a cross-examination? I expect your questions to show that."

"Yes, Your Honor."

Mario glanced at the jury, affecting a knowing nod of his head. He had not expected the questions to go unchallenged. Still it was worth the risk of irritating the judge to remind everyone that Wisocki had been wandering the streets with a loaded gun in his hand and had pointed it at someone other than Francisco. He turned back to Wisocki, glowering.

"Did you have a license for your gun, Mr. Wisocki?"

"No."

"Did you have any reason to believe the gun you possessed was a legal weapon?"

"I just didn't think much about that."

"You must be a very poor shot, Mr. Wisocki. Is that true?"

John, looking perplexed, mumbled, "I suppose so. I know very little about guns, or shooting them."

"Is that why you couldn't manage to shoot yourself, but instead shot an innocent man?"

"Objection."

"Sustained."

"Was it ever truly your intention to kill yourself?"

"Yes."

"But somehow, you just couldn't get around to it because you were too busy worrying about the man you had just killed instead?"

"Objection."

"Sustained."

"Did you dislike Mr. García?"

"I had no personal dislike for him at all."

"Is that why you wrote that he was a 'pain in the butt'? Is that why you called him a self-promoter and a selfish foreigner, a leech and a parasite?"

"Nothing I wrote was directed at him personally."

"No," Mario roared. "You don't believe that using insults and ethnic stereotypes against a Latino co-worker is getting personal?"

"That's not what I did. I don't have anything against the Spanish people."

"I'm not asking you about the Spanish people, Mr. Wisocki," thundered Mario, summoning up the righteous indignation of an avenging angel. "I'm asking you about your feelings toward Mr. García, and toward other Hispanic Americans."

"I have nothing against any group."

"Have you ever used the word spick?"

Felicia rose to object and abruptly sat down, seeing no harm in having him answer.

"No. I don't use language like that. Ever."

"But you do use language like 'self-promoter' and parasite when talking about Latinos you consider undeserving?"

"Objection."

"Sustained."

"Is it your practice to keep track of the weekend hours of your co-workers?"

"No."

"But you did manage to find out from the secretary that Mr. García worked on Sundays. Why were you so interested in his weekend hours?"

"I was merely making conversation."

"A host of witnesses have testified that you rarely just made conversation, Mr. Wisocki, that you were a withdrawn, insular, resentful misfit. Is that image of you not correct?"

Felicia again was on her feet, barely able to contain her rage. "Your Honor, we object to the people's characterization. In fact, we object to the people's entire line of questioning. It's beyond the scope of the direct, and totally irrelevant."

"You want to wrap this up, Mr. Santiago," said the judge.

"Yes, Your Honor."

"So it's your testimony, Mr. Wisocki, that you wanted so badly to kill yourself that you managed to fire an unlicensed gun two times, totally missing yourself, and shooting an innocent man in the chest? Your testimony is that you killed Mr. García because you were a bad shot? That you became a murderer by accident?"

"Objection."

"Sustained."

Alone in the taxi en route to her office, Felicia assessed the day in court. John had acquitted himself well. He had shown the requisite remorse and exposed the jury to his inner anguish, while offering a coherent account of how García ended up dead. He had also withstood Mario's cross. Any time you could put your client on the stand and end up relatively unscathed was an occasion for celebration. Yet, Felicia felt not all celebratory. She was haunted by Muriel's misfortune. The fact of Muriel's rape was bad enough, but that she partially blamed herself made things even worse—all the more so since Felicia had apparently contributed to Muriel's feelings of culpability.

Usually Felicia was proud of her quicksilver mind and debater's glibness. She depended on them in court and in the world at large. Yet, she couldn't shake the feeling that she had misused her gifts in responding to Muriel's question. Their exchange over dinner had replayed repeatedly in her mind. *"What about things you have no control over?"* *"If bad things happen to you, it's usually because you allowed them to happen."* But how could she have known what Muriel would make of that?

When she got to her office, Felicia dialed Muriel's number. Mrs. Johnson immediately put her on.

"So how are you doing today?" Felicia asked.

"All right. I guess."

"Anything I can do for you."

"I don't think so. But that friend of yours, Mrs. Dorset, called. We talked for a long time yesterday. She seems real nice."

"Yeah. Alyssa's real cool. I thought you two might hit it off. Are you back in school?"

"Yeah, I went back today."

"Things all right there?"

"I think so."

"Good. Well, I have to get back to work. Just wanted to check on you. Let me know, if you need anything."

"Thanks, Miss Fontaine."

"See you soon."

Felicia leafed through the messages on her desk—several from reporters, one from Frank, and one from a Reverend Williams. Nothing urgent, she surmised, as she flipped through her Rolodex, looking for Alyssa Dorset's card.

Wednesday morning's lead-off witness was the building maintenance manager, who testified that, during the weekends of the summer months, the building's air conditioning was turned off at 3 P.M. Next was Stefan Montiel, the psychiatrist and Columbia University professor. Felicia had briefly considered using Albert Strober, John's treating psychiatrist, but had decided ultimately to use someone accustomed to testifying, someone who came with a list of publications and an array of fancy academic credentials.

After having him qualified as an expert witness, Felicia asked Montiel to explain the process of psychiatric assessment and the so-called multiaxial assessment system.

"Having examined Mr. Wisocki and reviewed his treatment records," she asked, "do you have an opinion, based on a reasonable degree of scientific certainty, as to whether Mr. Wisocki, on or directly prior to August twenty-forth of last year, suffered from any psychiatric disorder?"

"Yes. He suffered from major depressive disorder."

"Could you explain? What is major depressive disorder, Dr. Montiel?"

"It is a mood disorder, an Axis One disorder. It is diagnosed if the patient has one or more major depressive episodes. Several symptoms are required for the diagnoses and Mr. Wisocki was something of a textbook case. He suffered from a depressed mood, insomnia, weight loss, feelings of worthlessness, and a diminished interest in those activities he once found pleasurable. He also had recurrent thoughts of and fantasies about death. The symptoms, which began at the time of Mr. Wisocki's job loss, worsened progressively over the next several weeks."

"Do you have an opinion, based on a reasonable degree of medical certainty, as to the seriousness or severity of the major depressive episode suffered by Mr. Wisocki?"

"Yes. It was very severe."

"Is major depressive disorder predictive for suicide?"

"Yes. It is strongly predictive. It is estimated that fifteen percent of individuals who suffer from major depressive disorder die by suicide. And it is worse if you are older."

"Is this disorder precipitated by specific events?"

"Yes, generally, it is precipitated by a severe psychosocial stressor, such as the death of a loved one, the breakup of a marriage, or the loss of a job."

"Is alcohol abuse typical of those who suffer from a major depressive disorder?"

"Yes, it is not unusual to find an alcohol abuse disorder contemporaneous with a major depressive disorder. The alcohol, unfortunately, aggravates the problem, and also interferes with the sleep cycle. It can, in effect, worsen the depression and the impact of that depression on one's life."

"Is there an effective treatment for major depressive disorder?"

"Yes, there is. Psychotherapy in conjunction with any number of different drugs can work wonders. There is fluoxetine, known as Prozac, or a range of other medications. Unfortunately, there often is resistance to the idea of taking medication, especially with people like John, who are not comfortable with the idea of seeking help. Taking medication can be perceived as a sign of weakness and can deliver a blow to self-esteem. So some people, initially at least, essentially reject the treatment. Often they self-medicate with alcohol."

"Do you have an opinion, Dr. Montiel, based on a reasonable

degree of medical certainty, on whether Mr. Wisocki was suicidal on August twenty-fourth of last year?"

"Yes. It is my opinion that he was suicidal. His deep depression, the recurrent references to death and suicide in his writings, his coming up with a plan, his possession of a gun, his substance abuse—all point in the direction of suicide. There is little doubt in my mind that Mr. Wisocki was suicidal. Events had diminished him nearly to the point of nothingness. He had already, in effect, suffered a form of psychologic death."

During the cross-examination, Mario forced Montiel to admit that he was being paid for his testimony and that he often testified for the defense. He also challenged Montiel's certitude regarding Wisocki's suicidal tendencies.

"To say that someone is suicidal, Dr. Montiel, is not to say that they actually intend to commit suicide. Is it?"

"One cannot be certain anyone will actually carry out a suicide until the act itself occurs," he replied.

"You have stated your opinion that Mr. Wisocki was suicidal," said Mario. "Would it be your opinion, based on the medical evidence, that he could also have been homicidal?"

"That would not be my opinion."

"But it is possible?"

"Yes, it is possible."

"Does it strike you as odd, Doctor, that a suicidal person could not manage to kill himself?"

"No, it does not. There are countless suicide attempts that fail."

"But many of those so-called attempts are not really attempts. Are they, Doctor?"

"Objection."

"Sustained."

Felicia's final witness for the day was her weapons expert, William Dillon, a clean-cut private consultant and former Marine Corps captain. Dillon had been head of the firearms unit in the FBI Laboratory and an adviser to numerous police forces, foreign and domestic. He was an expert's expert, and Felicia spent several minutes going through his qualifications, subtly making the point that her gun guru was a hell of a lot fancier and more impressive than Mario's.

A graduate of the U.S. Naval Academy and a Vietnam War veteran, Dillon was tall, stolid, and sturdily built. Even dressed in a dark business suit, he looked like a soldier and spoke like someone accustomed to giving commands.

"Are you familiar with the Glock Model Seventeen pistol?" asked Felicia.

"Yes. I own one and have advised several police departments on its capabilities. It was a weapon originally designed for the Austrian Army, and was introduced in the United States in 1986.

"Are you familiar with the Glock Model Nineteen?"

"Yes. I am very familiar with that model as well. It is in the same family of weapons as the Model Seventeen."

"Does that mean the two models are similar?"

"Yes, they are quite similar, but they are not identical. The Model Seventeen is a slightly bigger and heavier weapon. It generally has a seventeen-round magazine capacity compared to a fifteen-round capacity in the Model Nineteen. Each model can be manufactured to accommodate two additional rounds. In the civilian market, however, both guns are restricted to a ten-round capacity."

Dillon went on to explain that the model recovered from the scene had been manufactured for civilian use and therefore differed in many respects from the gun used by the New York Police Department.

"Could you explain the differences?" asked Felicia.

"The Glock Model Nineteen used by the NYPD is a police model. It is a smaller gun than the Model Seventeen, but also, since it is a police version, it handles more rounds of ammunition. It has a fifteen-round capacity, compared to ten in the civilian Model Seventeen. Also, the NYPD Glock was altered from the basic model."

"It was altered in what ways?"

"The NYPD has what they called a New York barrel, a barrel specially machined to make it easier to identify which bullet came from which gun. With a conventionally rifled Glock barrel, it can be difficult to match up the bullets. Also, the trigger pull on the NYPD guns was increased above standard factory specifications. Factory standard is five and a half pounds. The NYPD ordered guns with a seven-pound spring. Later, the NYPD moved up to a nine-pound trigger pull. It is known as the New York pull. The effect is to make the weapon significantly more difficult to fire."

"I see," Felicia said, nodding gravely at the jury to underscore the point. "Were there problems with the lighter trigger pull?"

"There were a number of accidental discharges when the gun was introduced in 1994 and at least one horrible tragedy. A sixteen-year-old died from a bullet fired into his head. The bullet was fired by a policeman using a Glock Model Nineteen. It was ruled an accidental shooting."

"So, the trigger pull on the police model was increased specifically because of the danger of accidental discharges?"

"Yes, it was. The decision rested on the common-sense assumption that if more force was required to fire a gun, it was less likely that it would be fired accidentally."

"Does the Glock pistol have an external safety?"

"No, it does not."

"Does that mean that, in order to shoot, you merely have to pull the trigger?"

"Precisely. The Glock fires double action only, which means you never have to cock it. You just squeeze the trigger and it fires."

"In your opinion, would it be possible for a Glock to be fired accidentally?"

"Yes. If the finger was in the trigger guard and the trigger was squeezed, the gun would fire."

"Are you familiar with the term 'stress reaction'?"

"Yes, I am. In a shooting scenario, when the adrenaline is pumping, or in similarly stressful situations, people often react by closing their fists. It is a reflex."

"Is it a reflex that can occur when someone has a weapon in his hand?"

"Yes, it can. There have been situations with police officers who are trying to control a situation. They may be using their left hand to try to maintain order, but because of the stress they end up squeezing both fists, including the one that has the gun. When that occurs, if the finger is on the trigger, the gun will fire."

"If, in such a stress situation, someone tried to grab something with his left hand, could this stress reaction cause him to close his right fist?"

"Yes, it could."

"In your expert opinion, is it possible that someone in a highly emotional state who is struggling over a Glock could accidentally fire the weapon?"

"Yes, that is quite possible, assuming his finger is on the trigger."

"In your expert opinion, is it also possible that someone falling in a chair, while attempting to catch himself with his left hand, could accidentally fire a Glock with his right hand because of the stress reaction?"

"Yes, that is possible, again, if the finger is on the trigger."

"Would a light trigger pull make that kind of accident more likely?"

"Yes, the less pressure required to pull the trigger, the more likely it is that it will be pulled accidentally."

"Is it your opinion that someone using the gun marked People's Exhibit Number Three would be more likely, all else being equal, to accidentally fire the weapon than someone using the Glock issued to members of the NYPD?"

"Yes. The Glock sold to the civilian market is an easier gun to discharge, and therefore it is an easier gun to discharge accidentally."

"I have no further questions, Your Honor."

Felicia politely bowed toward the jury and returned to her seat, feeling as jubilant as a schoolgirl who had just won a spelling bee. She glanced at Mario's table and noted that he was looking her way. She grinned triumphantly and silently mouthed the words: "Checkmate, lover."

14

Felicia's first impulse was to put Jotun Berge on the stand. As the pastor of John's church, he could credibly vouch for John's good character. Yet there would be risks in using him. For one thing, Berge had only been the pastor for three years—during which time John had rarely attended. Also, as the administrator of the Fund for Justice and Good Works—as Berge had ultimately decided to call it—the minister would make a tempting target for both the prosecution and the press. Mario undoubtedly would insinuate that Berge was standing by John solely because of the money the fund brought into his church.

It was Sophie who suggested a solution. Instead of using Berge why not use the Reverend Jonathan Dotson? The retired minister had served as pastor when John was a teenager. Dotson, who still lived in the community, had presided at Wisocki's marriage and was someone in whom Wisocki continued to confide.

Dotson was a tall, thin man, of regal bearing, who wore his shock of white hair like a crown. When Felicia called him to the witness stand, she made a show of assisting him. It was her way of playing to the jury for sympathy. But though Dotson walked slowly and with the help of a cane, he did not appear feeble.

Dotson's mission was to wrap Wisocki in the mantle of the

Church. And with Felicia's guidance and over Mario's objections, he got his message across: "Even when John was in his teens, and many of the other boys were acting out, everyone always considered him a gentle and caring soul. He is basically the same person today as he was forty years ago."

Mario confined his cross-examination to one question: "Do you have any direct knowledge of the events that occurred on August twenty-fourth of last year that resulted in the charge of murder against the defendant?" Dotson admitted he did not.

The final defense witness was Linda Wisocki. Although her testimony would be short, Felicia considered it crucial. Her job was to inoculate Wisocki against the charge of racial bias.

Felicia began with questions that introduced Linda to the jury. She concisely covered Linda's life story, including her marriage to John: "It was his gentleness that drew me to him. He made me feel serene and secure." Linda, who appeared nervous but poised, also confirmed the circumstances of their temporary separation. As to her reason for returning after John's arrest: "I realized John couldn't have done such a horrible thing, and I thought that he needed someone who loved him to be there for him."

"In your years with John Wisocki, did you ever hear him utter the word spick?" asked Felicia.

"No. He never uttered such a word."

"Did you ever hear him use any racial or ethnic slur?"

"Absolutely not. John was incapable of such language. It disgusted him. One time, when we were out together, John overheard a man call somebody a 'dirty Jap' and it upset him for the rest of the night. Any sort of bigotry made him terribly sad."

Mario also kept his cross-examination short.

"Do you love your husband, Mrs. Wisocki?"

"Yes. He is a wonderful man."

"Please answer the question yes or no, Mrs. Wisocki. You would never intentionally say anything to harm him. Would you?"

"No. I would not."

"You have no desire to implicate your husband in murder, do you?"

"No, I do not."

"Do you have any direct knowledge of the events that occurred on August twenty-fourth of last year that resulted in the charge of murder against the defendant?"

"No."

"I have no further questions for this witness, Your Honor."

Following a short recess, Mario got his turn to rebut, and recalled Francine Martin, the secretary from Computertronics. A bespectacled woman with a jittery, breathless manner, Martin was overly eager to talk. She barely gave Mario time to get out his questions before spewing out her answers.

"When did the conversation with Mr. García take place?"

"It was August twenty-second, the Friday before he was killed. I remember it because—"

"Do you remember what time of day that was?"

"It was in the afternoon, around three or three-thirty."

"Where did the conversation take place?"

"It was right outside his office. He was on his way back from a meeting, and mumbled something about having to go to another one."

"Who was present during that conversation?"

"Just me and Mr. García, but we were only a few feet outside of Mr. Wisocki's office. And he was sitting inside with his door open. So I think—"

"What did Mr. García say to you at the time?"

"He said he would probably be coming back to work after dinner on Sunday and wanted to know if I could talk to the maintenance people about keeping the air conditioning on."

"Did the defendant's office door remain open during the entire conversation?"

"Yes. He was sitting at his desk looking at some papers, as I recall."

"Can you generally hear a conversation in his office from your desk?"

"If he's talking loud enough. Yes."

During her cross, Felicia focused on the only relevant point.

"Prior to August twenty-fourth of last year, did you discuss this conversation with Mr. García with anyone else in your office?"

"No. I did call the maintenance people and ask them about turning on the air conditioning, but they said they could not do it for just one office."

"Did you ever discuss this conversation with Mr. Wisocki?"

"No."

"Did Mr. Wisocki ever indicate to you that he had heard this conversation?"

"No."

"And you have no concrete reason for believing that he did overhear this conversation. Is that correct?"

"Yes. That is correct. But he did ask me once, as I testified before, about whether Mr. García worked Sundays. And—"

"Please, just answer the question, Miss Martin," demanded Felicia, impatiently. "As far as you know, Mr. Wisocki had no specific knowledge that Mr. García would be in the office that Sunday, August twenty-fourth. Correct?"

"I guess. I don't really know what Mr. Wisocki knew."

Mario's final rebuttal witness was Harold Jameson, a psychiatrist who had taught Stefan Montiel, the defense expert, when Montiel was a medical student at Columbia University. Jameson did not dispute the diagnosis of major depressive disorder, but questioned the presumption that it was very predictive for suicide.

"In fact, most people who suffer from major depressive disorder don't commit suicide," he said in answer to Mario's question.

"Is there any way, Dr. Jameson, of determining with a reasonable degree of scientific certainty who among those who suffer from this disorder are most likely to commit suicide?"

"There is no precise way. In general, however, you would look for something other than merely a diagnosis of major depressive disorder. You would look for something like a personality disorder as well."

"Could you please explain, in layman's terms, what a personality disorder is?"

"A personality disorder is a set of behaviors or modes of thought that are considered abnormal or maladaptive. There must be a certain pervasiveness to the behaviors, a certain intensity, and a recognizable pattern. Someone who suffers from borderline personality disorder, for instance, might well be suicidal. Indeed, suicidal behavior is one of the markers for that disorder, along with recklessness, self-destructive behavior, lack of control over anger, and instability in interpersonal relationships."

"Can you say, with a reasonable degree of medical certainty, whether the defendant suffered from such a personality disorder?"

"I would be reluctant to make that diagnosis. It is not clear to me that he did."

"Can you say, based on a reasonable degree of medical certainty, whether or not the defendant was suicidal on August twenty-fourth of last year?"

"No, I cannot, although the fact that he stopped well short of the act may indicate that he was not. Many suicidal people who don't manage to kill themselves nonetheless do themselves serious bodily harm. The defendant did no harm to himself whatsoever."

Mario asked his next question almost as if it were an afterthought, though in reality it was anything but. "Dr. Jameson, are you familiar with the term stress reflex?"

"I am familiar with a range of stress reactions: combat-stress reaction, post-traumatic stress disorder, and a variety of anxiety reactions that stem from fears, reasonable or unreasonable, or from traumatic events. But I am not familiar with a stress reflex as a recognized symptom, syndrome, or disorder."

"Have you heard of or seen a body of reputable scientific research that explores or validates it?"

"No, I have not."

"No further questions, Your Honor."

Felicia eyed Jameson coldly as a fighter might eye an unworthy opponent, attempting to intimidate him with her stare. Mario's case, in her view, had crumbled. She had no intention of letting Jameson repair it with some academic mumbo jumbo.

"Can you say with a reasonable degree of scientific certainty that Mr. Wisocki had no intention of committing suicide when he went to his office the evening of August twenty-fourth of last year?"

"No."

"How many patients have you treated, Doctor, who were directly implicated in shootings, accidental or otherwise?"

"None."

"How many papers have you published that deal specifically with the subject of physical reactions in stressful situations?"

"None. That is not my field of research."

"Is it fair then, Doctor, to assume that you would not necessarily be aware of the most recent research as it relates to the stress reflex and other physical stress reactions in connection with hand weapons?"

"As far as I know, there is no refereed journal that—"

"Doctor," shouted Felicia abruptly, cutting him off, "the question is not whether you know about journals, but whether you know, specifically, about the latest research in the area of physical stress reactions and hand weapons. Have you conducted any research in that field? *Yes or no*, please."

"No. I have not."

"No other questions, Your Honor."

Since the beginning of the trial, Felicia's phone had been ringing relentlessly, so she had instituted what amounted to a triage policy in handling the calls: only those that seemed critically important got returned. By mentioning the name of Larry Roberts, her old Washington mentor, the third message from the Reverend Eddie Williams got her attention.

Her first assumption was that Williams must be calling with bad news: a heart attack, or perhaps something worse. So she returned the call with apprehension, but Williams immediately set her mind at ease. No, he said, he wasn't calling about Roberts, but about her. It seemed that Roberts was an old buddy and had asked him to look her up.

"I appreciate that very much," Felicia replied, "and I'll be glad to set some time aside once this trial is over."

"I was hoping we could get together this evening."

Felicia laughed. "I don't think that will be possible. I have a closing argument to review and a hundred other things to deal with. What I can do is have my secretary—"

"I don't think you understand, Miss Fontaine. It really is important that we get together soon. Look, I know you're busy, but even you have to eat. I don't live very far from your office. There's a diner called Burger Joe's two blocks from you."

"Yeah, I know the place."

"Why don't we meet, say fifteen minutes from now."

"But—"

"I won't take but a few minutes of your time."

"What the heck. Why not," Felicia replied in capitulation. "A bite to eat probably wouldn't be a bad idea."

Williams, an elderly dark-skinned man wearing a conservative gray suit, arrived seconds after Felicia and smoothly slid into the seat across from her.

"I recognize you from television," he said, smiling. "Eddie Williams. Glad to meet you."

They both ordered turkey sandwiches, which arrived almost immediately, whereupon Felicia stared at Williams and said, "So, Reverend Williams, why does Larry Roberts think I need to see a minister in New York?"

Williams smiled. "Could be he's concerned about your soul. But seriously, I think he's concerned about more worldly matters. Larry and I go way back. We were both active in the movement, and we've kept in touch ever since then. Larry keeps in touch with a lot of people, as you probably know. That's just his style."

"Yes, I do know. He's a very attentive friend."

"I'll get right to the point, Felicia. You are obviously a very capable woman, but I get the feeling, from my conversations with Larry, that you're not very plugged into the church community here."

"Yes?"

"Then you probably don't know just what Reverend Flores is up to, at least as concerns you."

"I know he's been marching practically nonstop for months outside the criminal courts protesting my client. But as far as I know, he has no personal grudge against me. Not that it would make much difference if he did."

"Well, apparently he does. He's been meeting with a number of ministers. And the long and short of it is he has cooked up what amounts to a two-pronged scheme."

"This I have to hear," she said, shaking her head incredulously.

"His hope, not to put too fine a point on it, is to make an example of you—to demonize you in the service of his cause. First he wants to ruin your reputation in the community, and then in your profession."

"Interesting. And just how does he plan to manage that."

"He's assuming, first of all, that you'll lose the case, which will make it pretty easy for him to portray you as a defender of bigotry and murder."

"A friend of mine mentioned that possibility."

"Perhaps your friend picked up some of the rumbles from Flores's camp. The man has been meeting with lots of people, you know, mostly ministers around town. He's been trying to rope them in to what he's calling a community crusade."

"The whole thing sounds pretty cockamamie to me."

"Perhaps. But I told this to Roberts, and he thought you should know. Step two of Flores's plan concerns this drug dealer named . . . Well, I can't remember his name. But according to Flores, there is some detective who can corroborate some kind of irregularity involving your tenure as a prosecutor."

"And who is this supposed detective?"

"I also don't know that. I get the feeling that Flores doesn't either, but apparently he's heard from some people in the media that this man exists and is willing to talk."

"Really," Felicia said, masking her alarm. "I don't see how that could be."

"I told all this to Larry. He suggested I share it with you. He also said you're one tough lady, that you were fully capable of taking care of yourself."

"I appreciate that," said Felicia, her face suddenly solemn, as she pondered the implications of this new information.

"Mind if I ask a question?" he asked, looking nearly as serious as she.

Felicia smiled sardonically. "Somehow, Reverend Williams, I get the impression that you have no problem saying whatever is on your mind. So go ahead, ask your question."

"Do you believe your man is innocent?"

"Of course I do," she replied, in a voice leavened with genuine sincerity.

He nodded and brought his hands together in what seemed to be a gesture of prayer. "Then I hope you win."

A closing argument, William Branegan had once told her, is a last chance to play God, a final opportunity to conjure up something good out of nothingness. In this case, Felicia felt her task was not nearly so overwhelming. Her only challenge was to weave into a seamless whole the scattered testimony heard over the past several days.

As she rose, following the lunch recess, to deliver her summation, she felt confident and at ease. She courteously acknowledged the prosecutor and the judge, expressed her appreciation to the jurors for their attention, and, moving the lectern closer to the jury box, focused on several faces she sensed were particularly friendly. Her voice was forceful and authoritative as she said, "Last August twenty-fourth Francisco García died in a horrible tragedy, a tragedy that my client, John Wisocki, will regret for the rest of his life. You must not compound that terrible tragedy by finding an innocent man guilty of murder."

She glanced upward, as if seeking guidance from God, then, speaking without text and with total conviction, Felicia continued.

"Let me take you back to when this trial began two weeks ago. At that time, the district attorney made a number of promises to you. He said he would prove that Mr. Wisocki was not suicidal. He said he would prove that Mr. Wisocki lay in wait for Mr. García, like a jungle cat waiting for the kill. He said he would prove that Mr. Wisocki was a liar and a cold-blooded murderer. He said he would prove that Mr. Wisocki was a bigot driven by racist impulses. He said he would prove all of this—*beyond a reasonable doubt*. In fact, he has proven none of it."

Gesturing passionately, she tore into Mario's gun witness: "a so-called expert who can't tell the difference between one model of a gun and another. An expert who is apparently ignorant of her own department's unfortunate experience with the Glock.

"I submit to you," she said, her voice ringing through the court-room, "that the only credible evidence on weapons heard in this court came from Mr. William Dillon, a man of impeccable and impressive credentials, who told you that the gun my client attempted to kill himself with requires roughly half the pressure to fire as the weapon used by the New York Police Department—a weapon which the New York Police Department had altered specif-ically because it was prone to fire accidentally. He told you also about a stress reflex that, in situations identical to the one in which Mr. Wisocki found himself, can cause a person to fire a gun acci-dentally. Mr. Dillon had no reason to lie. No motive to embellish.

"Let's talk about some more evidence," said Felicia, punctuating her points by pounding the lectern with her fist. "Mr. Santiago charges my client is a bigot, and that, as a result of that bigotry, he set out to kill a man. What is his proof? His only proof is the word of a *convicted felon*." She stared at the jurors as the words lingered briefly in the air. "A *convicted felon* who is also a notorious liar whose story changes by the minute," she continued, rocking slightly, rhythmically, as she talked, "a felon who lies about being a student, a felon who can't remember that he was drunk on rum the evening of the inci-dent, a felon who associates with known drug dealers. Compare Mr. Santiago's statements to the testimony of Linda Wisocki, who hap-pens to be a member of a racial minority group. Linda Wisocki finds the charge of bigotry ludicrous. Reflect on the testimony of Jonathan Dotson, Mr. Wisocki's longtime pastor. The Reverend Dotson also finds the charge of bigotry ridiculous. *Whom do you believe?*

"Let's look at some more of the evidence," shouted Felicia, clearly warming to the task. "Mr. Santiago claims my client knew Mr. García's work schedule, that he anticipated he would be in on the Sunday that he died. And yet, the log books Mr. Santiago himself presented into evidence confirm that, previous to last August twenty-fourth, Mr. García had never been at his office on a Sunday *evening*." She strongly stressed the last word of the sentence, pausing before adding: "Yes, Mr. García did work some Sundays, but, as his secretary has testified, he always left when the air-conditioning was turned off. And, as the maintenance crew has testified, the air-conditioning—on Sundays—was always cut off in the afternoon. John Wisocki had absolutely no reason to believe Mr. García would be present that Sunday evening. I ask you again: What is the credible story here? Whom do you believe?"

Felicia revisited Wisocki's testimony about his depression and ridiculed the prosecution's psychiatrist: "a so-called psychiatric expert who doesn't know the research on the very subject about which he testified." Then she dramatically re-created the evening of the shooting, inviting the jurors to try to imagine themselves in Wisocki's frame of mind.

"No living person, with the exception of John Wisocki," she said somberly, "can say with total confidence exactly what happened in that office on West Thirty-fourth Street last August twenty-fourth. Mr. Wisocki told you, in detail and under oath, exactly what happened. He did not duck any question, or shirk his responsibility. This is a man who called the police to the scene. This is a man who never attempted to flee, or to cover up the facts of the case. And with what does the prosecution refute his story? With a lineup of witnesses who are simply not credible, or who are credible but support Mr. Wisocki's version of the story.

Felicia reviewed the testimony of the medical examiner, stressing the fact that García may well have died of a heart attack. "Mr. García's death was tragic," she conceded. "But if you examine the evidence you will conclude that Mr. García was not murdered.

"The people indicted my client on two contradictory theories.

Why? *Because they don't know what happened,*" she said, and repeated the phrase a second time for emphasis. "They can pretend they know, and in a few minutes Mr. Santiago will make a great show of knowing. But if they, in fact, knew, they would not have gone forth with two opposing theories.

"One theory is that Mr. Wisocki shot Mr. García intentionally. There is not a shred of evidence to support that and, as you have heard, a great deal that refutes it. The second theory is that Mr. Wisocki shot Mr. García with a depraved indifference to human life."

Felicia shook her head, as if mystified by the foolishness of it all. "You must understand, first of all," she said, "that Mr. Wisocki was not at all indifferent. He pleaded with Mr. García to leave as he struggled with the demons of depression and suicide. *Depraved indifference?* What is depraved indifference? It means being so morally corrupt, so wicked, that you don't care what happens to another person. That does not describe my client. Mr. Wisocki, as we acknowledge, was ill. He was suffering from clinical depression and suicidal tendencies. But *wicked?* As his pastor, a man who has known him all his life testified, he is a gentle, moral man. His entire life has been lived honorably. He is a bulwark of his church and his community. Depraved? There is not one piece of evidence that supports that. So we are back to the question of intent. And that brings us to a simple equation. If there was no intent, there was no crime. *Let me repeat that.* If there was no intent, there was no crime. If he did not intend to kill, he cannot be found guilty of murder.

"By the same token, if Mr. Wisocki did not intend to use a weapon unlawfully against another—and let me stress that, *against another*—he cannot be found guilty of criminal possession of a weapon in the second degree. If there is no intent, there is no crime. If a crime is not proved beyond a reasonable doubt, there can be no verdict of guilty."

Felicia took several deep breaths before moving to her final points: "Look to the evidence, Mr. Santiago said. And in that he is absolutely right. You must look to the evidence. And based on that evidence and the instructions of this court, I ask that you return the only reasonable verdict you can reach: that John Wisocki is not guilty of murder in the second degree, that he is not guilty of unlawful possession of a weapon, that he is not guilty of any crime under the laws of the State of New York.

"As we put our trust in God, and put our trust in you, I implore you, look to the evidence and then search your hearts and find John Wisocki innocent of all charges. Thank you."

Felicia returned to her seat, breaking eye contact with the jury only as she sat down and placed a supportive hand on John's shoulder.

She could finally relax. Yet, in contrast to what she normally experienced at this juncture in a trial, Felicia felt no sense of impending triumph. Instead her mood was dark, almost gloomy. That was due in part, she knew, to the conversation with Eddie Williams. Though she had dismissed much of his talk as foolishness, she had been shaken by the mention of a detective. Eric Preston, the detective with the snitch on the Murphy case, had retired and was living in Florida. They had agreed at the time to keep the secret between them, and she could think of no reason why he would change his mind. Any revelation, after all, would be as embarrassing to him as to her.

Then there was the matter of Muriel. Somehow—and to whatever degree—Muriel had become a victim not only of the odious Glen Thompson but of an adult war of ideas. In the context of Muriel's problems, Wisocki's, for reasons Felicia could not confidently explain, seemed not quite as serious. Perhaps it was merely because John himself—whatever had really happened in García's office—was not nearly as innocent as Muriel. Felicia tried to put such musings out of her head as she focused her attention on Mario—and on the jury's reactions.

Mario approached the lectern and, after ritually acknowledging the judge and defense attorney, turned his full attention to the jury, eyeing them closely, as if he were about to share a grand confidence.

"You know, I was shaking my head with admiration during Ms. Fontaine's summation," he said, smiling slightly. "She is fiery and eloquent. She is a good lawyer. But it is important that we, that you the jury, separate fancy lawyering from law, that you separate fancy words from truth, that you separate clever arguments from facts, and that most of all you separate injustice from justice."

He turned in the direction of Isabel García, allowing the jury time to find her in the courtroom, and then continued his summation.

"I ask you to focus first on one irrefutable fact: Francisco García is dead. Mrs. García will go home this night, as she has every night since last August twenty-fourth, without her husband by her side."

Mario moved from behind the lectern and stepped closer to the jurors, striving for a feeling of intimacy. "One person you have not seen in this court is Blanca García, the beautiful daughter of Isabel and Francisco. You did not see her," he said softly, "because to subject a child of six to the awful details of her father's death was not something the people, or Mrs. García, could allow. One crime has already been committed. We would not compound it with another outrage.

"Nor," he said somberly, "are we willing to concede any portion of the defendant's case. Ms. Fontaine made much of the fact that two psychiatrists disagreed on a diagnosis of suicidal intention. The simple fact is that psychiatrists often disagree. If you pay one enough money, you can usually get the answer you seek, but the answer that is bought and paid for is not necessarily the right answer. The defendant paid for his psychiatrist. The people did not. We served Dr. Jameson with a subpoena, but we did not tell him what to say. He had no incentive to lie, and yet he told you that he doubted the diagnosis of suicidal intent, that he doubted the defendant actually tried or intended to kill himself.

Mario walked over to his table and picked up Wisocki's gun, carefully extracting it from the plastic bag. "Throughout this trial one question has lingered in the air," he said. "If the defendant was truly trying to commit suicide, as his attorney suggests, why didn't

he succeed? That is a question you must ask yourself as you consider
the evidence of the defendant's crimes. Killing yourself with a semiautomatic weapon is not terribly difficult—if that in fact is your
intention. *Why didn't he do it?"*

Mario held the weapon in front of him, allowing the jurors to
take a good look, then he dramatically touched it to his head.
"Bang," he shouted, causing several jurors to jump.

"This is a lethal weapon," said Mario, as he held the gun aloft.
"And, as you just saw, it is very easy to use, especially if you are aiming at yourself."

He lowered the weapon and replaced it on the table with an audible thud. "We read all the time of people who, even after killing others, manage to kill themselves," he said. "Why didn't the defendant
do that?

"There is only one logical answer. He never intended to kill himself. His intent was simply to commit murder. And even, assuming
for the sake of discussion, he was not intending to commit murder,
he clearly killed an innocent person. I submit to you that entering
someone's office with a loaded gun and pointing it at that person
surely indicates an indifference, a depraved indifference, to human
life.

"A second question has lingered in the air during this trial. If the
defendant was truly trying to kill himself, *why would he do it in such
a hostile way? Why would he select another man's office in which to
commit the act?"* Mario turned to face Wisocki, as if inviting him to
answer, before again turning his attention to the jury. "At the very
least, such conduct indicates a hostility toward Mr. García that rises
to the level of hatred. You heard from a number of the defendant's
co-workers, who testified to the defendant's envy and dislike of Mr.
García. You heard, in his own words, in his personal memoranda,
documentation of that envy and animosity. You heard from Mr.
Hernández that the defendant had used racial slurs. Mr. Hernández
is admittedly a convicted felon, but you must ask yourself the question: Why would he lie about this? He didn't know the defendant.
He had no more reason to lie about that than he did about the fact

that the defendant pointed a gun at him—a fact that the defendant himself admits to.

"Ms. Fontaine made much of her weapons expert," observed Mario, in a world-weary tone. "Mr. Dillon is indeed a very impressive man. He has a lot of fancy credentials. But in everything he had to say, he did not refute Ms. Gattling's main contention: that no gun, including the Glock Seventeen, fires itself. No gun shoots someone by itself. And certainly no gun fires itself two times in a row. The only logical conclusion is that the gun was fired on purpose. The defendant missed his first shot and therefore took a second—and obviously not at himself," he growled, sarcasm dripping from his voice, "but at Mr. García.

"Ms. Fontaine made a great deal of the fact that the defendant testified," continued Mario, fixing Wisocki with a look that fell midway between disgust and pity. "But what did he testify to? The defendant testified that he had no personal animosity toward Mr. García, when his own words show that he did, when his own words show that he called Mr. García a selfish, self-promoting foreigner, a leech 'living off our blood.' The defendant openly fantasized about Mr. García 'hanging from a tree in the middle of the desert as bugs and buzzards devour his body.' It's all recorded on his own computer," said Mario, lifting a floppy disk from his desk and slamming it down again. "I ask you: Are those the words of a person who had no personal animus?

"Ms. Fontaine made a great deal of what she claims to be a heart attack." Mario grimaced. "As if Mr. García simply walked into his office and dropped dead. Miss Fontaine hopes that if you conclude Mr. García died of a heart attack, you will also conclude he could not have been murdered. But I will ask you the question she asked you. Where *is* the truth here? It certainly is not to be found in the impressive double-talk of the defense. Mr. García didn't just have a heart attack; he had a bullet go through his chest. But even if you accept that a heart attack may have caused his death, the fact remains that that heart attack was set off by a bullet fired by the defendant from his illegally acquired gun. Even if you accept that

Mr. García technically died of a heart attack, that does not change the fact that he was murdered by the defendant—a man consumed by rage, by envy, by hatred. A man who had convinced himself that he was a victim of some generalized injustice perpetrated on white males like himself. Ladies and gentlemen, a sense of victimization does not excuse murder. Drinking does not excuse murder. Depression does not excuse murder. Nothing excuses murder.

"Where, indeed, is the truth?" he roared, finally unleashing his passion at full throttle. "Ms. Fontaine talks of truth. But she does not reveal it to you. You have to look behind the obfuscating words to find it. Once you do, it is staring you dead in the face. The defendant admitted to having an unlicensed weapon. He admitted that it was loaded. He admitted pointing that gun at Mr. García. He admitted firing it in Mr. García's office. In short, he admitted to nothing less than murder. There is simply no more that needs to be said."

Mario again lowered his voice dramatically, causing the jurors to lean forward in their seats. "We have proved that the defendant, last August twenty-fourth, committed murder in the second degree. We have proved the defendant had a loaded firearm, that he had every intent to use that firearm unlawfully against another person, that he in fact did use it unlawfully against another person, and we have proved all these charges beyond a reasonable doubt. We have proved, in other words, that the defendant is guilty of criminal possession of a weapon in the second degree. I ask, in the name of the people of the State of New York, that you find the defendant guilty as charged.

"Thank you."

Mario clasped his hands to his chest and leaned forward slightly from the waist, then he pivoted, and slowly walked toward his seat. And as he sat down, he glanced in the direction of Isabel García.

During Mario's closing statement, Felicia had scrutinized the jury, searching for signs of a positive response. She had looked particularly closely at two of her favorites—the black retired grocer and the

white travel agent. She had no reason other than instinct for sin-
gling them out, but she was convinced that wherever they went, the
others would follow. Although both had been fully engrossed in
Mario's monologue, there had been no smiles, few nods of encouragement, and little indication that they shared his intense indignation. But juries, she reminded herself, were always capable of surprises, and there was no reason to believe this one would be an
exception. Nonetheless, she squeezed John's hand and bid him to
"keep the faith. We're just about home," she added.

During the brief recess, before the judge gave the jury its instructions, Felicia reached Hector on her cell phone.

"So what can you tell me about Glen Thompson?"

"Not much you don't already know. But I did talk to some of the
guys. They're going to pick him up and have a chat with him. By
the time they're done I'm sure he'll understand that rape can be
extremely detrimental to his health."

"Good."

"There's something else you ought to know."

"Yeah."

"Remember your old friend, Eric Preston?"

"Of course," she said, suddenly apprehensive, "the detective on
the Carl Murphy case."

"Well, apparently, he's surfaced. Channel Three has him holed
up somewhere. Word is he's discovered the Lord, become reborn,
and is itching to get something off his chest."

"I see," she whispered, suddenly finding it difficult to breathe.

15

For Mario, waiting for the jury's decision seemed worse than waiting for a surgeon to complete a life-threatening operation. At least surgeons got their business done relatively quickly. They didn't leave you lounging outside the operating room forever. But a jury could go on for days.

Immediately after delivering his closing argument, he had begun to worry. Why hadn't he found a better psychiatrist? Why had he put Hernández on the stand? Could he have made more of Wisocki's computer-documented fantasies about Francisco García and death? Could he have done a better job of revving up the jury, or showed more righteous indignation?

After the jury received the judge's instructions and was swept off into sequestration, Mario and María Cristina went to Erizo, a place in SoHo that served Nuevo Latino cuisine and would offer, they assumed, an opportunity to relax. Despite the exquisite food and pulsing music, Mario was unable to unwind. María Cristina attempted to reassure him.

"Should we have the victory celebration now or later?" she asked. "Whichever it is, that promotion is yours—assuming you really want it." The comforting words, however, made no difference.

Mario's mind remained in the courtroom, reliving the trial.

The weekend was no better. He reread his summation more than a dozen times, each time finding a new reason for aggravation. *I should have attacked the minister's credibility directly. I should have reviewed the ballistics evidence in detail. I should have hit that possession count harder. I should have demonstrated just what Wisocki did.* The running commentary from Court TV and the local pundits didn't help his state of mind. Much as he abhorred the uninformed blather ("What do you think, Lloyd, about the odds of a hung jury?" "Feels like that's where they're headed to me. This reminds me of a case I tried in Texas . . ."), he could not resist watching it.

He was at his desk an hour early Monday morning, mostly because he had been unable to sleep. He certainly was in no mood to work. So he sat there, fiddling with paper, trying and failing to put the case out of his mind. He was relieved, but also apprehensive, when the news came from the clerk later that morning that the jury had a verdict. "Finally," he said softly, recalling that Mrs. García had spoken the same word, very much like an invocation, the day the trial began.

His first call was to María Cristina. "How long before they do it?" she asked.

"An hour or so. They need time for Felicia's side to assemble."

"I'll be there," she said. His next call was to Isabel García. She picked up the phone on the second ring, and he knew instantly, from the tension in her voice, that her weekend had been much like his—hopefully waiting, and yet fearful of the outcome. *Could she be in court in an hour?*

"I would be there in a minute," she said determinedly, "if that would mean that animal would go to jail."

Felicia was in her office when the call came, trying to make sense of her suddenly topsy-turvy world. The previous evening Channel 3 news had announced it had a special guest for tonight: "someone who will be able to shed light on the allegations of impropriety involving Felicia Fontaine." Since then, scores of reporters had called, wanting to know about the Carl Murphy affair. She had not returned a single call, and had instructed Tracy and Tanya to tell any media person who called that she would have nothing to say today. The news of a verdict was a welcome distraction, giving her something to focus on other than Eric Preston—whom, despite the efforts of Hector and some friends on the force, she had been unable to locate.

Linda answered the phone at John Wisocki's house and Felicia told her straightaway, "The verdict's in. It's going to be read in an hour."

"What do you think?" asked Linda.

"I think it's in the bag," replied Felicia.

When John came on the line, Felicia was even more emphatic: "I sense a victory. They came in too quickly for anything else." As she hung up, she prayed her prognosis was correct.

Reporters were notified shortly after Mario and Felicia got the word and several radio stations immediately begin issuing news bulletins. Shortly before the appointed hour, Mario decided to take a walk to calm his nerves and clear his head.

Even before he set foot on the sidewalk, he could sense the excitement in the air. A reporter he knew zoomed past him, apparently oblivious to Mario's existence. A defense lawyer he had opposed several times in court grinned and shouted, "Good luck, buddy." The crowd that was milling around in front of the Criminal Courts Building was abuzz with chatter—creating a sound that, to Mario's ear, seemed like the flapping of a thousand birds. "Buzzards circling the prey," he whispered to himself.

A camera crew spotted Mario seconds after he stepped out of the building and a blinding light suddenly assaulted his eyes.

"How is it going to go, Mr. Santiago?"

Mario smiled, held a thumb high up in the air, and quickly escaped into 1 Hogan Place.

The rendition took place shortly after 2 P.M. Judge Campbell initiated the ritual by solemnly declaring, "Ladies and gentlemen, I understand the jury has reached a verdict. Madam forelady, please rise. The defendant please rise."

John rose along with the forewoman, a nursing administrator in her mid-thirties named Wanda Latillis. Often, during the trial, Mario had sought in her eyes a sign that his case was prevailing. She had always responded with a nod or a smile, with enough of a reaction to provide a sense of hope. Now, his eyes begged her acknowledgment, but her face was unreadable as she solemnly stared at the judge.

"Madam forelady, please listen carefully to the clerk of our court as he asks you questions concerning the verdict," ordered Campbell.

The clerk, standing at his desk to the right of the judge, spoke in a loud bass monotone: "Has the jury agreed upon a verdict in the case of the people of the State of New York against John Wisocki, the defendant?"

"Yes we have," said Latillis.

"How does the jury find as to the first count of the indictment which charges the defendant with the crime of murder in the second degree? Guilty or not guilty?"

"We find the defendant not guilty."

There was sudden rustling of paper near the front of the courtroom. Both Mario and Felicia ignored it, keeping their eyes fixed dead ahead.

"How does the jury find as to the second count of the indictment, which charges the defendant with the crime of murder in the second degree. Guilty or not guilty?"

"Not guilty."

John lurched forward, but caught himself on the table, as the courtroom erupted in whispers. The air became heavy, almost impossible to breathe, and Mario struggled to suck it in.

"How does the jury find . . ."

The clerk and jury forewoman continued to talk. Mario heard them, but dimly—as they worked their way through the remaining charges. When the recitation was done, he was in shock.

Wisocki had been exonerated not only of the murder counts but also of the aligned "lesser and included" manslaughter charges. On the gun charge, of which he was convicted, the jury opted to go for the less serious offense. Instead of convicting him of criminal possession in the second degree, they found him guilty only of possession in the third. Still a felony, but not much of one. Wisocki could get away with a year behind bars, maybe less.

The clerk polled the jurors and recorded the verdict. The judge thanked the jurors for their time and effort and set a sentencing date four weeks away. He agreed to let Wisocki remain at liberty pending sentencing.

Mario, with effort, pushed away from the table and made his way over to Isabel García. "I'm so sorry," he mumbled.

She embraced him and replied, in a voice heavy with grief, "I know. I know. I'm sorry, too. You did what you could. I thank you for that. I thank you for caring."

Wisocki, who had collapsed into his chair following the reading of the verdict, suddenly came to life. He leapt to his feet and hugged Felicia, murmuring his thanks between sobs. Then he simultaneously hugged his mother and his wife, the tears continuing to flow.

Felicia felt a surge of satisfaction, but nothing remotely approaching elation. Instead of savoring the moment, she thought mostly of escape. But with the television cameras whirling and photographers circling, a quick getaway was not an option. So she grabbed Wisocki by the arm and announced, "Time to meet the press."

16

Several of the jurors held their own press conference, which Mario watched on television when he got home. As he listened to their rationale for the second time—the first was when he had interviewed them earlier in the day—he shook his head in dismay. They hadn't been able to see beyond the smoke Felicia had blown in their eyes.

"In order to convict him of murder, we had to believe he intended to kill Mr. García," Latillis explained. "We just didn't see enough evidence that he did. Wisocki was mad as hell at the company, and he was mad as hell at García. But intent? We just didn't see it. That was a big barrier for us, the biggest one. We couldn't get past it. Also, being so timid and all, Wisocki just didn't seem like a murderer. It was hard to imagine him looking someone in the eye and shooting him."

As for the manslaughter charges: "We spent a lot of time thinking about that, more than about anything else, but the judge's definitions were real precise, and what Wisocki did just didn't fit. I mean, it looks like he probably caused the man's death, but he didn't mean to do it. There isn't proof, at any rate, that he meant to. So that killed the whole intent thing. And it wasn't even all that clear that he was reckless. He testified, after all, that he asked Mr.

García to leave. So that seemed to make him pretty concerned. At any rate we couldn't say beyond a reasonable doubt that he wasn't concerned. And that's the standard we had to adhere to. And then there was that heart attack. It's possible, you know, that Wisocki didn't even kill Mr. García. So we just didn't feel comfortable convicting him of that."

Even the criminal possession of a weapon charge had not been easily resolved. "For one thing," said Latillis, "the count they indicted the man on, criminal possession in the second degree, well, that charge requires intent too. For us to convict of that, we would have had to conclude that he was intending to hurt somebody, or at least intending to use the gun against somebody. At the end of the day, we just couldn't see that. We then had to look at criminal possession in the third degree, but there were problems with that. You see, if he only had the gun in his home or in his place of business, then we couldn't convict him of it. And the shooting, as you all know, took place in his office, in his place of business. To be more precise, it took place in his colleague's office, but they were part of an adjoining suite. So the way we read the law, that made Mr. García's office pretty much the same as Wisocki's office. As you can see, that was a real problem—for us, anyway.

"What allowed us to go ahead and convict him on that charge was Mr. Hernández's testimony. You see, Hernández was in the street. Wisocki didn't live on the street, and he sure wasn't conducting business there. If we could establish he had the gun on the street, that would get us around the home and office exception. Once Hernández placed Wisocki in the street with the gun, and once Wisocki admitted to having the gun in the street, then we had him. You see, without that, how could we be sure that the gun wasn't in his office all the time? And, like I said, it ain't against the law to have a gun in the office. But the Hernández testimony really made a difference. Hernández let us convict the guy of something at least. And we wanted to do that, because, well, Mr. García did die. So Wisocki had to be held accountable some kind of way."

"Jeez. Can you believe that shit?" fumed Mario. "They're saying

Hernández saved the goddamn case. *Hernández.* Give me a fuckin' break."

Still shaking his head, Mario switched the channel, just in time to catch the end of an interview with Nelson Flores. "We have no intention of giving up this fight," said Flores. "We will be at the sentencing, and we will demand that he be put in jail for a substantial period of time. And tomorrow we're going to be marching on the office of the U.S. Attorney to demand that Wisocki be prosecuted on federal civil rights charges. Wisocki clearly violated Francisco García's civil rights. Take my word for it, this is not the end of this case. We will haunt Wisocki for the rest of his life. And we are putting the city on notice, and Wisocki's apologists and his attorney on notice. We won't stand by as our Latino and black brothers are used for target practice by paranoid white men."

"Do you expect riots as a result of this verdict, Reverend Flores?"

"Riot? Are you nuts? What kind of fool riots in the wintertime?"

Mario clicked off the television and turned to María Cristina, who was sitting beside him on the sofa. He squeezed her hand and sighed. "Well at least it's over, all but the sentencing. But I sure as hell could use some time off."

"So why not take it? Hard as you worked on this case, you surely have it coming."

"You know, that's not a bad idea. What do you think of taking a week, maybe going to the island? We can see the grandfolks in Ponce and then head for the beach. We've both got a bunch of time piled up. And I need the sun. I need the heat. I need some time to recoup. And I need in the worst way to be away from here."

"That's the second best idea I've heard all day," she replied.

"What's the first?"

"When you began unbuttoning my blouse and suggested we go to bed."

At Wisocki's post-trial press conference, Felicia did most of the talking. She and Wisocki were considering following up with a civil suit against Infotect, she said. She personally was still considering a libel suit against Brenda Noel and the *Journal*, she added. How did she read the jury's verdict?

"The fact is Mr. Wisocki did not commit a murder," she replied. "That charge was always ridiculous, and the jury said as much. The conviction on criminal possession of a weapon is unfortunate, but there may be grounds to have it set aside. It's not clear to us that the instructions to the jury were proper on that count. Nor is it clear to us that the jury fully understood the requirements of the law on that count. We never denied that Mr. Wisocki had a gun, but he had it in his place of business, which is an exception under the law. So we are looking into that."

Wisocki confined his comments to expressions of gratitude and thanks—to his wife, his mother, the jury, and his attorney. "It will be good," he said, "to finally be able to put this behind us."

When several reporters attempted to ask about the Murphy case and the upcoming Channel 3 broadcast, Felicia bluntly cut them off. "This is not the time to address those issues. This is Mr. Wisocki's day," she announced through a tight, combative smile.

Following the press conference, the Wisocki family headed to Carmine's, a family-style Italian place for a celebratory dinner. Felicia declined the dinner invitation, but agreed to join the family for a toast. She was not surprised that neither Frank nor Stephanie wanted to go with her. So, later that evening, Felicia found herself alone with Linda, Sophie, Wisocki, and her cell phone, sipping chardonnay and reflecting on the letdown she already felt. Much of her mood, she concluded, had to do with the tension generated by Muriel's woes and Eric Preston's apparent resurfacing. Much of it had to do with her feelings for John Wisocki, or more accurately her lack of any feelings for him. He was unworthy of her efforts—and the principle his case represented somehow receded into meaninglessness when connected to the actual man. Nonetheless, she raised a glass and toasted their triumph and beamed at Sophie when she asked, "Have you ever considered becoming a Lutheran, Miss Fontaine? I think you would really enjoy belonging to our church."

Felicia winced at the thought.

True to her word, she didn't linger, but soon escaped to the solitude of her office. Although it was after hours, the phone rang constantly. For the most part the callers were reporters on deadline in need of quotes—which she tried to supply, provided the quote had nothing to do with Carl Murphy. Eleanor Lamont also called to let her know that producers for *Good Day New York*, *The Today Show*, and *Larry King Live* were all interested in having her appear. The most intriguing call came from a woman identifying herself as Elaine Jones, an adviser to conservative moneyman Mike Smith.

"Congratulations on your great victory," said Jones, after introducing herself. "I realize you have a lot on your mind right now, but Mr. Smith wanted to plant a seed of a thought. As you know, New York has a Senate race next year and we are in the market for an interesting candidate. We think you might be that person. Don't respond now. Just think about it."

"Right. I won't respond now," said Felicia, as she replaced the receiver, feeling too worn out to think of much of anything at the moment. As she was on the verge of leaving, the phone rang yet again. It was a producer from Channel 3, inviting her to be on the late night news.

"I'm sorry," Felicia replied. "Not tonight. I've said all I want to say about the Wisocki case for today."

"Oh, this is not about the Wisocki case," replied the young female voice on the other end. "It's about someone you know named Eric Preston. We thought you might want to go on the air with him."

"Why in the world would I want to do that? I don't think so," said Felicia, in her frostiest voice, and eased the phone back into its cradle.

She met Frank at a wine bar near her home, but was still unable to shake herself out of her somber mood. Indeed, the final call had worsened her spirits. Now, in addition to being mildly—and unexplainably—depressed, she was more apprehensive than ever. *What in the hell could Preston be planning to say? And why now?*

"Are you feeling all right, honey?" Frank asked.

"I'm just tired," she replied. "And I guess I was also thinking about some things."

"About the case?"

"Not really. I was thinking about me, about where I am. Do you realize I'll be forty next month?"

He hesitated, causing her to add with a laugh, "It's not a test, Frank. It's okay if you don't remember my exact birthday. But it's true. I will be forty years old. It's kind of scary."

"That's a milestone. We'll have to do something special."

"That would be nice. I'm generally not big on birthdays, but forty, that's a big one. It's one of those things that makes you sit back and take stock. You know, I got a strange call a little while ago from a woman who works for Mike Smith. Wanted to know if I wanted to run for the Senate."

"Jesus Christ. Do you?"

"I can't even think about that right now. There's too much else on my mind. Politics, I don't think so. But who knows?"

"Well, one thing I think we both know is that you don't want to become a pin-up girl for Mike Smith."

"Probably not, though I don't think pin-up girl is what anybody has in mind. Anyway, another thing to think about. Guess I have some things to sort out now that this Wisocki case is pretty much done."

"You'll certainly have a lot more time."

"I suppose I will. You know, we should do something fun, really fun, even before my birthday."

"Like what?"

"I don't know." She paused for several seconds, looking into his face, and realized, with a twinge of sadness, that she didn't much associate Frank with fun. "Do you think we have a future, Frank?"

The surprise in his voice underscored his bewilderment. "Why do you ask?"

"I don't know. Was just wondering."

"To be honest," Frank said, his voice now grave, "I don't really know. I used to think we did. But now I'm not so sure."

"Oh?" she said, trying hard not to show her surprise.

"It just seems, lately at least, we're having a hell of a hard time connecting," he continued. "I'm not sure why, but something just isn't right."

She stared at him for a long while, not trusting herself to respond at first; but as anger welled up inside, she could no longer hold her tongue. "I really don't need this tonight, Frank," she murmured. "I think maybe I just should go."

"Honey. What I was—"

"*Please, Frank*. I'm just not in the mood to talk."

"All right. I'll walk you home."

"No. Don't. I'll talk to you later."

Upon arriving home, Felicia took the phone off the hook and sat in front of the television. Since the news would not come on for another half hour, she switched to a situation comedy, hoping it would lighten her mood. Instead, the show's stupid jokes merely aggravated her, so much so that she finally pushed the mute button and simply sat there staring at the silent figures on the screen.

The buzzer from downstairs sounded. She grimaced and ignored it, figuring Frank would soon go away. When it blared for the fifth time, she finally answered, fully prepared to tell Frank to go to hell. But instead of announcing Frank, the doorman told her Geneva was waiting in the lobby.

"The guy downstairs told me you were home," said Geneva, as she entered the apartment. "When you didn't answer, I told him to keep ringing. I figured that sooner or later you would decide to pick up. I also figured you might need some company."

"So have a seat," Felicia said. The two of them took their places on the sofa together, just as the news came on.

Channel 3's news led with a recap of the trial and pronounced the verdict a great victory for Felicia and her client. It took another ten minutes, and two promotional teasers, before Eric Preston finally appeared on camera.

He was a bit heavier than Felicia remembered and there was a softness to his facial expression, a Zen-like look of peace. Retirement apparently was treating him well. The nighttime anchor, Jim Blain, conducted the interview.

"I understand that you're now retired and living in Florida, Detective Preston."

"Yes, that's right. I always wanted to live near the ocean. It makes you feel closer to life."

"I suppose it would. You told our producer that you regard yourself as a completely different man than when you were in New York and on the police force. What do you mean by that?"

"I have taken Jesus Christ as my personal savior. I am not the same person in any respect now that I once was. I have given my life totally to Christ."

"I'll be," mumbled Felicia, and suddenly fell silent.

"And you were willing to come on television tonight because you wanted to set the record straight about some things," said Blain.

"Yes, that's true. Although I have renounced much of my past behavior, I have to take responsibility for what I did. There are some people I put in pain. I want to try to make amends. This is a first step."

"To whom in particular do you wish to make amends, Detective Preston?"

"A few years ago I did something horrible," he said, visibly struggling with his emotions. "I disgraced the NYPD. I want to acknowledge the wrong, and I want to apologize. I want to try to set things right."

"Yes?"

"I arrested and framed an innocent man, someone whose only crime was getting in the way of my ego."

Preston lowered his head, as if in prayer, and added, his voice cracking, "As I humble myself before Jesus Christ, I must humble myself before the man I have wronged. His name is Johnny Robertson, and I intend to do everything within my power to clear his name."

"Johnny *who*?" muttered Blain, as astonishment flashed across his face. "I mean, this isn't what you talked to our producer, Ms. McClymont, about."

"Johnny Robertson," repeated Preston. "He never laid a hand on me. All he did was to call me a name. For that I destroyed his life. I owe him much more than an explanation."

"Yes, I'm sure you do," said Blain, clearly unsettled. "But you also worked with Felicia Fontaine when she was an assistant district attorney. Isn't that correct?"

"Yes, it is."

"On the case involving an alleged drug dealer, a man called Carl Murphy. Right?"

"Yes. I did some work on that."

"And, as you may know, there have been allegations of impropriety around that. Is there anything you can tell us about it?"

"In fact, I can. I know Carl Murphy. I arrested him. He is not an innocent man. I have thought a great deal about his situation, and I have asked my Lord for guidance."

"Yes?"

"Carl Murphy, I can tell you, is the worse kind of human being imaginable. He's a killer and a leech. He has a great deal to answer for, before God and before the families of those people he killed."

"Yes, but the allegation is that he is not guilty of the specific crime with which he was charged, that Ms. Fontaine fabricated evidence—or, I should say, withheld exculpatory evidence."

Preston sighed. "It is not my place to judge Miss Fontaine. There are some values higher than the law. There is man's law and there is God's law. Carl Murphy is a murderer. He deserves to be in jail. God put him there. That's where he ought to stay."

"But what about Ms. Fontaine?"

"She's a very good lawyer, and I wish her only the best."

"Praise Jesus!" Felicia said softly, wiping tears from her face.

The next evening, Felicia picked up Muriel and took her to Brasilia on Forty-fifth Street, where they shared a large casserole of a meat-heavy stew called *feijoada*.

"Do you have a boyfriend?" Muriel asked out of the blue.

"That's a good question," Felicia replied. "I *had* a boyfriend, but I must admit I'm not sure where we are right now."

"Relationships don't get easy when you're old?"

Felicia grinned. "I'm not old, *yet*. So I don't know. But something tells me they always take a lot of work. So . . . How are things in school?"

Muriel muttered something noncommittal and promptly took advantage of a lull in the conversation to change the subject from schoolwork. "Some guys beat up Glen Thompson pretty bad the other day. They had to take him to the hospital."

"How do you feel about that?" asked Felicia.

Muriel smiled shyly. "Pretty good. *Real good.*"

After dinner, they stopped at Felicia's apartment for ice cream, where Muriel confided that the conversations with Alyssa, the therapist, were going well. "I gathered as much," Felicia said. "You no longer blame yourself for what happened. And that's good."

Muriel nodded wordlessly and continued to eat.

Later that evening, as they said their good-byes, Muriel hugged Felicia and suddenly began to weep. When the sobs finally ended, she looked up and softly said, "Thank you."

Felicia walked into Jason's at half past five and immediately spotted Mario at the bar.

"Want to buy a lady a drink?" she whispered. He turned in surprise and she quickly added, "Better still, why not let a lady buy you a drink?"

The slightest suggestion of a smile flickered across his face. "Why not," he said with a shrug, and followed her to a booth.

"Looks like you've been hanging out under a sun lamp," she said.

"María Cristina and I are just back from two weeks in Puerto Rico. We spent a lot of time on the beach pretending it was summer."

"Good for you."

"I needed it. I needed to get away. There was a lot built up inside of me that I needed to let go of. Talking of which, I never congratulated you on your victory."

"No," she said, "you didn't."

"The fact is, you tried a good case. Maybe a bit underhanded at times, dishonest at points, but nonetheless you did good work. I hope your client is happy."

"He's dealing, though I suspect he won't really know what he feels until after sentencing. But you know, I'm glad it's over. Somewhere along the way it stopped being fun. It got way too serious."

"A man died, Felicia. It was always serious."

"You know what I mean, Mario. It got serious in the *wrong* way. It got personal. You must have tried a few dozen murder cases. How many of them got really personal?"

"Every one of them. I couldn't try a case I didn't care about. It's always personal. It's always serious. I think that's one of the big differences between you and me, Felicia. You see a case just as a game. For me, it's not about that. Maybe your way is better. Fact is, you're probably a better lawyer than I am."

Felicia winced. "You say it like an accusation."

"Maybe that's the way I feel," he said, an unfamiliar sadness in his tone." I mean, you're damn good at playing the game, but you don't particularly care about the people involved. Sometimes I wonder whether you even care about right and wrong. You obviously don't have to. The fact that you sometimes don't may be part of your strength. It may be why you're such a good litigator. The problem though, it seems to me, is that it leaves you without a center. It leaves you very open to manipulation, by others and by yourself."

A look of incredulity swept across her face. "That's bullshit, Mario. I'm one of the most centered people I know. I came up, like you did, without a whole lot of advantages. I've had to make my own. And I've managed to do so without giving up who I am or what I believe in. If I say so myself, I think I've done pretty damn good."

"I can't deny you've done well, Felicia. I guess you deserve to. But I don't think you're being honest, least of all with yourself, about what really motivates you, or even about who you are."

He leaned forward and peered deeply into her eyes, speaking in a voice not much louder than a whisper. "The Wisocki case was not about some grand ideal, much as you might want to pretend that it was. It was about you, and about being rejected by the crowd you came up with. It was about trying to have it both ways—about trying to fit into a club that is not sure it wants you, while thumbing your nose at the people who could get you in. You are one complex piece of psychology."

"We all are, my friend," she shot back. "You certainly are. I mean, talk about self-deception and illusions. Do you really believe being a prosecutor makes you a knight in armor? Are you supposed to be some paragon of truth and virtue?"

"Compared to you?"

"Don't even go there, Mario. I know you way too well," she said, fury flashing in her eyes. "That little back-stabbing trick you tried to play, planting that item in Brenda Noel's gossip column, was not what I would call chivalry in action. And don't claim it wasn't you—"

"You're right," he glumly admitted. "It was me, and it was a very stupid thing to do, which isn't to say that you didn't deserve it. But it was stupid, and it was mean-spirited. And I apologize for it—for what it's worth. Anyway, it doesn't seem to have done you any harm. Just the opposite. Damn near made you into a hero. Go figure."

"No thanks to you. And talk about craving acceptance. I think you may be referring more to yourself than to me. Remember, years ago, when we went to Ponce?"

"Sure, I remember."

"I know your grandfather didn't know that I overheard him, but I did. It seems that all he could talk about was acceptance, was about how, if your children were too dark, they would not be accepted in the right circles. About how, if you married me, you would be ruining your chances for acceptance. I don't recall you lecturing him on the folly of the notion of acceptance. It seems to me you were buying into most of what he was saying. I guess he must really approve of María Cristina."

Mario sighed. "The fact is, I did lecture him, Felicia. Old ideas in old heads die hard."

"I guess they do. Old relationships sometimes die hard also."

"Meaning?"

"I don't know, Mario," she said, her tone gentle as a breeze. "I miss something that we had. It would be nice to have it back."

"I thought we had pretty much concluded that whatever we had wasn't working worth a damn."

"That's right. It sure as hell wasn't working the way we were going about it. Maybe we weren't ready. I don't know. Maybe we've both changed enough to make it work. You have to admit that's possible. And if you ever get rid of that wife of yours, it might be something to think about. In some ways, we made a pretty good team. We might make a better one now."

Mario shrugged, fighting the tug of nostalgia.

Felicia placed her hand on the table, palm up, next to his. Mario looked away, staring into the distance, flashing back to the moment of their first encounter, then he pulled back his hand, wrapped it around his glass, and took a sip of his Stolichnaya.

Epilogue

John sat silently in front of his computer, wondering whether Linda would leave him as soon as the sentencing was over. He had been afraid to press her on the subject, thinking it better to let her know—as subtly as possible—how happy he would be to have her back, how miserable he would be if she were to depart. She seemed to have appreciated the Valentine's Day card he had given her: a caricature of a computer nerd on front and a greeting inside that read, "You're always resident in my RAM."

"Kind of cute," she had called it.

Linda still insisted on sleeping in her own bed, but she usually joined him for dinner, though sometimes she would vanish in the evening and not return until very late at night. "You have to tell her you care," he typed into his new laptop computer. "Maybe she doesn't realize how important she is to you."

He stored that file, and retrieved one labeled "Sunday." It was a file into which he typed random thoughts about the day Francisco García died. He had replayed the incident hundreds of times in his mind, and tonight he replayed it again.

He recalled gulping a mouthful of Scotch just as Francisco walked in. He remembered thinking that his problems were all Francisco's fault and shouting, "Get the hell out."

But instead of leaving, Francisco had walked toward him and demanded to know what was going on. And then Francisco had presumed to psychoanalyze him. "I know you're going through a rough period, John, but it can't be worth this. Rough times pass. We all have them," he had said.

John had scowled, making no attempt to mask his contempt. *How dare Francisco patronize him. How dare he pretend that he understands.* Francisco, now directly in front on him, had leaned across the desk and said softly, almost as if talking to a child, "John, give me the gun. *Please.* John, give it to me." He had touched the hand holding the pistol, but John had pulled away and tightened his grip.

"Damn you," he had shouted. "Get away from me." But instead of leaving, Francisco had grabbed his hand.

At that moment, weeks of resentment had swelled up inside and exploded into hatred. At that moment, he had wished nothing so much as to see Francisco dead. He had willed with every fiber of his being that he die on the spot. Yet, he had not pulled the trigger. At least, he could not recall pulling the trigger—although he could recall, very clearly, the gun firing once, and then again. But it had fired on its own, as if commanded by God.

The ways of the Lord, they always said, were mysterious. And who was he to question God?

John leaned forward and typed into the computer. "I owe a great debt to Felicia Fontaine. She opened my eyes in so many ways. She helped me to see and to accept what really occurred that night. A heart attack. A stress reflex. They are things over which we have no control. As forces of nature, such things are in the hands of God, who, in His infinite wisdom, decided Francisco's day had come."